TRUTH IS A GIFT OF LOVE

MARK ATLEY

TRUTH IS A GIFT OF LOVE

TULSA UNDERWORLD

4 Horsemen
Publications, Inc.

DEDICATION:

To those who deserve second chances.
And my wife for loving me.

ACKNOWLEDGMENT:

I'**VE RECENTLY READ SOME EXCELLENT** acknowledgment sections, and I believe Jack Carr does it best. His acknowledgments are often the most enlightening and educational parts of his books. I admire his accomplishments and the stories he shares because people often forget that civilization is built upon the sacrifices of brutal individuals. Society remains safe only when some are willing to endure hardships for the sake of others. This perspective is why I strive to feature law enforcement or law enforcement-adjacent characters in my writing. It also explains why my books have clear and distinct "good" guys and gals; they may not always make the right decisions, but they do what's necessary when it counts.

I don't craft my acknowledgments quite like he does, but I want to express my gratitude.

Thank you to everyone who keeps others safe: our military, police, firefighters, dispatchers, jailers, EMS, and many more.

Thank you to everyone who contributes to making the world go around. Without you, nothing would be possible.

So many people are to thank, as writing isn't a solitary endeavor. My writing is woven from countless snippets of my everyday life, which means I couldn't be who I am without everyone around me. I am grateful to everyone I work with, live with, and share my life with.

I want to thank 4 Horsemen Publishing for taking a chance on my books. I also thank Matthew McConaughey for his advice about having a baby and not saying no to opportunities. I'm glad I didn't decline 4 Horsemen's challenge to write and release ten books in five years.

Most of my books in this series are finished. I enjoy referencing characters and events from previous stories and trying to present them in new and exciting ways. It's my way of rewarding dedicated readers.

And that brings me to whom I am most thankful for: my readers. Regardless of how few or many, every one of you makes this journey possible.

I started writing because I wanted to read stories about complex characters and relationships that treat the reader as an equal, not someone to write down to. My first and only promise to you, dear reader, is to entertain. I want every story to satisfy you by the end. You might not like every ending—I certainly haven't expected some of the endings in my favorite books—but that doesn't mean I wasn't satisfied.

I am incredibly grateful for my writing community: Craig, Douglas, and Martine. Without you three, I would have failed long ago. Craig and I discuss craft and storytelling; he's older and wiser, always encouraging me to stay grounded. What he's doing with Luke Fisher is fantastic, and I hope you find his work if you've read my books. Douglas championed my work when few others did. His summaries and insights into my writing are among the best marketing materials I've ever seen—something I struggle with. If you want to understand my work, read his reviews; he truly gets me. And to Martine, my first reader and editor beyond myself, I appreciate her keen grammatical instincts. I value her insights when she points out a section that feels slow, doesn't work, or needs rewriting. Often, I just delete the problematic parts, keeping only the essence of the passage. Martine is a writer in her own right, and her character, Declan Shaw, who is looking for a publishing home, is one of the most unique characters I've encountered. I can't wait to see him in print. I encourage you to read and support their work, just as I'd love for you to do the same for mine.

There are others, too; you are not forgotten.

My last few books have presented challenges. Life often gets in the way, as it does for many writers. During downtime, I've spent the last few books typing chapters on my phone and using my free moments for hasty edits—during naps. I could not be a writer without the unwavering support of my family, from my parents and grandparents to my wife and three daughters. I am incredibly thankful for everything they have done and continue to do for me, especially my wife, who keeps me grounded and challenges me in new and exciting ways. None of my books would be possible without her.

TABLE OF CONTENTS

CHAPTER 1:

LAMAR HENRY PRACTICES BOXING WITH his cellmate in their prison cell while waiting for the doors to open for breakfast. The two are half-shadow boxing, half-slap boxing, in the slim aisle between everything else: the narrow walls, the bunk beds, a small desk built into the wall with a metal stool, and Lamar's added an extra plastic chair so they'd both have something to sit on when they played cards after lights out, which Lamar shoved into the corner, so he didn't have to sit on the toilet.

He's in prison, not an animal.

There isn't much room to move around, but Johnny Hudson, the white man, and Lamar, the black man, make it work. They are two cellmates who've only bunked together for a few months, but long enough for Lamar to trust Johnny, and since Lamar hasn't tried to kill Johnny, he's coming around to Lamar.

One is a convicted bank robber. That's Lamar. And the other used to be a cop, Johnny. Leading to the other inmates telling Lamar they have some *real* unique cops and robbers bullshit going on.

"If you were in a boxing gym," Lamar Henry says, "they'd tell you that you don't start with the roof when you build a house. You start with the foundations. They'd have you working on your stance, stepping forward and back, to the sides, while maintaining a certain width between your feet."

"But we're not in a real gym," Johnny Hudson says. His oranges are two sizes too big for his frame. "I can't exactly move side to side here."

"No, we are not," Lamar says, accepting Johnny's point. It's hard to argue when he can damn near touch both sides of the cell by extending his arms out like he's flapping them like a bird, fingertips inches from the cinderblock. "But what I'm saying is, fighting's a lot about the body. Everything has to work together. Has to make sense— much like life. You've got to keep the dominant arm in the back so when you throw it, it comes from way back there, shoulders rotating, hips snapping, legs thrusting it forward. Let your body do the work. You have to have time to build up speed, using all the weight and leverage from the entire body, like a batter does in baseball."

Johnny twists his face and drops his hands, defeated, mumbling, "But this isn't baseball."

Lamar swipes at Johnny.

"Pick up your hands."

Johnny throws an arm up to block, but his arm is too low, too slow. Lamar slaps Johnny across the cheek before patting his right side with his other hand in a one-two combo.

Lamar could take Johnny apart like a surgeon and have just as much feeling as those butcher doctors about it doing it.

"You know what your problem is?" Lamar says. "You don't do the foot drills. You never do; none of you guys here like to do them." Lamar means the guys he teaches boxing to, especially his cellmate. "And you don't want to put the work in. Not the real work. You don't want to get up with me, do the workout. Do the cardio. It's all about that. Cardio. Cardio. Cardio. The work. You don't do it."

"What's cardio going to do for me here?" Johnny asks, dropping his hands again. "I'm surrounded by walls. I can't take a shit by myself. And showering's a hair-raising experience."

"As long as it ain't raising nothing else," Lamar jokes, but a quick read of Johnny's face tells Lamar he's not into the banter this morning. "The cardio would help you get out of that situation if you happen to find yourself in the shower in a *raising* experience."

"It's not funny, Lamar. You don't know what it's like for me here."

"I know what it's like to be here," Lamar says. "That's something. I *never* said I wanted *to be you,* but none of that means nothing. It's an excuse. And it's beside what we're trying to do right now. You live too much in other moments. You need to be in this moment. You can't go around thinking about the past, thinking about what's going to come. You're going to miss what's happening. And what's happening right now is your shit discipline. You have to put in the work if you want to learn how to box. It's all about the cardio because with the cardio, or the work you put in for the cardio, comes the discipline. You have discipline, right?"

"I have discipline," Johnny says.

"Then show it to me."

"How do I show it to you? That's not something that just comes out on my face."

"Well, then put in the cardio. Get up, do the sit-ups, and quit complaining."

"I hate sit-ups on the concrete floor," Johnny says. "Hurts my tailbone, rubs it raw. I've got a bruise."

"Well then, do them in your bunk."

"I'll hit my head."

"It's not my fault you're getting to be a fat fuck." He's giving him sarcasm; if anything, Johnny's losing weight. "Why don't you do this? Stop eating food, and maybe you'll be able to do a crunch without banging your head on the bottom of my bunk. Why don't you miss today's breakfast? Stay here; I'll get you a banana or something?"

Johnny steps back from Lamar. "You don't know what this is like."

Lamar frowns, realizing Johnny's about to enter one of his moods, where he gets all mopey and sad. It's depressing and is happening more and more. Once Johnny starts down this road, it's hard to get the guy out of his funk.

Lamar drops his hands to his side, "I guess we're done then," not being nice about it.

Lamar likes these sessions. They give him purpose. Give him exercise and keep him sharp. Johnny may lack the discipline, but Lamar doesn't. It's what's kept him alive. He won't stay safe. Nothing in here keeps him safe. But busy, sure.

Johnny sits at the foot of the bunk and glares at Lamar. "Don't."

"Don't what?" Lamar says, settling on top of the stool. "You come to me, you say, 'Lamar; I see you over in the yard teaching guys how to box.' You say, 'I'm a cop.' Which let me stop you right there." He holds up his left hand. "You're not a cop, not any fucking more, no longer. You used to be a cop. But that's that past bullshit I'm talking about. You're a fucking nobody now. All that's over—that's your old life. You don't have that life no more. You aren't that person no more. All we are is who we are here. Do you think I go around telling people I was a bank robber? Like that's some sort of qualification for an introduction? Hi, I'm Lamar Henry; you might know me as the Dapper Desperado—"

"I thought it was the Thonged Thief."

Lamar hates that moniker.

"I *prefer* the Dapper Desperado; it's more accurate. Just because I robbed a bank one time in flip flops—"

"Thongs make me think of something else," Johnny interjects.

Lamar talks through the interruption, "A spur-of-the-moment type of deal."

Johnny asks, "Why spur of the moment?"

Lamar pauses. He thinks about what he's going to say. How can he explain the way his mind works? How he can't resist a challenge. Even stupid ones. Ones that end up here.

"It was a dare ... from a girl," Lamar starts to say, mind turning it over. It's a good question. It landed him here—not planning, not having discipline—going with it, a spur-of-the-moment deal. That's what the girl said. She said, "Go with it. Be cool."

This place, life, this fucking cellmate, is what he gets for being cool.

This fucking life. This fucking cellmate.

It was cool for about a fucking minute until he tripped running while doing a *cool* (by that, his mind now associates that word with idiotic) end-zone dance.

"You know what? It doesn't matter. What matters is that it was one time. I wasn't caught, and I wasn't wearing no thong. 'Cause you're right, people think I had a G-string up my ass, and that's all I was wearing. I even heard the judge joke about asking the prosecutor where I'd put the money. That bitch... No, it was a one-time deal. Every other time, I looked nice, like a businessman. That was the key. It's not your money I'm stealing; it's the banks. And their money's insured. It's not personal; it's business. Hence the suit. I had all sorts of suits, real nice pieces, bright colors, and clean. Even had a top hat and cane for one robbery, which made me feel like a villain from some comic book or something. Robbed banks in forty-nine of fifty states: it's not what you're thinking. I got one in Alaska once when I went on a cruise, and we stopped off—it was perfect. It's Utah; I never pulled a job in Utah, because what's in Utah? Nothing but a damn salty lake. Never mind, I'd stick out like a sore thumb. I'm smarter than that. I can walk into the bank like the freaking Planter's Peanut, top hat, cane, monocle, and all, but I can't rob a bank in Utah."

"If I'm not a cop anymore," Johnny says, turning back in on himself and ignoring Lamar's soapbox moment, "then what am I? You say I'm nobody. I can't be that."

Lamar leans forward, close enough to smell the man's morning breath. His last cellmate was a rollie-pollie kid with rotten teeth. At least Johnny doesn't have bad teeth. He needs to brush his teeth this morning, but Johnny's routine is to eat breakfast and then brush his teeth. Lamar points a finger in Johnny's face.

"No, what you are is depressed."

A weird, pitiful hope dawns on Johnny's face. He says, "That's somebody, right? I don't want to be a nobody. Nothing. Forgotten. I liked being a cop. It meant I was somebody. I was something. Like it was my identity. Now who am I?"

Lamar shakes his head, dropping it some.

What the hell's wrong with this guy?

He says, "Wrong, that's not an identity. That's nothing."

Johnny raises his head so that when Lamar finishes speaking and brings his eyes back around, Johnny's staring at him now, features flat. "A real poet is what you are," Johnny says.

"What's up your butt this morning?" Lamar says, pushing back from Johnny, getting out of the loser's face.

Johnny shuts his eyes and drops his head into his hands. "I think my wife's going to leave me."

Now, Johnny's getting to the real reason for his morose-ass attitude.

Lamar reengages. That makes sense. If Johnny thinks his wife's leaving him, that would explain the man's mood. It's not like Lamar hasn't seen it before; he has seen it happen to other inmates.

"Why do you think that?"

"I'm two years into a twenty-year sentence."

"She hasn't left you yet," Lamar says, like that means something. It means nothing, but he can't say that. Lamar's seen too many men come in with someone and go out with no one. "Did you do that thing where you told her to leave you... as a test because we both know you didn't mean it... and she passed, saying, 'No baby, I'll stick with you'?"

Johnny nods.

"Well, why do you think she's going to leave you?"

"First, she visited every month, called once a week, sent letters."

Johnny stops talking, falling into a solemn silence, which means only one thing.

So, Lamar takes up the rest of the story. "But now, you're lucky if you hear from her."

Johnny's eyes flash toward him, the old cop's strength flaring in his irises, or maybe it's the change in light. Lamar's not sure.

"I love her," he says.

Buying time to think of what to say, Lamar glances to the underside of Johnny's bunk, his eyes going to the picture of Johnny's wife stuck on the cinderblock wall next to Johnny's mattress. She's a white woman, slim, and might even be considered petite. It's hard to tell in the picture—no frame of reference for Lamar; it's just her in the photograph, not much in the background that's discernable. It's all out of focus—it looks like a park or something, with lots of flowers and greenery. She's a brunette with dark eyes and bright red lips. In the photograph, she wears a slim black dress that is nothing but shoestrings at the shoulders, showing off musculature that has spent time being sculpted. If Lamar had sculpted the woman of his dreams, she might have looked like this woman. Maybe not. Still, he supposes that a seventies nudie mag photographer might like a woman like her to grace those pages—that being before silicon was invented and became a housewife staple, except she doesn't look like a woman who would appear in that type of magazine. There is nothing fake about this woman, maybe that smile. Nothing else. If she's tall, she'd be more of a model on the catwalk than lay in some creased and sticky centerfold. She seems too wholesome. She's just got that look and authentic flavor of the month-type. She's not anorexic, and she wears a light amount of make-up. She's natural, and Lamar likes that.

The expression she's giving to the camera is playful and serious. For example, did she want her picture taken? No, but she's not going to fight it either. So, she is half-turning in the photograph to look over her shoulder at the photographer, presumably Johnny, the lines of the dress highlighting her natural curves as she does it. She's raising an eyebrow and puckering those lips, creasing her cheeks, playing for the camera like she's seductive. In the photo, she looks younger than Johnny by a whole yard, maybe ten. She stands there and makes eyes with the camera, and in that look, Lamar loses himself in the photograph. The entire time, Johnny's been his celly, this is probably the best thing about bunking with Johnny.

Lamar switches his attention back to Johnny. "If you love her, what are you doing here?"

"I was trying to make a life for us," Johnny explains. "I had everything set up."

"What's everything? What are we talking about here, a golden parachute?"

Johnny says, "Yeah, kind of." And then says, "They did this score, and it was big, but it was also the score that ended up taking us down." Johnny never explained to Lamar who "they" and "us" were or what happened for someone like Johnny to end up in prison. Shouldn't it be "we"? All Lamar knows is that Johnny was a cop, and if he's here, he was a dirty cop or did something he wasn't supposed to do when he wasn't working, but Johnny isn't the type. He's too Captain America for Lamar's taste. No, he was led astray. Lamar's gotta make him the victim in his mind, so it's easier to talk to the guy. He just assumes whatever Johnny did had to do with other dirty cops. "I even bought a retirement home in Costa Rica. I have this nice piece of land, a house mostly built, and a woman to care for it."

Lamar, who has seen this man take a shit, can't believe what he just heard. This isn't the Johnny he's come to know. Maybe Johnny isn't as square and helpless as he appears. Still, he can't believe Johnny would have a woman in another country.

Lamar asks, still unable to wrap his head around it, "Like a side piece?"

"I wouldn't call her that to her face."

"What about to your wife?"

"I wouldn't call her that in front of her either."

"What is she then?"

"Someone to handle my affairs."

"And your cock?"

Johnny smiles, looking all bashful. He admits, "That too."

Lamar whistles. "*Jesus.*"

Maybe Lamar misjudged Johnny.

Maybe he ain't Captain America. Maybe he's the guy that wears the suit but can't fill the position.

Johnny says, "I was a year out from retirement; I had everything going for me and set up. All I had to do was pull the plug. I wanted this marriage to go right. Third time's a charm, right?"

"I guess so; it's your life."

Lamar doesn't mention how sidepieces can mess up those plans, figuring the man has already discovered that.

Johnny says, "All I had to do was make it one more year, then move us down to Costa Rica."

"So why didn't you?"

"I wanted more," Johnny says. "I got greedy. It bit me in the ass, and once the news broke about what we were doing," again, Lamar doesn't have an earthly clue what that was, "I wanted to do the right thing."

Johnny stops talking.

Lamar waits for him to start up again, but he doesn't. He says, "How did that work out for you?"

"One of the other guys got eight years. He only had to serve two. I heard he's out on parole. The other didn't get anything."

"Nothing?"

Johnny shakes his head in disbelief, as if he can't believe how it all shakes out. "Nothing."

"How'd the fuck you get what you got, and he got nothing?"

Johnny's lips stretch into a grin like everything's a sick joke, and maybe it is. Lamar isn't in the know. Johnny says, "I bet you've seen him on TV, too. He's hosting one of those live body camera shows, or he was. I don't know if he still is. I can't watch them. They make me sick, but the guys in the dayroom had him on a few months back. I couldn't believe it."

Lamar can't believe it, either. "The Wrench? You're talking about the Wrench, that guy?"

"Yeah, that guy."

"You were with the Wrench," Lamar clarifies. "Wait, wait, wait, that guy's dirty?"

Johnny clasps his hands together. "We're all sinners, Lamar."

"Don't give me that bullshit," Lamar says.

So, Johnny nods.

Then, it hits Lamar. Johnny was the fall guy, but he can't say that to the guy.

Lamar says, "Let me guess. I know how you ended up here. If I had to bet, you're the nice guy in the group, and you didn't do nothing—whatever it was you were doing—but you didn't say nothing to anyone either. You probably just took the money envelope 'cause it's always an envelope, right? And you looked the other way. Am I right?"

"You're right," Johnny says.

"Which is why you want to learn how to box. So, you don't get beat up anymore in the yard... Yes, I know you work in the library and all that while most everyone is out there walking around in circles, staring at the sun like some sheep. If it rained, they'd all drown. Leave their mouths open, thinking it's a free drink. I know you've been hiding in the library since you're not in protective custody anymore."

"That's it."

"Okay, I have to tell you, you're a shitty boxer," Lamar says, mind still reeling from the revelation. Lamar doesn't know what to think about the guy now, so he switches back to something he knows how to discuss. "You do what's instinctive like most guys. I'd say, though, you are getting better. You put your dominant arm out front, dangling it there for anyone with any skill to disassemble it in moments. I fixed that. Then I gave you my five points. Teaching you how to jab, throw an uppercut, block a punch or two, move, and protect yourself, but you have to do the cardio."

"Why?"

"In case you ever get out of here... or end up in a fight. Why do I have to do all your thinking?"

"You don't," Johnny says.

"That's right, I don't," Lamar says.

The cell door unlocks and slides to the side like a ghost has yanked it back.

Time to go. Breakfast.

Lamar places a hand on Johnny's shoulder and squeezes it three times to reassure the guy and cheer him up. "Look, there you go, breakfast time. Why don't you do me a favor and eat something so you feel better, and then we can come back here and work on your cardio? Yeah, you're doing your freaking sit-ups. I'll throw a towel on the floor if that helps you, and then I'll get the guys around to talk to you about how being here isn't conducive to married life. An entire therapy session."

And Lamar does know just the guys.

He says, "This isn't something new; any guy over the age of twenty-five knows what it's like to have some woman walk out on them or, in this place, walk away from their man."

"I don't know if I can do the time by myself. I love her."

Lamar just looks at the man.

Johnny stares back.

"What about your side piece?"

"I love my wife," Johnny says with some feeling. Maybe he does have a backbone. Lamar hadn't met a cop afraid to wrestle, but he figured that was just a mixture of his luck, profession, and skin color. He's got to believe in a better world. Some guys don't think of moving their fists without first trying to wag their lips. "She didn't deserve to go through any of this."

"Well then, you got to show her what's what," Lamar says, not knowing what the hell that means but thinking he needed to say something to the guy.

Johnny stands up and steps toward the cell opening.

"Good news, partner," Lamar says, standing to follow Johnny, thinking of something better. "You're not alone. You have me."

Glancing back at him, Johnny genuinely smiles for the first time this morning and looks at Lamar as he steps out of the cell, takes a right, and steps right into a shank. Lamar sees a hand with the shiv, an old toothbrush sharpened to a plastic point, stabbing one, two, three, six times. All Lamar focuses on is the shiv, like many people in a robbery focus on the gun, seeing nothing of the wrist beyond, acknowledging it's a human male's wrist, and then Johnny's freezing in surprise, head lolling back as the shiv falls to the floor. Johnny's eyes open wide, asking Lamar what the hell just happened.

Lamar rushes forward, catching Johnny as he falls backward, and lowers him to the ground, Lamar scooting out from underneath, careful to limit the amount of blood that gets on him and his clothes. Then, an idea of a plan for escape leaps across Lamar's mind. Without thinking about anything else, he snatches up the shiv and stabs himself in the chest, just to the left of his right nipple.

CHAPTER 2:

LUCILLE HUDSON MEETS WITH HER HUS- band's attorney, Dickie Johnson, in his office located on the seventh floor of a building downtown, two blocks from the courthouse. Dickie had Lucy come to the office to discuss some troubling news, so she is seated at the conference table, papers and folders laid out in front of her as she thumbs a paper clip.

"Sorry I have to be the bearer of bad news," Dickie starts, "but Johnny was stabbed yesterday."

Even though he's a pretty good lawyer, he dresses like shit. Today's outfit is loud golfing attire over gaudy pants, with his gut hanging over the belt and his salt and pepper hair greased back in place. He doesn't own the office; he shares it with several other attorneys.

He explained two years ago: "We help each other out occasionally with rent and cases. If I'm unavailable, they will appear in court for me. Sometimes, I need an expert in tax law or contracts." Dickie's specialty is family law—aka divorces—but he dabbles in everything. "Like how Erin Moorcock handles criminal law. Remember her daddy, Bob, worked on Johnny's case? Served as co-counsel during the trial. He started this little co-op. Bob's gone now, but as I used him, sometimes she uses me on some of her family matters. We all do a little bit for everyone else and even chip in for the secretary out front."

The room looks like a magazine-perfect country club retreat, with blonde wooden paneling covering everything and tables and chairs to match. Maybe to go with Dickie's golfing attire, make him feel right at home. Or he dresses that way to match the space. Regardless, there's even a large fireplace, which is Lucy's favorite feature. During Johnny's trial, they spent many evenings here, and it would have been unbearable if not for the fireplace and the flames. If it wasn't in the heart of downtown Tulsa, Lucy might be able to shut her eyes and pretend it is some hunting lodge out in the woods.

Behind her are a law library and a fully stocked bar. But if that's too far to walk, a drink cart with a handpicked selection of Lucy's favorites is at the head of the conference room table. Lucy knows it's Carrie's, the secretary, job to pre-stock the cart when a client comes in for a meeting and fill it with everything the client likes. How Dickie and the others know what she likes without asking is beyond Lucy; she's never figured it out. Sure, they'd asked for some drink recommendations, but even on the first day, she was surprised to find that they had everything she liked, every brand, no matter what it was: coffee, tea, soda, alcohol, whatever she desired, it was there on the cart. So, either Dickie hires a private investigator for every retained client to find out what they like and don't like, or Carrie's exceptional at her job.

Carrie strikes Lucy as exceptional.

To Lucy's right, beyond where Dickie's seated at the head of the table, are normal-looking square windows—old and out of date, which is uncharacteristic for the space. The blinds are open outside the windows, and Lucy can see the terrace and a fantastic view of downtown Tulsa. It's afternoon; the sun is setting and casting an incredible warmth across the canyon of buildings.

"Lucy, did you hear me?" Dickie says. His yellow legal pad, divided down the middle into two columns, is on the table in front of him. He drops his pen on the pad and reaches out his left hand to place it over hers to comfort her. He says in a soft voice, "Johnny was stabbed."

Dickie's hand is warm, but she's not sure she heard him right, even if he said it twice. Lucy blinks. "Stabbed?"

"Shanked is the common vernacular."

The words stumble, coming out of her mouth. "Where...?"

"In the abdomen, or so I'm told." Dickie pats her hand and then retracts his hand, now that the hard news is over. He only does just enough and sometimes not even that.

Lucy shakes her head and keeps her hand on the table. "No, I mean, where was he stabbed, like where in the prison did it take place? Where was he... is he now?"

"His cell," Dickie tells her. "He and his roommate... *cellmate*? He's currently in the infirmary. I'm not sure how it happened; they didn't get into details."

Lucy doesn't know who *they* are, probably the prison staff. She still can't believe it. "Is he alright?"

Dickie doesn't understand the question. "No... he was stabbed."

Lucy gives him a tired look and tries again. "Is he going to die?"

Dickie understands now and smiles softly to show it. "Not if the doctors can help it," he says. "Johnny's cellmate was there, was able to apply pressure to the wounds, keep Johnny from bleeding out."

"Wounds, as in more than one?"

Dickie doesn't answer right away.

He stands and places one hand on his hip while extending the other toward her like he's inviting her to dance.

"Would you like a drink, some coffee, beer, wine, something stronger?"

Which is Dickie's way of saying he's uncomfortable with the situation. The guy can't sit still when he is uncomfortable.

Lucy squeezes her eyes closed. She is trying to process what's happened. She sits still, exceptionally still.

"No," she says and then, after a moment, rethinks the offer. "Actually, yes, I'll take a glass of wine."

"Red, correct?" Then, without waiting for her to respond, Dickie steps to the drink cart near the windows. He picks up a bottle of wine and stares out the blinds as he says, "Merlot?"

"That's correct," Lucy says.

Dickie uncorks the bottle and sniffs the opening while Lucy says, "This wasn't part of the plan."

Dickie speaks as he pours, saying slowly and confidently, "No, *it was not*."

Dickie pours the wine the same way he does it every time, like he's doing a tableside presentation. It gives Lucy time to think. Think about the plan, her plan. How waiting two years is long enough? How people still remember. How they remember the scandal. Bring it up with her when they hear her name. "Lucy Hudson?" they say, "Hudson... as in Johnny Hudson, the cop? That you..."

She's tired of explaining herself to others. Yes, her husband is Johnny Hudson, now in prison. And yes, she'd like a job. She despises how that sounds. It sounds like she's begging, and she hates explaining how the hospital cut her hours. Before Johnny, she was a rad tech, took X-rays, and did CTs. After the story broke, the hospital fired her outright. The hospital didn't want the publicity of someone like Lucy Hudson working for them. She was married to the dirty cop, Johnny Hudson. So, when the media did catch on to her employer, the hospital director, in a confident press release, said, "No, she doesn't work for our health care system."

But thank God she's friends with Charlie, the lead tech. He pulled some strings. So yes, they fired her, but then they hired her back after the first wave of publicity subsided, which considering all the time she spent in this office with Dickie, Johnny, and Bob going over Johnny's case, was a godsend, but not only a godsend for her, giving her some extra time with her husband, but for the hospital too. They hired her back under her maiden name, Lucille Proctor.

Charlie throws Lucy shifts when he can. The problem is the shifts come and go: two one week, four the next, and none the week after. That's not enough because her bills come on the first and middle of the month like clockwork, not here and there.

The only places she can find steady employment are in the food industry. They don't seem to care who she is because half the kitchen staff are felons, which is fine by Lucy; they seem more honest than the hospital director and the board. But working in food, when she had a promising career before she met Johnny, is demeaning and a step backward. Now, she asks people what they'd like on their bagels. It's not the same thing as shooting them with radiation.

Lucy met Johnny at the hospital. He was a detective and worked in a Street Crimes Unit (SIU). Johnny called himself an aggressive detective, explained how SIU works cases, and took it to the bad guys by serving warrants and doing drug buys. Johnny was at the hospital because they had arrested a guy for a gun charge; he resisted and got banged up on the car hood. Maybe that's true. At the time, Johnny had joked about how they got pancakes after the arrest, so who knows? Johnny brought the bad guy in for an X-ray. Lucy did the X-ray. Johnny was the most charming man she'd ever met. He was married then, so she should have known he wasn't the most honest man. But that was before the scandal—dirty cops, crooked cops, disgraces to their uniform, the whole lot of them, but not Johnny. He just wanted to be part of the boys. Well, look where that got him. A year out from retirement, he was newly married to his third wife, Lucy, and is now spending the next twenty years of his life behind bars.

Lucy met Dickie through Johnny. During the court case, Johnny hired Dickie to represent him because Dickie had done so with Johnny's divorce. Dickie was adept at handling Johnny's other wives. So, Johnny trusted him and had Dickie on retainer. Johnny didn't trust anybody else to represent his interests. Johnny always considered Dickie a friend, even going so far as to have him over to the house.

This is why Lucy hired Dickie; she thought it would be easier coming from him, her intention for a divorce. She never intended to hire him for the divorce if Johnny wanted to fight it; she'll do Johnny that courtesy and let Johnny be with Dickie. But she thought it would soften the blow.

While Dickie goes through all the pomp and circumstance of opening the bottle of wine, Lucy's mind turns over everything that's come before and what will come next. Finally, she says, "Did you serve the papers?"

Dickie hesitates before answering. "I was going to, that's why I was going out there, but seeing him in the infirmary—I didn't have the heart."

"No, I suppose that would be considered cruel."

Dickie turns and hands her the glass. She swirls the glass and sips it.

"I did speak with him..." Dickie pauses to consider his words. "Have you discussed this with him?"

No, she hasn't, but she doesn't tell Dickie that. There's no reason the man should know more about her marriage than she has already offered. Besides, if Johnny did choose to contest the divorce, she didn't want to give Dickie any ammunition he could use against her, and ammunition is precisely what he would use. Dickie's morals, or code of ethics, is that of a trial attorney, which is just a fancy way of saying, because Dickie has, on many occasions, *by any means necessary*.

Lucy says, "When he was first arrested."

But that's all she says.

Johnny had begged her to divorce him. He said it would be better that way. He told her what the papers said wasn't true, not all of it. Okay, some of it was true, but she would hear a bunch of nasty things he and his friends supposedly did... and most of it was not true.

"Terrible deal," Dickie says with regret. He looks away, purposely avoiding her gaze. "I advised him to stay in town. I told him if he went to Costa Rica—"

"I never wanted to live down there," Lucy says. "He was obsessed with the idea. He came to me and said he'd love to retire down there and have a coastal place and talked about some island that looked like a monkey... on the one visit he took me, the island looked like a gorilla head, but they call it monkey island... We were on this boat, drinking wine." She holds up her glass and inspects it. "He pointed to a cliff near the horizon. The sky was so beautiful. The sun was blazing yellow, dipping into the water, bisected by the ocean, the clouds running from purple to pink to white, beautiful, and he says, 'Lucy, you see that right up there where the pickup is parked, that's going to be our new home.' I thought he meant the pickup, but he had to clarify. I then asked him who had parked the pickup there. He told me when he left me at the resort we were staying at, Sandy Shores, he went to park the pickup so he could show it to me... He said he was marking the spot... the whole trip was foreplay for that moment... except earlier in the day, he said he'd left to pick up a gift and gave me a gold watch."

Lucy pauses to touch the watch on her wrist.

"This watch," she says. "The whole thing with the pickup, the house, was the whole reason for that trip. He wanted me to give up everything here to go live there, telling me they had hospitals and were the most stable democracy in the region."

"And what did you say?"

"I said I liked being American," she says. "I wasn't sure I was ready to stop being American... it has a pretty good democracy, too."

Lucy finishes the drink.

She says, "I asked him, 'Did you rent that truck?' He told me he bought it. I asked him when he bought a truck and why did he buy a truck. He said he'd owned it for over a year. I didn't know that. I didn't know he'd been going to Costa Rica when he would take off for weeks. All he told me was it was for work. I don't know what he was thinking—living down there."

"So, you knew about the house?"

Lucy nods. "That's how I found out about the house, that one trip. I knew about it from then on. I don't know if I approved it, but I knew about it. I still don't think I like it. It's still down there, paid for, and sitting empty."

She doesn't know what to do with the house. She supposes she needs to visit it. Maybe enlist some locals to sell it, but doing so means facing the truth. Sure, she can sit in any potential employer's office to tell them how she didn't know, wasn't involved, and wants to move on with her life, but none of that is facing the truth. It is the opposite. It is distancing herself from it.

"Have you been back since?"

Lucy looks at Dickie—stares. "He got arrested the moment we got back, right after getting off the plane."

That's the truth she doesn't want to face—the past.

Dickie probes further, displaying his *any-means-necessary* nature. "So that's a no?"

"That's a no," she says. "When he was arrested at the airport, Johnny yelled at the marshals, telling them, 'I want to take the deal,' but the guy he'd been dealing with, checking in with and all, told him as he put the cuffs on him right there in the terminal in front of all the other passengers that the deal was off the table. Said someone else took it. The deal, that is. He had to clarify that for Johnny right there and then. Course, we didn't know it was Craig Jentsch who took it until the trial."

Dickie sighs and shakes his head as if the thought of the memory troubled him too. "That's why I told him not to go to Costa Rica."

Dickie shakes his head some more as he sits back down. He picks up the pen from the legal pad, ready for work.

"I said, if you go to Costa Rica, even to think about their offer, they'll find someone else, and then you're going to be left out in the cold."

"What'd he say?" she asks.

"He said he needed to get down there to check on his property, show it to you," Dickie says, stressing the last word, *you*, to add some weight to his feeble attempt at controlling his client as if everything that happened and has happened was her fault. "He said he planned that trip for months and didn't want you worrying about things. He wanted one last moment with you before the lid blew off everything. I was surprised they let him leave the country, but he told the AUSA that he would be back. Still, I can't believe they let him go."

Dickie breathes in through his nostril, making a whistling noise. He shuffles in the seat before he asks his next question.

"I have to ask, just between you and I, you didn't know about the investigation?"

Lucy shakes her head. "No, I didn't know... I should have known, but I didn't. He was distracted the whole trip. I don't know what he was thinking. I would have taken the deal, not gone down there."

Dickie lifts a page of the legal pad and reviews his hand-written notes, which are upside down and, from where Lucy's sitting, look like chicken scratch. Dickie returns to the original topic of conversation. "The prison did let me meet briefly with him."

"Did they?"

Dickie nods. "He asked me to hand you a tape."

"What tape?" Lucy asks.

"That was my question as well."

"So, you don't know about the tape?"

"I didn't, but now I do. That's what he wanted to tell me."

She considers her interest piqued. "Where's the tape? What's on the tape?"

Dickie reviews his notes silently, sighs again—something he's good at—and says, "That's the thing, I'm not sure. He said there's a key, a safety deposit key, and that key goes to another box, and in that box is a tape he made for you."

"Made for me?"

Lucy doesn't understand. This is the first she's heard about some safe deposit box or some tape, and she thought Johnny had told her everything. That's what she made him promise when he begged her to leave him two years ago. The condition she placed on him then was the whole God's-honest-truth. Something he supposedly fulfilled. It was the only reason she hadn't left him then, because he said he'd told her everything or was in the process of telling her everything, including things he wasn't charged with and what he was found guilty of. At the time, she was disgusted at what Johnny had allowed to happen, that he was a witness or party to, but at the same time, that type of intimate honesty is admirable, and it bought him two more years with her.

It's everyone else trying to get her to look at the truth that's finally worn her down.

Now, there's this tape?

Dickie reaches into his pants pocket and withdraws a key. He sets the key on the conference table and slides it to Lucy.

"He made me get this key from a PO box I didn't know about. Did you know about a PO box?"

Lucy shakes her head again. "I guess there's a lot I didn't know."

"I don't like playing these games with my clients. Typically, I don't like discovering hidden assets, but Johnny and I have known each other for a long time. The key to the box that contained this key was hidden in the paper-weight he bought me; he knew I wouldn't throw it away because of the embedded coin, which was recovered from Abraham Lincoln's person after his death, affixed to the top of the box. Johnny hid the key inside the box. I didn't know it opened. He told me how to open it."

Lucy accepts the key, which is still warm from being in Dickie's pocket, but is not sure what to make of the rest of Dickie's story. She remembered Johnny buying the little wooden box with the dinky-looking coin and how he promised it was an investment in their future. He told her he wanted to thank Dickie and Bob, who had another gift, which makes Lucy wonder if there's something to that one, too, for their vigorous defense.

"This key's for me?" she says. "Why did he want me to have it? What's on the tape?"

Dickie consults his notes. He says, "A contingency if they got to him."

"If who got to him?"

"He didn't say."

"Where's the box?"

"He didn't say," Dickie says. "Although, he did say you would know his favorite bank and that if I handed you *that* key, you'd know where to go. So where is that?"

National Federal Bank of Oklahoma, NFBO. Johnny has had an account with them since he was sixteen. His stepmom opened it as a goodwill gesture when she married Johnny's father.

But Lucy doesn't tell Dickie.

Looking up from the key in her hand, she asks, "Did he say what was on the tape?"

"He didn't say."

"Did he tell you why he wanted me to have it now?"

"I don't understand."

"Why now, after two years? Wouldn't something like this be important when he first went to prison?"

"I do not know."

"What do you know? Did he tell you why he wanted me to have it?"

Dickie says, "Because you're his wife and you should be taken care of."

"Taken care of?" she says. "What's that mean?"

"He didn't say."

"Well, what did he say?"

"He loves you," Dickie says.

Lucy is quiet for a long time as she digests her husband's recent revelation and how it fits in with her plans. She slips the key into her purse and clarifies, "So, you didn't deliver the divorce papers?"

CHAPTER 3:

MORRIS WOODFORD STANDS IN TOM Cooper's real estate office wearing a white wife-beater with black and gold suspenders and black slacks, pacing back and forth in front of Tom Cooper's desk. Morris goes by Woody. His dress shirt and jacket hang on Cooper's closet door on a wooden hanger to avoid wrinkles. Also in the room, the attorney Dickie Johnson, wearing one of his many shitty golfing outfits, sits in one of Cooper's chairs drinking Cooper's whiskey—Bulleit to be exact; Woody already downed his—acting as if he belongs in a room with Woody and Cooper.

Dickie doesn't.

"So let me get this straight," Woody says, mid-step, "she didn't tell you where the box was?" Woody adjusts the suspenders by pulling his thumbs on the straps at the shoulders.

Since he got out of the joint, Woody's been Cooper's driver. Cooper owns a series of apartment complexes, which he manages with an iron fist. That iron fist is Woody. Cooper cares about a lot of things; he can be pretty partic-ular. One of those things is looking nice. He makes Woody wear a suit, but Woody doesn't, won't, and refuses to wear a tie. Not even a clip-on. He refused to wear a tie during and after his trial—even though his attorney didn't care and made him wear one anyway—because dressing in a jail cell with the guards watching him was humiliating, especially when he had to have his attorney tie his tie on the first court appearance because he never learned.

Tying the tie for an unhappy Woody, the attorney said, "Jesus Christ, you never appeared in court?"

Woody said, "I'm appearing now."

The attorney said, "Not now, dimwit, I meant to testify."

Woody shot back at him, "I'm not a rat."

But the attorney shook his head. "I'm not talking about that type of testimony; I meant for any cases in which you worked."

Woody said, "I never wore a suit to court, a black leather jacket with a polo and some slacks. Had so many different colors of polos it was like I was the Easter Bunny. Suits were for church, and I don't even wear one with my ma."

The attorney said, "Well, after today, I'm getting you a clip-on."

Woody said, "If you make me wear a clip-on tie, then you'll have to figure out how to unclip it from your balls." He told the attorney he'd never wear a tie again. The attorney told him that's something he won't have to worry about if he goes to prison.

So, now out of prison, Woody wears a suit to work, although modified to fit his persona—no tie. This is a frequent point of contention with Cooper, one he eventually lets go of—Cooper, not Woody.

For Woody, it was good to be back among friends. The two years behind bars were long and lonely—Woody spent most of it in protective custody or solitary confinement for fighting. The time turned the temples of his once-prized jet-black hair snow-white, giving him these wings that most people assume are dyed. They aren't, or at least he isn't going to admit it to anyone and let them live.

When Woody got out of prison, Cooper was there waiting for him outside, standing in the bright sun with the really freaking green trees around him. Of course, the trees could have been regular green trees, but not seeing any green for two years heightens one's color perception; it's like not getting to see for a long time, and then suddenly, he could. Cooper looked at him and said, "What, are you letting a skunk live on your head now—or is it supposed to remind me of a badger?" Which he followed up with, "Seriously, you aren't worried Pepe Le Pew's going to try to ass-rape you?"

Per the agreement, and for being a stand-up guy, Cooper set Woody back up in life, helping him get back on his feet and access most of the money he squirreled away or *skunked,* as Cooper now says, the money the government didn't get their grubby little hands on, giving Woody his rundown apartment complex to manage. Except Woody lives in one of the lovely apartments, works as security and landlord, and has free rein of the workout facility, which he puts to good use, and no one seems ever to use but him. That's fine. Being alone's something he got used to on the inside. What he got sick of on the inside was the body-weight bullshit only available in prison, and he was happy to see a full-weight rack.

Woody's apartments may not be the best in Cooper's stable, but Woody selected some of the best weights and equipment Cooper was willing to buy to stock *his* workout room.

Now in the office located downtown off Denver, and not too far from Dickie's office—Cooper's building used to be an Abstract company—Dickie looks from Coop, who motions for him to answer, then back to Woody, and then shakes his head. Dickie says, "No, she didn't say."

"That was your one job," Woody says. "You were to find out where the key goes, meaning—I guess I'm going to have to fucking spell it out for you—which bank."

A day ago, Dickie had called Cooper in a panic, telling Cooper he might know where the missing moola was— the moola Johnny had hidden from the rest of the group. Dickie told Cooper about the safe deposit key but said he didn't know what bank it went to. Cooper asked Dickie to get the wife to tell him. Expressed to him that they needed to recover the shit Johnny stashed but neglected to tell anyone where he stashed it. When Cooper asked Johnny about the money, right before Johnny went away, Johnny called it his insurance, but Woody figured it was because after it was all said and done, Johnny got screwed over. So, Cooper let it and him go.

But hearing Cooper on the phone with Dickie, Woody disagreed with the plan, reminding Cooper about what they did to Johnny, saying, "Every group has to have a fall guy." Woody asked Cooper, "What if the wife doesn't say?" Cooper said they should play it slow; trust Dickie. He's come through in the past. Woody said, "When was that?" Cooper said, "You saw what he did for you with Johnny; you better be happy it's his ass sitting in prison for another twenty years and not you. You got eight, eight years is all; you've only had to serve two—that's doing something for you."

Woody didn't say to Cooper then that Craig "the Wrench" Jentsch made sure Johnny got more time, painting the whole enterprise as not Woody's idea, although in a way it started that way, but as Johnny's. Woody then agreed with the AUSA to knock some time off his sentence. Still, two years is two years. All of it as a cop. It's not easy time.

Now, staring at the two men, eyes hidden behind bifocal lenses perched on the edge of his nose, Cooper has the top button of his yellow dress shirt unbuttoned, his tie loosened, and in one hand, grasps a cigar while, in the other, a glass of whiskey. Cooper's face darkens as he thinks everything over for a moment, doing that thing where he drops his chin, giving himself double chins or more. In Woody's mind, the whole scene—Cooper, the look, everything—reminds him of Winston Churchill, Cooper's favorite.

Cooper points the cigar at Dickie. He says, "You did give her the key, right?"

"I gave her the key," Dickie says. "I didn't know Johnny had a PO box."

"You couldn't give us that key first?" Woody says. "Jesus, if we had it, we could have figured out what bank it went to, but now, we must rely on her."

Coop tilts his head up to look at Woody. "What would you have done?"

Woody places an arm out on the bookshelf to prop himself up.

Cooper says, "Get your dirty hands off the shelf."

Woody drops his arm to his side.

Cooper goes back to what he was saying. "Would you go to every bank, hold the key up, and ask them if this key went to their vault?"

That's precisely what Woody would have done.

Woody says, "Look, we—and by that, I mean you and I, not that shit stick—used to be trained investigators."

They were police officers, highly trained, highly dedicated, and highly underpaid. When Cooper approached them, offering membership into the fraternal brotherhood of The Brass, Woody jumped at the opportunity.

Woody says, "We could have found that box had Dickie Boy come to us sooner. But he didn't."

"No, he didn't." Cooper levels his gaze at Dickie. "I'm still struggling with this part of the story."

Dickie shrugs. "What was I supposed to do? I'm bound to some ethical considerations here. I didn't know Johnny had the PO box. He never said nothing. Lucy never said nothing. I knew nothing about it."

"What would he have said?" Woody says, aggravated with the attorney's blah attitude. "Hey, there's a tape in a safety deposit box. It's got all my dirty little secrets on it. I left it to my slut. Go fuck yourself."

Cooper snaps to get Dickie's attention, pulling Dickie's eyes from Woody to Cooper. "Do we know what's on this tape?"

Dickie shakes his head. "*Apparently*, Erin's dad did the tape. He's dead now. Erin doesn't know anything about it. She said she'd check his notes—the guy took prodigious notes."

"Oh, I bet you asked her about it when you were done letting her peg you in bed," Woody says.

Cooper sets the glass down. "Woody, control yourself."

But Dickie engages. "I don't get pegged... wait, what is that?"

"Where you like to take it up the ass, woman controlling everything," Woody says, smiling. "Where she wears a prodigious dildo to fuck, and goes in nice and smooth, cuz you're greased up all the damn time from the preparation H you apply to your asshole for them dingleberries causing you problems... No, you know what, I bet you don't have to even use any lube... you get wet just thinking about it. Like a squid shooting ink. You like that, you sick fuck, don't you?"

"Woody," Cooper says again, trying to regain control of the conversation, but it's clear to Woody he's gotten under the shit lawyer's skin.

"Isn't that more your thing?" Dickie says, giving Woody some attitude. "Seeing you're the one who went to prison."

"If this wasn't my boss's office, I would beat the shit out of you, but Coop doesn't like any violence happening around him. He says he got through all that kid stuff when he rose through the ranks, and he doesn't need to be connected to anything unsavory no more."

Almost absently, Cooper, resigning to letting the attitudes play out, banking on them fizzling, reminds Woody, "This is why I hired you, so I don't have to get involved."

Woody throws a thumb at his chest and stares daggers at Dickie. "You better start showing me some respect, you fuck head; I'm the reason you have that home in Vale."

"Calm down, Morris." Cooper leans back in the high-back leather chair, a deep maroon. He crosses his hands over his chest.

But Woody isn't calm, far from it. The money Johnny squirreled away—for his insurance—should have been

Woody's money. He's not going to lose two years of his life for nothing.

Woody points a finger at Cooper. "Don't tell me what to do."

Cooper cants his head to the side. "What do you mean, *'don't tell you what to do'*? That's my job," he says, volume raising some. "What are you going to do about it if I do? You're a two-bit fuck, and I'm still an upstanding citizen of this great community." Cooper glances at Dickie. "So is Dickie, but you, you went to prison because you couldn't be bothered to wear a goddamn ski mask on your last operation. Like I told you to do. Had you shown just a little consideration, some fucking forethought, none of this would be an issue."

Woody turns around to face the bookshelf and a bunch of leather-backed spines that appear to have never been opened. Not one of them is broken or creased. Cooper reads, but not these books. Woody wants to shake the shelves, knock all the books off, and let them fall on the floor. He shoves both hands into his pockets and rocks on his heels. He shuts his eyes and counts to ten before saying in a softer voice, "It's not my freaking fault there was an undercover in the room."

"It is your fault," Cooper says without pause. "You were supposed to deconflict your operations with the rest of the department so nothing like what happened would happen. You didn't. It happened."

They've had this argument many times since Woody was released from federal custody in the last six months.

"Now we are two years down the line and have an opportunity here. We couldn't just kill Johnny; I wanted the money back, and I knew we could wait him out. Well, here we are. Someone's gone and delivered us a chance. I don't want to lose it. Not after your list of fuck ups."

"Yeah, well," Woody says, turning. "I made a mistake."

"One that cost you," Dickie says.

"Years," Cooper adds. "Years, you cost us all years. I was expecting my cut to set some things up…" Cooper pauses mid-thought and looks at Dickie. "How much of what happened did Johnny Boy discuss with you?"

"Privileged information," Dickie says, looking smug. "I can't tell you even if I wanted to."

"Do you want to?" is all Cooper asks.

"Fuck this," Woody says. He can't take it anymore. The guy's like ten steps away, sipping on his boss's alcohol, and he won't even show an ounce of respect.

Woody jumps across the room in two strides, coming on him like a freight train, and grabs Dickie by his throat before Cooper can intervene.

Woody lifts Dickie from the chair, squeezing, spilling what's left of Dickie's drink, and growls, "You stupid bastard, you don't get no privileged information in this office. When the big man asks you a fucking question, you answer his fucking question."

Cooper, trying to usher some calm into the room, says, "Morris," not raising his voice. He uses Woody's real name, and Woody realizes he's overstepped, but Woody isn't listening.

Woody brings Dickie's beady little fucking eyes closer and stares right into them, his breath hot as it bounces back into his face off Dickie's cheek. "If you don't answer the fucking question, then I'm going to fuck you up."

"*Morris,*" Cooper says again.

"And if that don't knock some sense into you, then I'm going to take you out back and put a fucking bullet into your brain."

"MORRIS!" Cooper yells, half-standing, pounding the desk. Hands flat on the desk. The little golden trinkets on Cooper's desk that Woody plays with while Cooper makes his phone calls rattle with reverb from the blow.

Woody, with one hand on Dickie's throat, skin to skin, and the other wrapped around Dickie's collar, tugging him out of the chair, closer to him, pauses. He turns his head toward Cooper. "What?"

"Put the counselor down," Cooper says, more reserved. He motions for Woody to sit in the other chair. "We pay good money for him and his associates' services. I need you to put him down."

Woody glowers at Dickie.

Cooper adds, "Unharmed."

Woody shifts the glare to Cooper and then relents. He pushes Dickie back in the chair.

"Sit," Cooper commands.

Woody challenges him by not sitting.

"Sit, Morris," Cooper says.

"You say that like I'm your fucking attack dog," Woody says, still not sitting. "I'm not a dog."

"You're my dog," Cooper corrects. "Now be a good boy and sit the fuck down so we can figure out how to fix this situation." After a beat, Cooper adds, "I'm not inclined to ask you again."

Woody stays standing.

Cooper sighs and removes his glasses. He tosses them on the desk and rubs the bridge of his nose. "If I have to tell you to sit one more time, I'm going to fire you, and when I say fire, what I mean is you're going back to prison, seeing working is a condition of your supervised parole, and when you get there, you can look forward to one of the many men you put away behind bars or guys sympathetic to those that you put away behind bars, coming for you the same way they got Johnny. Now sit the fuck down."

Woody stares at Cooper slightly longer, considering how far he can push the situation.

Woody asks, "Can I get a fucking drink first?"

Cooper sighs. "Sure, get a drink first, but then sit the fuck down and shut up."

Woody steps to Cooper's desk, picks up the bottle of Bullet whiskey, and pours some into his glass.

Woody offers it to Dickie. "You want some?"

Dickie looks at him curiously as Cooper starts to say something.

But Woody adds, "Considering I spilled your drink, you want a refill?"

And when Dickie doesn't respond quickly enough.

Woody says, "I'm trying to be fucking nice here and fix you a fucking drink. Say yes, you fucking faggot."

Dickie doesn't move. Doesn't speak.

So Woody snatches Dickie's drink glass out of his hand, refills it, and shoves it right back in that same hand. "Now, here you go. Are you happy?"

Dickie doesn't say anything.

Almost sing-song, Cooper says, "Morris."

Woody flips Dickie off as he sits down in the chair next to him. Woody crosses a leg over his knee and sips his drink.

"Now, counselor," Cooper says, relaxing back into the high back. "What do you think we should do next?"

Dickie sips his drink, side-eyeing Woody, giving him a full helping of an eye.

Dickie gulps once. "I think someone should go talk to Lucy," he says. "Maybe a friendly face. See if that person can get her to tell them what bank Johnny would've used."

CHAPTER 4:

ERIN MOORCOCK SADDLES UP TO THE bar next to Craig Jentsch, wearing red flannel over blue jeans. Erin has dark, chestnut-colored hair with blonde highlights, bobbed at an angle to hide her one flaw or what she considers her flaw, a long-repaired cleft lip, giving her a Joaquin Phoenix-like grin, which is more attractive than most men let on or expect at first glance. She still wears court attire: a salmon-colored blouse under a black blazer, a black skirt, and pale pink heels. The shoes announced her presence.

Hearing her coming, Craig acknowledges Erin, half turning his head and lifting his hand. He says, "I don't want to hear it."

He sits hunched over at the bar, drinking a beer from a bucket of beers. Three unopened Bud Lights are in the ice bucket, and two empties are turned over on the bar—the sixth in his hands.

Erin drops her purse on the bar, which plops with a dense thud. The bag is black and as large as her torso, which doesn't say much.

"You don't call," she says. "You should call."

They, other cops, and now everyone else and their dog call him the Wrench and have for many years. Erin's asked Craig about it, but Craig doesn't talk much. He tells her he doesn't like how he got the name. Now that he's been on national television, it's become a water cooler topic of conversation. People are asking, "Why do they call you the Wrench?"

When Craig appeared on her morning show, Kelly Rippa did it once. Grinning, acting humble, he told her, "It's just a nickname... Do we ever really know where nicknames come from? It's not like I gave it to myself. I guess you'd have to ask the guy who gave it to me."

Kelly Ripa didn't like that answer. No one did. But it shows you can't control what it reveals when you spotlight yourself.

Craig's learning, learning that the hard way, and judging by his look at the bar, he's not taking the lessons too well.

Erin settles on her seat and orders a Crown and Coke. She kicks off her pumps and bends over to pick them off the floor while the bartender makes her drink. The bartender sets the drink down on the bar next to her purse. Erin puts the shoes on top of the bar next to the glass. The bartender raises an eyebrow, and Erin gives him a look. The bartender shrugs and moves away to the next customer.

Then Erin withdraws a pair of black flats from the purse and bends to slip them on her feet.

She asked Craig to meet her, and he suggested Gold's Bar. Gold's is across the street from a strip club, named after a type of pubic region haircut she once tried out before going bald out of frustration—she didn't like the look. *When she showed the new look to Dickie, the night she tried it out, he said, "What the hell happened to all... where'd it all go?" Erin spread her legs and played with herself for him, putting on a show, not that it would amount to much. Most of the time, Dickie gets too drunk to be of any use. But that night, she'd counted his drinks and figured she might as well give it a shot. He said, "I thought you were going to leave just a strip... it's all gone... you look like a teen—you got nothing!" Erin said, "I figured if I was going to go all that way and leave just a strip, I might as well go all the way."*

Which might as well be Erin's mantra.

Later, when she showed Craig, he liked the new look. He said it helped when he was down there. Said his nose hair didn't get so tickled, intermingling with her hair. Easier to breathe, too. But all of that was before Craig went and got famous, or as close to famous as a veteran cop can get.

Erin knows from many post-coitus conversations: Craig likes Gold's because it is across the street from the strip club, and Craig spent a lot of time working with informants who happen to be strippers. He said it's easier to be in here, "drinking," putting the word in air quotes, than trying to meet them someplace or be covert about it. He said, here, they can come, saddle up to the bar, like Erin just did, and talk to him, all while on their break or at the end of the night, and no one would be the wiser.

Not that Craig has ever tried to disguise his Richard Gere good looks. Tall, slim, with sinew so tight it pops and rolls under his skin when he moves, chiseled jaw with a premature gray head of hair, all give Craig the appearance of someone who should be in Hollywood. But that was before Craig went to Hollywood and dated a pop star. Craig's not a cop now if he ever was. Craig's freshly retired or "released," as he jokes. He's a TV star. Except he's not that and not retired, which is the joke. He is currently on a leave of absence as the department tries to figure out what they will do with him. The publicity they receive from his show's too good to straight out fire him, and Craig's too close to retirement to walk away when there's money on the table. So, the city and he worked out an agreement, one Erin arranged, that benefits all involved and allows Craig to appear on TV without repercussions from the city. So once Tulsa stopped participating in that *one* show, the Wrench didn't. He started flying out to New York, hosted, and worked his charm so much on the small screen that he was eventually given a program. It ran for one season and was a smash hit. Then, a man got killed in Minneapolis, and then a whole helluva lot happened nationwide for years, and Craig's flavor expired. Right now, the first program won't happen, and they placed the other show on hiatus, too, so no hosting.

Craig is back in town and drinks here for comfort, familiarity, and the "good-times'" sake—his words. Erin thinks it's because he's an idiot, the smartest one she knows, but still an idiot. She tells him all he does is feel miserable, thinking about what could have been versus what could still be.

Settled in her seat after slipping the flats on, Erin asks Craig, "Why do you still come to this shithole? There are so many better places you could go to drink."

Craig doesn't look her way as he answers her. "No one acts as if they recognize me."

"It's a bunch of old-timers; how do they not recognize you? All they do is watch TV," she says. And then she adds, "Knowing most old people around here, there is no way these Fox News-loving, Donald Trump-voting people don't watch the type of show you starred on as a cop. How do they not recognize you? You were a fan favorite."

"Until the dickweed of a mayor canceled us because he didn't like the perception it gave the city. The network wants to use me on another show, but I don't know."

Erin knows it's a sore subject, but it's a joke, anyway. "Is it canceled? I thought you were on a break?"

Craig doesn't dignify the jab with an answer.

Then he adds, "Usually, a break this long is labeled as a sabbatical."

Erin says, "You know the media said the mayor didn't like the show 'cause it showed you only going after black people. If you and your team decided to arrest other colors, it might go a long way to salvaging what you have."

"Gang bangers," Craig corrects her. "It was the gang unit. That's what we are supposed to combat. Not my fault most of the gangs hang out north of Admiral."

"You didn't see you all terrorizing the nice white wanna-be black boys in South Tulsa; no, you all liked rolling around with the cameras in North Tulsa."

"That's where the crime is."

"In North Tulsa? There isn't crime anywhere else in the city?"

Craig ignores the dig. "I have a theory," he says. "I think it has to do with the lack of supermarkets. It's all the processed foods. If the South were a food desert, you'd also start getting crime. All they have up north is Dollar Trees—"

"Isn't crime *down there* too?"

"—and Dollar Generals, but those aren't grocery stores. I think fresh produce is important."

"I do, too," Erin says, not knowing where he's going with this and not believing his bullshit, but Erin doesn't care about where the crime is as long as there is crime. There is no other way for a defense attorney to make money than to defend people accused of committing crimes.

"I think people need to be cops to understand cops."

"I think that type of thinking is why you don't have a show," she says. "Still, I'd expect…"

She looks around the room. A group of three older men is seated at the bar, wearing clothes two sizes too big, all neutral colors. Two of the three wear hats with different wars on them. A raggedy older woman sits in the corner with what Erin can only assume is her daughter and her daughter's friend, both good-looking but quickly pickling themselves to catch up to their chaperone. Some younger people play pool on the far end, near the jukebox, laughing and smiling.

Erin forgot what she was going to say. She says, "This place reminds me of the Elks Lodge when my father was a member. I still remember when the elder Moorcock would take his lovely, horribly coveted daughter by these lecherous old men, *me*, to the lodge to hustle the old guys in pool… Let me tell you, I've thrown up in those sinks a time too many. But I'm surprised the Gilf Parade over there isn't throwing themselves at you—or at least unrolling a titty to get an autograph—you have a sharpie?"

Craig shakes his head. "If they recognize me, they know better than to say anything," he says, responding to Erin's previous thought, picking it back up; he was always good at figuring out what she was thinking, even if she moved on.

Erin says, "I guess I can't argue with that. I once heard Johnny Depp liked to walk the streets of Paris because no one bothered him, and if they did, they didn't say anything to him."

"You see him lately? He looks like a meth head."

"Doesn't mean people recognize him on the streets."

Craig swigs the Bud Light bottle. "Why should I call you?" he says, returning to her opening. "All you ever do is bust my balls."

Erin tugs at her purse, slipping her hand inside to dig out a pack of cigarettes, and then searches the bag for the lighter, mumbling to herself, "I can never find my fucking lighter."

Erin notices Craig watching her from the corner of his eye. He says, "Maybe you should get a smaller purse."

Frustrated with the elusive lighter, Erin snorts. "But I can't carry my stuff around if I don't have a bigger purse. I need most of what's in here."

"What about the other stuff that's in there?"

"The other stuff is the stuff I want. Not need."

Craig drinks more of the beer, finishing it off. He turns the bottle over and sets it next to the other three. He reaches into the bucket, fishes out a fresh one, undoes the cap, and drinks it while saying, "Yeah, but if you carry everything you want ... and need ... and can't find what it is you want in a moment, at your fingertips, what's the point?"

Craig's tone could be better.

"I understand; you're upset about the TV gig. In today's environment—"

"When are you going to leave Dickie?"

So, he's not upset about the TV gig. Or that's just Craig's weak attempt to change the subject. That's okay; she'll come back to it.

"I'm sorry. I wasn't aware I was on a timeline," Erin says.

"I'm not saying there's a timeline; I'm just saying, we've fooled around for what... years now?"

"Two years, to be exact," she says.

It started when Erin represented Craig in the corruption trials. Craig's participation in the prosecution was conditional on his name staying out of the paper. If his name found its way into the paper, he wasn't testifying. The government could try to make its case without him, which wasn't possible. Sure, they'd get something on the guys, but not what the government wanted.

Craig says, "I say it's about time you leave him and come be with me."

"And just what would we do?" Erin finds her lighter. "And you haven't exactly been available yourself."

"Don't," he says, flicking fingers her way without lifting his hand.

Erin bites her tongue. "Don't what?"

"You're going to talk about the show, and I don't want to talk about the show anymore. That's all anyone ever wants to talk about."

Erin makes a baby "wah" noise and mock rubs her left cheek with a fist. "What, are your feelings hurt now?" she says. "And no, I wouldn't talk about the show anymore. I was going to say you were dating that pop star."

"Erin," Craig says. He sounds so severe.

She doesn't like severe. He's in it now, whether he knows it or not.

Erin asks, "Did she discover why they call you the Wrench?"

Craig doesn't respond.

"Did she think it was because of that thing in your pants? Because I want to know why, so you know. I want to know the story."

"It's not because of the thing in my pants."

"Are you going to tell me why you're called the Wrench, then? Confirm what I've heard."

His supposed friend, Woody, told her a story. Maybe Woody told her to scare her. Maybe Woody told her so she acted right and treated everything with the correct level of seriousness; Woody thought she needed to hear the scary tale, but Woody's a thug in her mind. Nothing more. Nothing less. Certainly not someone credible. Besides, she can't see Craig doing the things Woody said he did to earn the nickname. That's not the Craig she knows.

Craig shifts in the seat. Erin catches him glancing at her in the mirrored backstop. "No, I am not," he says.

Erin nods and tries to lighten the mood. "It's the thing in your pants; you're just too humble."

Craig doesn't do light, not after the pop star and the implosion of his career. "Erin, it's not the—"

"Well, it should be," Erin says before pausing to jam a cigarette in her mouth to light it and shut him up. "No, you were dating that girl... what's her name?" Erin thumbs the wheel on the lighter. Nothing happens. "You know who I'm talking about, that bitch."

Craig says, "We don't have to mention her name."

Erin tries the lighter again, rolling the tip of her finger across the cog, this time some sparks. She wants to make him say it. "She took you to award shows and everything. The press covered you like you were a regular Bennifer."

Craig sets the bottle down and turns on the stool. "We weren't a Bennifer. We weren't nothing; we never had a cute name."

Erin glances at Craig. "I take it the tabloids didn't care much about your breakup. She dumped the cop, good riddance. In this atmosphere, this country at this time, it was just a matter of time. Cops, who needs them? Bunch of nobodies is what they are, can only bring down cheap bimbo, badge bunnies—that's what they're called, right?"

"Erin," Craig says, "you're starting to do that thing where you get your way without telling me what you want."

"You know she got married, right? Lost a bunch of weight, too. It looks good on her."

"Most women do when they get married."

"Yeah, but he wrestles gators."

"You're avoiding."

The cigarette hangs out of her mouth as she speaks. "Oh, honey, I always get my way. She made a song about you." She pauses and slips the pack back into her purse, giving her thumb a break. "'Tulsa Jesus Freak', now who do you think that's about?"

Erin works the lighter's initiation wheel again, trying to get the lighter to work. The damn thing must be out of fuel.

Craig says, "I wouldn't know."

A cigarette is in her mouth, and she pauses, looking at him. "Did she date anyone else in Tulsa?"

"Not that I know of."

Erin cups the lighter with her hands. "I never took you for one of those kinds."

"And what kind would that be?"

Erin looks up at him with the cigarette dangling from her mouth. "A Jesus Freak."

Craig removes the lighter from her hands and motions for her to come closer. "I'm not a freak, per se, I just… with what happened… I feel like I have a second chance at life. Ever since I met you, the trial, things have been going nicely for me."

Erin leans in; Craig flicks the wheel with his thumb once, sparking and lighting the flame. He meets her halfway and lights her cigarette.

"Until now," she says. "It's funny how things can change in a moment … or with the flick of a wheel."

"I don't want to talk about the show."

"You don't want to talk about the show, though; get over it, I do," she says. "*And why do you want to talk about the show, Erin?*"

"Erin, stop."

She acts innocent. "Stop what?"

"I know I owe you," he says. "I thought if we were together—"

"You wouldn't have to pay me?"

"I am working on it," he says. "I've been making my payments."

"But how much were you making on the show?"

"Enough to live, not as much as you would think."

"How do you know how much I'm thinking? Is this some new party trick? Did the hippie jazz chick teach you to read minds?"

"Erin, I'll get you the rest of the money. You know I'm good for it. I haven't missed a payment, but two hundred thousand is a lot of money."

"In legal fees," Erin says. "Don't I know it? But I would like you to settle your bill sooner rather than later. It's been two years."

"I think this is bullshit," Craig says, feeling the shakedown.

"What? I'm here shaking you down for the rest of the money you owe for me defending you or that you just filed for retirement and now have a lot of money at your fingertips."

"I did the right thing," Craig says, looking at her now. "That should count for something. Yeah, I waited. I wanted to see how things shook out and how much information they had. With Gordon getting killed, Johnny fleeing to Costa Rica only to later come back, and Woody not saying nothing, I thought I'd see where they went with it."

"But then you listened to your high-priced attorney and decided to play ball."

"Clear my conscience is what you said."

"I'm glad one of us has one." Erin breathes the smoke into her lungs. "I sure don't—but I *do* have a man who will collect my money in the most unpleasant ways. Even if it is from a man, I like to fuck."

"I'll get you the money, but things are a little tight right now," he says. "I may have a second chance at life, thank you for that, but with the show on hiatus, the other one canceled, and now I'm forced into retirement…"

"You did lie," Erin says, taking another drag and letting it out. She might as well be sticking a knife into Craig. "You can't do that and wear a badge, and if you do that like you did, you can't wear it forever; eventually, no matter how good your attorney is at fucking, and attorning, it will catch up to you. What did you expect?"

"For everything to go away, that's what immunity is."

"But it didn't."

"And then the paper found out about the Giglio because I lied and came clean. You'd think coming clean would erase the other."

Erin chuckles. "You're so naïve. It was bound to happen sooner or later. What makes you think the new chief and the mayor weren't just waiting until you hit your twenty to quietly usher you out the door by putting pressure on you? 'It's not us doing it,' they'd say. 'It's the judge. Swear, you can't testify in court or work for us. Why don't you retire and become a TV star.'"

"Stop it," he says. "I'm already feeling down."

"Then you don't want to hear why I wanted to meet with you," she says, letting the smoke out. "It's funny you mentioned immunity. You know what the condition of immunity was?"

"I tell the truth."

Even though she knows the answer, Erin says, "And did you do that?"

"Tell the truth?" Craig says. "Sure."

Erin pauses to pick up her drink. She sips it.

"Craig," she says, "don't bullshit me, okay. You told most of the truth. You told the convenient truth. You left out Tom Cooper. You left out Woody's real involvement, blaming everything on Johnny. And seeing Johnny got the brunt of the US government, I'd say you were pretty successful, but you know immunity comes with conditions. Those conditions are unconditional... I know, but it's the only word that works for me right now... you should have called me back."

"Why?"

"I mean, I like seeing you, and I want to take you out back and fuck your brains out, but you should have called me back sooner."

"Why?"

"Johnny made a tape," Erin says. "I heard about it from Dickie and then went looking for my father's notes, which I found. The problem is my father took a lot of notes, and the best I can figure out from the notes is that the tape Johnny made contradicts nearly everything you testified to, which means an argument could be made that I knew what you said wasn't true because I was my father's co-counsel. That's an ethical issue if you aren't keeping score. I could be disbarred, which means my ass is on the line here. Johnny made that tape with my father, where he admitted to everything... supposedly including where he hid the money and guns from your last score. Now, the tape, I can fight. Hard evidence, such as guns, that's a bit harder."

Erin pauses to see if Craig will say something. He doesn't.

"Now—those guns aren't going to tell a different story than what you sang for your immunity, are they? Not back up whatever Johnny said in his tape?"

CHAPTER 5:

L**AMAR HENRY STRUGGLES TO THE SUR**-face of consciousness to find himself handcuffed to a hospital bed, machines whirring and beeping around him. One whooshing as if it is breathing like Darth Vader. He awakens from his opioid-induced dreams every few hours, thinking the machine's trying to kill him. Lamar jerks the cuff with his left hand. His right hand is free. His bed is shoved in one corner of the room at an angle. Johnny Hudson lies in another bed, shoved in the opposite corner. The window on the wall behind Lamar gives him plenty of light throughout the day to sneak peeks at the goings-on in the rest of the room.

Considering the instantaneousness of his plan, this isn't the wrong place to be. It's where he hoped to be—outside the prison walls. But puncturing his lung wasn't part of the plan; although it didn't hurt to sell the idea, it did make it look good.

Lamar still can't believe he stabbed himself. Holding Johnny in his lap, telling him things like "it's going to be okay" when it wasn't going to be fucking okay—the guy bleeding all over the place, making the floor slippery, and that toothbrush lying there. He didn't think much about it. He picked it up like he was admitting to his Japanese shame, boom, shoved it in, not concerned with where except there was no one behind him to take his head off with a samurai sword—leaving the whole crime scene just two men attacked in their cell before breakfast.

And like always, inside the prison walls—any prison Lamar's been in, or neighborhoods growing up, too—no one saw anything, no one said anything, no one knew anything, which is how Lamar prefers it.

The doctors patched Lamar up all right. They said he'd be a little winded for a few days when he came to enough to open his eyes and track the penlight. Have a hard time catching his breath, but the wound could have been worse. It should heal on its own without much intervention now that they've stopped the bleeding and stitched him up. They said he could have had a drain in his side or gone septic.

Johnny, on the other hand, isn't doing so well. Not that the doctors told Lamar that. Johnny's out in the bed across from Lamar. The doctors said the worst of the wounds was a ruptured intestine, and Johnny had gone septic before the prison could get him to the hospital. The doctors explained it to the marshals who transported and guarded them. "Your bowels hold a lot of nasty stuff, and if that nasty stuff makes it into the rest of your body, then it can be deadly."

So far, two marshals have been assigned to watch them at all hours. The hospital thought, and the marshals agreed, it would be easier on the government to house both inmates in the same room; that way, the marshals only had to worry about one door and one set of nurses and doctors, which makes a sick sort of sense.

Although he's been awake for two days, Lamar lets the marshals think he's out of it like Johnny. The good part is that Lamar can hear everything the marshals say—listening to all the gossip and rumors and what will happen with him and Johnny. The worse part is watching what they want to watch on the one TV, which consists of a lot of game shows: *The Wheel of Fortune*, the *Price is Right*, *Let's Make a Deal*—fuck Wayne Brady; Lamar used to get compared to him way too often; perhaps it's the bald head and clean smile—and *Family Feud*—Steve Harvey is alright. Now, there's a smile. The other bad part is he's always thirsty, having to sneak swigs of water when the marshals aren't in the room or waking just enough when the nurses are around to take a quick drink.

But the worst thing is one of these marshals, named Rafferty, likes to shit in the room's bathroom, which wouldn't be that big of a deal, but the guy takes epic movements, most of which stink up the room to the point they burn Lamar's nose hairs. It makes his eyes water. Lamar knows his name because the last two days, the guys coming in to relieve him have asked, "What the fuck did you eat, Rafferty?"

Now, the two dayshift marshals come into the room. The night shift marshals greet the new duo, Rafferty, one of them, and then the night guys exit. All the while, Lamar plays like he is asleep, looking at everything through narrow slits.

In the room, Rafferty informs the other marshal he will step into the bathroom. The other marshal, a good-looking

Chicano, says, "I'll go get a cup of coffee; text me when you're done."

Rafferty smiles a big fat smile, bunching his rosy, puffy cheeks, and snaps the day's paper. "I'll let you know when I make it to 'Sports.'" Rafferty's wearing a tan polo over blue cargo-type pants and has a bit of a gut. Big jovial guy.

Not like the other guy. The Chicano marshal.

The other guy is someone Lamar could get to know. Judging from his style, he's a laid-back dresser dressed in a bowling shirt with a Panama hat. Lamar could drink with the Chicano marshal and hear what stories he might have to tell 'cause a guy who holds himself like this has stories to tell.

The Chicano marshal says, "Any chance you'd let me borrow the funny pages first? I don't want them once you've shit all over the place."

Rafferty clutches the paper tightly to his chest. "How would I loosen up if I'm not laughing? You don't want me to have to strain, do you? Ever heard of a hernia? Ruptured ulcer?"

"Whatever," the other man says. "Just let me know when the room airs out. I'll send Susan up to sit outside the door."

"Why are you going to torture her like that?"

"I'm not the one eating and then shitting roadkill the next day. You might need to see a doctor."

"We're in a hospital," Rafferty says. "I've seen them everywhere."

The Chicano marshal says, "Seriously, there's something wrong with your gut. It's rotted or something."

"Why do you care so much? These two aren't going anywhere," Rafferty says. "At home, I have four girls. I never get the bathroom to myself; someone's always banging on the door, telling me to let them in, or asking me to get their hairbrush. My house has six dozen hairbrushes, yet I always have to get one where it shouldn't be or where it is because they can't find the backups. Found one in the back of my truck the other day. I don't know how it got there for the life of me. Found one on the couch; I thought it was one of the four, only to find out it was my wife's. They all share them. I say, don't you know you're not supposed to do that, and my wife just looks at me and says, do what? Share their brushes. It's how lice gets spread around—happened once—not a pleasant experience, shampoos, combs, stuffed animals in plastic baggies, laundry for days, then weeks of wondering if you'll have to do it all over again. Not pleasant. And getting up off the toilet to hand a brush out the door, cracked, so they don't see man parts, isn't the worst. The worst is winning the chance to use the bathroom, and I say win because I have three shitters, and I feel like it's a battle royal to claim one. Either I have to wake up early or stay up late, but even then, it's too difficult to claim a porcelain throne, and when I do, all the banging on the door, heavy sighs, questions, and demands about taking a shower, so what am I going to do while we are on this cushy detail? I'm taking a shit."

"Every day?"

"Every goddamn day until this detail's over." Rafferty slaps the paper against the Chicano's shoulder. "My colon thanks you for your patience."

The other marshal acts like he can't believe it. "What are you doing, not shitting any other time, saving it up for this?"

"That's exactly what I'm doing; I'm relaxing," he says. "Catching up on my reading, my current events, see what's going on in the world. These guys aren't going anywhere. Let the colon clean out; be as clean as a whistle. I'll go home and pass gas during movie night, and everyone's going to ask why someone whistled in the living room. Maybe even get one kid to come running down the stairs. Yeah, that's what will happen. I'll go outside, spread my cheeks apart, let a fart out, and it'll sound like a whistle, like my mom used to do when the streetlights came on, telling me to come home, a real loud thing, where she stuck fingers in her mouth, sharp. That's what it will do: tell the kids to come running. Sound out throughout the entire neighborhood. Get them all running home."

"You're disgusting," the Chicano says.

"I'm honest," Rafferty says. "In China, they talk about digestion all the time—other places, too. Italy. France. As a nation, we're behind the times—or heathens, take your pick. In those places, this isn't a taboo subject... you know you learn a thing or two when you get up in the morning, four o'clock in the morning to be exact, to shit, shower, and shave in peace, no elbowing for the use of the sink or bathroom, no bitching or complaining about taking too long. I put in one of those tankless water heaters, so I didn't have to worry about running out of hot water. You can't believe the length of the showers these girls take."

"Well, we aren't in China, Italy, or France. Don't get too comfortable there. We're taking the punctured lung back this afternoon. That's why Susan's coming, and I'm going down to the in-house Starbucks to grab a cup of coffee."

"Why do you think I'm trying to get into the shitter now?"

"Just keep an eye on them."

"You want me to shit with the door open?"

Oh God, no, Lamar thinks.

"Just ensure they're not too long out of sight."

"Why? Where are they going to go? They're both doped up and stupid. One's this close to death." Peeking through slits, Lamar sees Rafferty hold up his index finger and thumb an inch apart. "The other not much better; sure, he's going to make it, but it's not like he's going to be winning any foot races any time soon. Even I feel like I could chase him down."

The Chicano squints at Lamar, and Lamar's heart catches in his throat for a moment. Does he see he's awake? The Chicano's eyes study his supposedly slumbering form, making Lamar feel like those little people in that movie that had the tower with the all-seeing eye his best friend in school tried to tell him was a vagina, but the Chicano shrugs.

The Chicano says, "Do you know who that one is?"

"I know who they both are," Rafferty says. "One's the dirty cop; I saw the Dateline special. Read about it in my favorite shitting magazines. The other... he's a nobody bank robber."

"He's not a nobody bank robber," the Chicano says, almost showing admiration, which brings a tear to Lamar's eye. The guy knows Lamar and speaks about how Lamar thinks about the Chicano marshal. "I was on that one's task force with the FBI. I didn't capture him. I was at his grandmother's when they got to him. I'd like to think I helped though, feel like I was this close to getting him." Again, peeking, Lamar sees the Chicano mimic Rafferty, holding up his fingers in Rafferty's face, messing with the guy. "He's a slippery mother. When they came for him at his aunt's house, not his aunt, but that's what everyone in his family called her, more like a godparent. When they came for him, the task force, he was in New Orleans, and he saw them coming, barricaded himself inside, and picked up a butcher knife. He was fortunate he didn't get plugged for that one. He jump-kicked the guy with the shield and cut the cords on the taser with the butcher knife. Somebody shot at him, causing everyone to back up, so Lamar thought he could go out the back door, but there was another arrest team there waiting. So, he picks up the microwave, rips it from the oven's vent hood, and uses it as a battering ram, chucking it at them to make a break for it. It took five guys to take him down."

"So what? He's laid out in a hospital bed," Rafferty says. "He's handcuffed to the bed. Where's he going to go?"

"I'm sending Susan up," the other says. "When she gets here, either have her sit in here, although I don't think she's going to be able to stand it—I'm not sure how the stench hasn't risen the dead and woke these two fucks up— or have her sit outside with the nurses, but she needs to stay close."

Rafferty waves the paper at the Chicano. "Whatever, go get your coffee. I'll try to make this a combat drop, which will be done by the time you return."

The Chicano leaves, and Rafferty steps into the restroom.

Now's Lamar's moment. In addition to robbing banks in forty-eight states, he's escaped custody twice. If he's getting out, now is the time to make a move.

As soon as the bathroom door clicks shut, Lamar lifts one eyelid and then the other, scoping the room out to ensure no nurse or anyone else is in it.

His mind is on the conversation he heard Johnny having with his lawyer in the prison's infirmary. Something about a tape, maybe some money for his wife—the same wife he thinks will leave him. The attorney didn't seem concerned with the money; he kept asking what was on the tape, and all Johnny said was, "The truth, man. The truth."

When Lamar stabbed himself, he was only set on escaping, but now that he's overheard Johnny's confession or preamble for a confession, Lamar has places to be, people to see, and money to find.

He flicks his fingers, uncovering the paperclip he palmed from some hospital paperwork the marshals had to look over. Using his bound hand, Lamar mangles the paperclip and uses it to pick the lock on the handcuffs, something Lamar learned how to do at age eleven when he thought he wanted to be an escape artist and magician. The skill's come in handy as a bank robber a few times too many. The silver bracelets loosen on his wrists, and he slips out of the cuffs.

Up and out of bed, the floor is cold against his feet. He rushes over to Johnny, who's sleeping.

"I'm sorry," Lamar says. "This will hurt, considering where you were stabbed."

Lamar punches Johnny's stomach, awakening the man and sending the machines crazy, beeping and whistling. The heart monitor shoots up, and so does blood pressure with other numbers Lamar doesn't recognize or understand.

Johnny groans, curling up some, feet coming off the bed, mouth opened in the shape of an O, hand straining against his handcuffs. Lamar slaps a hand over Johnny's face to keep the man from screaming, surprised that it worked.

With watery eyes, Johnny looks over at him. Lamar shushes the man with his finger and removes his hand slowly.

Johnny says, "What the fuck?"

"I needed you to wake up."

Johnny's head turns side to side, taking in the room. "Where are we?"

"Hospital," Lamar says. "You got stabbed."

"I did?"

"Six times," Lamar says. "You weren't going to make it."

"I'm dying?"

"Not now, but it's always a possibility and potentiality."

"So, I'm not dying?"

"Not yet," Lamar says. "But I don't have much time to argue this with you." Lamar pauses, thinking of how he's going to get what he wants to know out of the man, considering the lawyer pleaded with him about it, and Johnny, even in his doped-up state, wouldn't say. "What bank?"

"What bank? What are you talking about?"

"You're going to live," Lamar says, backing up some, "but I'm getting out of here; you getting stabbed gave me an idea, and so far, it's working." Lamar shows him his cuffless hands. "Listen, when you were back at the prison before we got shipped over here, your attorney came to visit you."

"Dickie?"

"Yeah, I guess, is your attorney's name Dickie?"

"Why'd Dickie come to visit me?"

"I'm not sure." Lamar thinks back on it. "The man looked like he was about to tell you about your puppy dying, but it doesn't matter. Listen, I'd take you with me, but you're not in any shape to move. I'm getting out of here, and I want your help."

"My help?"

"Do me a good deed," Lamar says.

"What sort of deed?"

"That money you got stashed away. Tell me where it is."

"I can't do that; it's for my wife."

"You told your attorney—Dickie—because you thought you were going to die. You said you stashed some tape away that told the truth, whatever that is, and would tell your wife where you hid the money."

"I did?"

"You did, meaning you hid the money? Or you did, meaning you don't remember telling him your secrets."

Johnny scrunches his nose and thinks about it for a second.

A long revolting fart sounds from the confines of the restroom.

Lamar glances at the bathroom door and then back at Johnny. He says, "There's not much time."

Johnny's eyes haven't moved. He says, "The second one."

Lamar tells him, "Listen, I can get your money. Make sure it's safe, but I need your help. I don't know you. I don't know your people. I don't know your wife, but what I've seen on your wall and what you've told me. What I can do for you is get the money, take a percentage; you know, a split of something is better than nothing, and I can stash the other bit away for you when you get out or give it to her. She won't have to know how much there was."

"Why would I tell you?"

Lamar lays it on thick. "Because I saved your life more than once, but this time specifically is what I'm referring to," he says. "Kept you from bleeding out—got stabbed for my troubles—but I held on to your wounds, holding everything in, trying to stop the blood, bleeding all over the place like a stuck pig... sorry, didn't mean it like that." Lamar pauses and prepares his final sales pitch. "Tell me where the tape is, and I'll make sure no one else sees it, and then I'll go get the money, hand-deliver it to your wife so she doesn't have to find out about all the nasty things you've done, and the Costa Rican missus."

CHAPTER 6:

EDUARDO CHAVEZ GAZES OUT THE window of the conference room. He likes the view. He doesn't have a view at his desk. This one is something, which is better than nothing: five floors up in the federal courthouse, buildings around, even if most of what he's looking at is the parking lot, with oblong mediums breaking up the asphalt with polite little trees there, dotting the landscape to give the gray some color. His desk doesn't have a window. His desk doesn't have an office for it. His desk is just that, a desk in a large room, one among many. Not even a cube. Windows are there, on the far side of the room. Just because he can see the windows doesn't mean he gets to look out of them.

There's a metaphor for his life somewhere in there.

Behind him sits Sharon Hadley, who shouldn't be here; she has no bearing in this, and John Rafferty, who should be here because it's his fault at the end of the day. He's the one who was supposed to be watching the inmates instead of choosing to take a shit.

But that's not right; Eduardo was in charge. He knew what he was doing. He shouldn't have gone for the coffee.

He should have waited for Rafferty to finish up in the bathroom. It's his fault. That's what he must accept. The last few days have been hectic. Now, things have settled. Rafferty has it right; it's like they shook a bottle of orange juice, and now the pulp, that's them by his account, has settled to the bottom to be discarded. Thrown away.

Rafferty's a talker. The guy can go all day. Likes to go on about nothing. On and on about nothing.

Eduardo usually lets Rafferty's voice wash over him. Has been doing that for the week or so on desk duty while the internal investigation ran its course.

Eduardo isn't a talker. He doesn't talk much. Likes to keep his thoughts to himself. Beyond Ving Rhames in *Pulp Fiction*, telling people he is pretty fucking far from okay, Eduardo's favorite movie line is that from Michael Corleone in *Godfather Part III* when Michael tells Vincent never to let people know what he's thinking. Eduardo likes Pacino. Loves Garcia, the strong man attitude. The look. The line was given after some shit had happened in the movie. Vincent's hotheaded attitude is coming out about how he wants to hit back. Michael and Pacino are doing an excellent delivery, grabbing him and telling him, "Don't let people know what [he's] thinking." Words to live by.

And right now, Eduardo thinks he's pretty far from okay. There's not a lot of room to recover from what happened. He's screwed. He knows it. There will be a punishment. It's not like the movies; he's not in the same state Rhames was in, and he's closer to Garcia in looks than Rhames, but it doesn't help Eduardo's embarrassment, hurt, and anger with himself.

He knew better.

He's on the hook and figures he can guess what's about to happen. The verdict.

"All I'm saying is it's not my fault," Raffety says. He's wearing a yellow polo with 5.11 boots, black, scuffed. They look like he's had them since he started with the marshals almost twenty years ago. Soles ripped. No shine left. Polo's similar, with his gut completing the general look of sloppiness where the shirt fails. "You knew I needed to use the restroom."

"I know," Eduardo says, hands behind his back, thinking about all that: the movies, the quotes, the trees that need support to grow. Thinking Rafferty is right. He shouldn't have left him there. "I should have waited for you to finish."

"Damn right, you should have. I told you I don't get to shit at home. I told you I had to shit. You knew that, and still you left. I don't get to shit at home. I don't even get privacy."

Sharon makes a clicking noise with her lips, followed by a huff, and holds up a hand. "Do you have to be so vulgar?"

She isn't sitting in a chair like Rafferty is. She is leaning back, feet up on the table, and her thigh is braced against the head of the table.

Rafferty eyes Sharon in her blouse, with a blue blazer, for a moment. He answers her slowly. "What do you mean, *vulgar*?"

Eduardo stays out of the coming confrontation. It is better that way. After a few days or so of desk duty and an IA Investigation, it's judgment time. So today, he decides not to take things too seriously, no matter the outcome. It's part of his way to buck the system.

He wears loose-fitting cotton slacks with a business casual shirt, black with a beige streak, which Rafferty says looks like a bowling shirt, and striping to match the pants. He says, "How the fuck can you walk around like you just stepped off the sun deck? Wearing those shirts like you're Charlie Sheen's double?" One of Rafferty's favorite lines.

Sharon places a hand flat on the table, speaking toward Rafferty but looking at Eduardo, who can tell because of the direction of her voice and the tone, and he can feel her eyes on his back. He can also see a reflection of the entire room, both sitting far enough apart to be framed on either side of Eduardo in the glass.

She says, "You keep saying the word *shit*. You have to *shit*. Saying you couldn't *shit* at home. With you, it's all about *shitting*. You are a *shit*. You talk more about your bowel movements than a Chinese medicine man."

In the window's reflection, Eduardo catches the raise of his arm as Rafferty points a finger at her. "You know many of those?"

"I know those people like to discuss digestion."

"How do you know?" Rafferty asks, cutting her off. "How do you know? You a Chinese agent?"

"No, I'm... seriously? Do I look like a Chinese agent?"

"That's what I'm asking," Rafferty says. "The way you're busting my balls, I don't know. How would I know? If you were, you'd take steps to hide it now, wouldn't you? What do you think, Ed? You think Sharon over here is a Chinese agent?"

Eduardo turns. He hates being called Ed, but Rafferty does it anyway because he thinks it's cute and endearing. It's annoying. Same reason he's messing with Sharon.

Eduardo says, "I think she doesn't want to hear about your shits. And neither do I."

Rafferty throws up his hands. "Well, what do you want me to say?" he asks. "You know they'll come here asking many questions about how this happened, even though we've been through it all before. You know how this goes." Rafferty looks from Eduardo to Sharon while making his argument. "They're going to come in here; tell us they've come to a decision. Make us go through the dog and pony show and tell the story again—it doesn't matter that we are all here. That they've done the divide-and-conquer bullshit already; sit down at this table, talk to the two investigators one at a time, and tell our side of things while everyone else is out there looking for Eduardo's famous bank robber. They want to make us dance like we are puppets. Like they're dangling our strings. Jerk us around. Makes us dread their decision.

"I do the same thing to my girls," Rafferty says. "I know what happened. I know what each told me. One will crack if I bring them together and get all righteous on them. Rat on the others or blame the others. I do it so they learn. See if they turn on that one, teach that one a lesson. Or see if they stand in solidarity and accept the outcome. That's what I want: kids that don't rat or tattletale. But with kids, they have to see the anger and the fatherly disappointment. Nothing is worse than a parent saying I'm not angry or disappointed. Sometimes, I am downright angry. But most times, in reality, I don't give a fuck. I'm just making sure they know I'm the top dog and that this behavior isn't going to stand. That's what they want all of us in here for."

Sharon says, "You don't know that. Can't know that."

"Sure, I do, that's what this is," Rafferty says, dropping his feet off the table. He leans across the table to add weight to his view of the situation. "This is their way of delivering judgment. It's all an act. So, what will happen is they're going to ask Sharon to step out; she's home-free. Not her fault. She's the driver. She was down in the car. Then they're going to ask Ed where he went and what he was doing; they're going to bury the lede with him, make it like he's not at fault, but we all know it's his fault. He's the head honcho; I should have known better. And he should have, but it's not his fault. I get stinky. He had to leave or suffer gas poisoning. Then it will be my turn. They're going to ask what I was doing. I'm going to tell them I was taking a shit, which I was. So how am I to answer them if you two don't want to hear about my shits? What am I supposed to say?"

Sharon chimes in. "You could just say restroom. That would work."

Eduardo nods. "That's a suggestion."

"I could," Rafferty agrees, nodding as if thinking it over for the first time. "But then they're going to be wondering two things." Rafferty holds up two fingers. "One, why the hell am I changing my story now? I said shit, then. I don't want to start saying restroom now. Shit is common vernacular and easy for people to understand. No misunderstanding with shit. Which is why I said it from the beginning. The only reason someone changes a story this late in the game is that they're guilty. I'm not guilty. Not my fault, but I wanted to stretch out and sit like this in a restroom for once." Rafferty scoots his chair back and holds both legs out straight, waggles his boots. "Have some room for once."

"What's the second thing?" Sharon asks, annoyed, breaking Rafferty's flow.

"Second thing," Rafferty repeats, trying to remember where he was, shuffling the chair toward the table. "Oh yeah, the second thing is that the restroom could mean a bunch of different things. My girls spend too much time in the restroom going to the restroom and having to be there, but I don't know what that means or what they are doing there. Restroom. What is a restroom?"

Sharon sighs and asks, "Are you trying to be a comedian right now? Try out new material on us. I don't want to hear it, not right now. I'm not in the mood."

Rafferty occasionally tries his amateur stand-up material on his coworkers, including Eduardo, his usual victim, to see what works and doesn't. If he gets Eduardo to chuckle, he says that means it's good stuff. Says he's going to be the next Dangerfield; he says that guy started at fifty and made it big. Says he sold the vacuum beforehand, so imagine what a retired marshal could say. To which Eduardo says, "Yeah, you can do the follow-up to the ladybug's movie, coach a bunch of girls in soccer." Rafferty says he's already done that; what did he think having all those girls was for—research, preparing for the role his whole life? "Bring it on," he says.

Rafferty doesn't confirm if he's doing a routine or not. He continues as if she hasn't interrupted. "Ever think about that? Better than the lavatory. Would you like me to say I had to use the lavatory? Maybe I'm conducting experiments in there—"

"That's a laboratory," Eduardo says. "Lab, with a b."

Rafferty pauses momentarily and then continues as if he hit a speed bump.

"Could call it using the water closet," he says. "That's a little closer to what I'm doing 'cause there's water in the name, in what I'm doing. I'm watering the bowl. Showering. But then, a water closet makes me think of this dark, dank thing with no space. I value my space. So, no, I'm not going to call it that. I go with my original statement. It's common—"

Sharon cuts in. "And doesn't leave anything to the imagination."

"That's right," Rafferty says, not slowing down. "Now you get it—that's exactly why I say shit. So yeah, you want me to use the word restroom. But now that could mean a bunch of different things. I go back to my girls. What are they doing in there? Are they showering, pissing, shitting? I don't know. The restroom is vague; it doesn't tell me what they are doing. Could be in there resting, for all I know. Knowing dear old dad needs to get in there but can't. Maybe it's a game, just to mess with me. Maybe they have a meeting there, deciding to gang up on me. All for one against me. Maybe my way of parenting is working, and they stick together. Who knows? Maybe they're getting dressed in the restroom? Maybe they're changing out their monthly feminine products in the restroom? Maybe... maybe they just sit in there. Rest."

"Maybe—" Sharon says as the door to the conference room opens. Miranda Arenado, their supervisor, cuts Sharon off and prevents her from saying anything more.

It also prevents Rafferty from saying more because he starts to say, "Now bathroom, that's better..." but when he sees Miranda, he straightens up and stops talking.

Sharon stands from the table.

Eduardo remains where he is.

Miranda surveys the room, each face, with a folder tucked under her arm. She dismisses Sharon with a curt head nod. "You may go. You are off desk duty and have returned to full duty. Thank you for being patient while we conducted our investigation and for waiting for me."

Miranda remains rigid, proper even, as Sharon glances at Eduardo and then leaves.

The two IA investigators step into the room. Dour guys who do a good job. Then, the US attorney behind them. The attorney stands next to Miranda. His first name's Mike. Eduardo's worked with him before. Nice guy. He remains quiet. It's Miranda's show.

Miranda turns to face Rafferty. She makes a disgusted face when she realizes what he's wearing. Then she dismisses it. She sits at the head of the table where Sharon had been. The attorney sits next to her. The two investigators remain standing off to the side.

Eduardo moves across from Rafferty, but Miranda says, "Eduardo, you don't have to sit down if you don't want to," stopping him. "We won't be here that long, and this isn't as formal as it appears. You can stand if you prefer."

"Yes, ma'am," Eduardo says. He stands next to the table. Rafferty offers him a smile.

Miranda organizes the folder on the table and opens it. She spreads her arms out across the table, motioning to both men. "I guess I'll start with the bad news."

CHAPTER 7:

LUCY HUDSON OPENS HER FRONT DOOR to find a dark-complected man wearing a Panama hat, a straw-colored thing with a navy-blue band that matches his shirt that isn't tucked in, standing on the other side, five steps from the door, but still on the porch. Lucy figures he did that so she could see him when she looked through the window, but not shoot him if she cracked open the door. It's a cop thing. Johnny taught her not to stand directly in front of the door.

The man straightens, comes to attention, and snatches the hat off his head, revealing the high shaved sides of his head, the edges following along the curve of his skull, and a mop of wavy, black hair on top held back with some sort of product. He's a good-looking man with sharp features and is clean-shaven. He is of average height and build but incredibly handsome, with a laid-back feel to his movements and posture. He reminds Lucy of the panther she saw at the zoo last year when she went with her sister and two kids. He has the same sleepy green eyes.

The man starts to say something but then thinks better of it. He closes his eyes for half a second and then begins again, almost like she surprised him, and maybe she did.

"Mrs. Hudson?" he says. "Lucille Hudson?"

"Yes," Lucy says. She opens the door just a bit wider and glances side to side to see if he is alone, which he is. A newer silver Chevy Impala is parked in the driveway, proving this man is a cop or a law enforcement officer. "Lucy's fine. Can I help you?"

"Ma'am..." He steps forward and lowers the hat over his heart. "I've come to talk to you about your husband."

"Oh God, is he ... dead?"

It will save Lucy a lot of trouble and legal fees if he is. She loves Johnny, but betrayal tends to tarnish one's feelings.

"Dead?" The man tilts his head to the side, not understanding. "No, he's not dead... Did you know he'd been stabbed?" The hat drops down to his side.

The man looks ready to pounce but is still loose. He gives Lucy those panther vibes, a cool cat stalking through the jungle, like the thing from that Disney movie about the boy lost in the wilderness. Paternal-like—knowing what's happening but patient enough to let the other characters figure it out, even if it means disaster.

Lucy relaxes in the doorway. She could toy with him and play the grieving wife, but other than not getting a job, life's been great without Johnny. Though, Lucy's ready to move on. She's been dutiful because the ring on her finger means something, not that there haven't been flings—that's what she tells her sister they are, flings. But flings lack the internal fire to keep burning to become full-fledged relationships, and the ring on her finger acts as a collar around her heart.

Lucy says, "His attorney told me."

The man raises an eyebrow. "His attorney told you he'd been stabbed?"

"He went to visit him. I guess he was in the infirmary before he got there." She catches herself wondering why she's telling a stranger all this. "Who are you?"

"Oh, that's right." He lifts the bottom of the shirt, revealing a badge and a gun, showing his stomach's smooth, defined, dark skin. Undershirt, something white, probably a tank top. "Deputy US Marshal Eduardo Chavez."

She shoves the door to the side. "Would you like to come inside, Deputy US Marshal Eduardo Chavez? I'll explain."

Deputy US Marshal Eduardo Chavez corrects her, hiding the mischievous crooked grin, "You can call me Eduardo."

"Not Ed or Eddie?"

He shakes his head. "No, Ma'am, Eduardo is fine."

"Fine," she says. "Mr. Eduardo, would you like to come inside? I just started a pot of coffee."

Lucy leaves him at the door and tells him she is about to get ready for work, and he can wait in the living room; she'll get the coffee. She moves to the kitchen, around the corner from the door, through the dining room. The entryway also leads to the living room, which rounds to the kitchen and breakfast nook. It's an open concept. Johnny's office is to the left of the front door, next to the stairs, and there is a whole section of the house she has to clean but doesn't use. There are three bedrooms and the garage opposite the living room and kitchen.

Moving through the house, Lucy undoes her ponytail and puts her dark hair up into a loose bun, securing it with a couple of flicks of her wrists to get the hair off her neck. Johnny was always a fan of her neck, telling her he liked how slender and graceful it was. She does it now because she wasn't expecting company, and she's a bit self-conscious about what she's wearing, consisting of a white t-shirt, no bra, and blue jeans, which hug her hips tightly. No shoes. She fights the urge to disappear into the back of the house to change clothes because she can't leave a strange man in her home unattended, and if she went to change, it might send the wrong signals.

"I hope you don't mind," she says over her shoulder from the kitchen; loud enough, he should be able to hear her in the living room. "I wasn't expecting company. I'm not what you would consider dressed for it."

There is a delayed reply, and then, from the living room, Eduardo says, "You're fine. I am sorry to just drop in on you, but we usually don't make it a habit to call first."

Lucy retrieves two coffee mugs from the cabinets and lifts the pot off the base. She pours coffee into the mugs. Still, loud enough, he can hear her in the other room; she tells him, "You can sit anywhere you would like."

"Thank you, but I prefer to stand," Eduardo says. "You said your husband's attorney saw him at the prison?"

"I did," she says.

"Why was your husband's attorney at the prison?"

Lucy returns the pot to the base and gathers up the mugs. She rounds the corner, entering the living room from the breakfast nook side, with both cups in both hands, arms bent, and elbows at her side. She finds him still gripping the hat in his hand down by his thigh, studying the photographs on the shelves next to the TV.

Eduardo senses her entering the space. He turns to her without turning his neck and looks at a photograph. "This Johnny?"

Lucy closes the gap to look at the photograph in question, but stays a few feet away to give him his space so she doesn't spill the coffee if he suddenly turns around and steps into her. That'd be too much like a movie, a rom-com: a cute guy in her house, she in this white shirt, no bra, him, turning to say something to her, awkwardly, bumping into her, sending the warm, wet brown liquid down the front of her shirt, exposing her to him, while he figures out the right thing to say after seeing what he saw.

Eduardo points one finger at a black-and-white shot.

Lucy approaches and looks like she's looking at the photo, which is silly. She knows what it is.

"Johnny on the day he graduated from the police academy," she says.

In the photograph, Johnny is wearing his dress uniform, which is pressed and starched, his hair tamed and slicked back like Eduardo's. Looking at Johnny's face, Lucy notices both men now have similar looks. There's a bit of Johnny's mischievousness in Eduardo's eyes. But where Johnny has bravado, what she sees in Eduardo is natural, as if he's been through everything life can throw at him, and he's handled himself well.

Lucy says, "I wasn't around then; I don't know if he was on wife number one yet."

Backing up, Lucy hands the mug to Eduardo. She stares into his eyes. He doesn't see her doing it, but she does it and can't help herself. She almost loses herself in them. So green. Emerald.

Eduardo accepts the mug and holds it even with his chest, still studying the photographs. "Wife number one?"

Lucy breaks the stare.

"I'm number three." She points to a different photo. "That one is of our wedding day. See, that's me in the white dress. He's in the tuxedo. We got married in a little ceremony in his grandmother's living room."

"In his grandmother's living room?"

Eduardo shifts his attention to the photograph. Eyes first to her in the dress, her cleavage, her face, and the dress, in that order. Then he transfers his attention to the rest of the picture, Johnny's smile, his hair. Eduardo comments on the fact that Johnny looks like Jon Bernthal in this photo, and then on the picture's background.

"That looks like this living room."

Lucy smirks. "That's because it is."

Eduardo turns his head to look at her and then looks beyond her at the rug. "You're wife number three? I'm sorry. And you are living in his grandmother's house?"

His eyes ask, *Where is she?*

"She's not here, you know." Lucy steps back from the photographs. "She's a couple of miles down the road at a home. She didn't want to go but couldn't take care of herself anymore. She didn't want the home to sit empty."

With the hat, he points at the ceiling. "But this was *her* house?"

"Is her house, technically," Lucy says. "Ours was seized by you all."

"Because of the trial?"

"Because of the investigation, the trial, and the conviction," Lucy says, like her priest growing up saying, "Father, Son, and the Holy Ghost."

"I'm sorry to hear that," Eduardo says as if he means it, making Lucy pause and look at him again. She notices Eduardo can't keep from glancing down at her chest; sure, he's careful about it, but he can't help himself, those sleepy green eyes sinking to her chest, the white shirt, semi-sheer, when he doesn't think she's looking.

To her chest. To her figure. Then, repeat to her clothes, the house, back to her face. It's like he's fighting himself. One half of his brain is saying peek. The other saying, no, be a gentleman.

The vibe Eduardo puts off says he leans toward the gentleman's side. Like he does alright with the ladies, but he isn't going to overstep his bounds. He seems like a natural rule follower, but if he were a rule follower, he'd be wearing a suit or something, not this... what is it, a bowling-type shirt?

He looks like he's wearing something from Charlie Sheen's wardrobe from *Two and a Half Men*, but jeans, not cargo shorts.

There he goes again, glancing down at her.

Lucy's heart beats a bit faster, and her cheeks flush with warmth because those eyes are looking at her, and—those eyes—and he doesn't bother her. She likes the attention. She doesn't have to trace his eyeline to see where he's looking now. She can feel it. She pops her chest out some more, playing with him, figuring he's already seen this much. Why be self-conscious about how she looks now? The cat's out of the bag, so to say, and he's eyeing his prey.

She drops her shoulders some.

If they met under different circumstances, maybe in a bar or the grocery store, she'd find it hard to tell this man no.

He's magnetic.

Lucy pulls her mind out of the gutter or the bedroom, returns to the conversation, and sips the coffee from the mug to hide her attraction to Eduardo. "It's okay. His grandmother let me come live here."

Eduardo shifts his eyes back to the pictures, staring at a photograph of Johnny's grandparents posing for a photo taken three days after they were married, his grandfather, twenty, about to ship out to Korea, and his grandmother, eighteen, both smiling and full of life. "Johnny's grandparents?" he asks, glancing to the side to see her nod. Then he says, "That's nice of her."

"She said she isn't using the house and didn't want to sell it yet."

Eduardo glances around the room. "Have you changed much?"

"Other than new furniture?" Lucy says. "No. I haven't changed much. I bought some new furniture because of a water leak. By new, I mean used garage sale finds. Even that didn't feel right. It's not my house."

Eduardo steps away from the photographs, giving her his back. He sips from the mug. Then he says, "What type of work do you do?"

"I wait tables."

Lucy tells him where she waits tables as she sits in the recliner, placing the coffee mug on the TV stand, acting as an end table next to the recliner, thinking comfort exudes from this man, so she might as well get comfortable. See where he and this conversation go. He's obviously here for a reason. He hasn't said that yet, but from the formality of the bit at the doorway and the conversation, it has to do with Johnny. He keeps circling to Johnny, but Johnny isn't here, and from what Lucy's gathered, he's in the hospital recovering from his stab wounds. So why is he here?

Coming inside, he didn't expect that, but when the opportunity arose for him to come in, spend some more time with her, look at her—ogle would be a good word—and slowly ask his questions, he didn't hesitate.

That says something about him. Says he takes what he wants, but he doesn't steal it. He waits until it's his turn to take.

Johnny's not like that at all.

Eduardo asks about the restaurant. "Any good?"

"Are you asking if I make good tips or if the food is good?"

Eduardo clarifies. "I'm asking about the food, but if you make good tips, I'd want to know that too, to know how much I need to tip. You know some guys; they don't like to tip? I have one coworker with four girls; he doesn't tip anything. Doesn't buy lunch either. He doesn't spend any money."

"That's because he has four girls," Lucy says, smiling. "They do that to you. Women take all your money like the bit on the *Jetsons*, in the opening when the wife and the daughter and the son all take the dad's money."

"You speaking from experience?"

"I'm female," she says.

"I noticed."

Lucy clears her throat. "I'm sorry, but did you come here for a reason or just to see me?"

Embarrassed at his manners, Eduardo sips from the mug, nodding, saying, "I came to see you."

"Me? Why?"

"To talk to you about your husband."

"But I already know he's been stabbed. Is there more?"

Eduardo tips the mug and says, "Yeah, I think so. I'm curious why your husband's attorney was visiting him."

Lucy hesitates before answering, considering how she wants to answer.

"I asked him to," is all she offers.

"Right," Eduardo says. He motions with his hat to the sofa adjacent to her. "Mind if I sit?"

"Not at all."

Eduardo sits on the sofa, places the hat on the seat to his left, and cradles the mug under his chin. "Seeing you know about the stabbing—"

"Do you know who did it yet?"

"No," he says.

"Do you know why he was stabbed?"

Eduardo shakes his head. "Officially? I do not."

"But if you had to guess?"

"Then I would say it would be the same guess you would make," Eduardo says. "Because he was a cop."

"Do you have any leads as to who stabbed him?"

"That's not my concern."

"It's not?"

Eduardo shakes his head. "No, I'm a marshal assigned to fugitive apprehension, but now and then, I work prisoner transports."

"I see," she says, but she doesn't see or understand. "Then why are you here?"

Eduardo leans back in the seat, getting comfortable on her sofa. He throws one arm across the back of the couch and crosses his leg over his knee. He sips the coffee and asks, "Did your husband ever talk to you about his cellmate?"

"Cellmate? I'm sorry, I don't understand."

Lucy doesn't tell the marshal that Johnny mentioned the black guy he was bunked with or that he said something about the guy being a bank robber or something. Johnny said he was alright, but snored. Johnny wrote letters about it. Lucy's got the letters in her room.

Her eyes float toward the hallway leading to the rest of the house, thinking about the letters, how Johnny's losing it, and how she doesn't know what to say to him anymore. She can read only so much about the food, the yard, the library, and this book he reads. And that book. How this guy said something. Or how the place smells. How Johnny misses her. Misses her body.

Life's not moving for him, but it's flowing for her, especially now.

Lucy likes this guy and wouldn't mind seeing him again.

When should she ask to see this marshal again? When he's leaving? Should she say, "Why don't you come back?" No, that'd be too obvious. No, it should be something like coffee, or she might drop in on him. But he's not said where his office is, and what would she do when she gets there? Tell him to jump her? No, that's not it, either. Oh, she's got it. She'll invite him to the restaurant on the way out. She'll walk him to the door, promise to call if she has any information, and then ask him to stop by the place—see her in her natural habitat. If he shows up there, she'll be a bit more forward and show him how happy that'd make her.

Eduardo says, "His cellmate is a fellow named Lamar Henry. Have you ever heard the name?"

Lucy shakes her head. "No, I can't say I have." She's not sure why she's lying to him, but she assumes it has to do with wanting to hear him tell her things instead of the other way around.

"Lamar, a black man?" Eduardo asks again. "A bank robber."

"No, Ed, I haven't."

"Eduardo, please."

Lucy catches the slight hint of frustration in Eduardo's face, the flush of annoyance, and a bent eyebrow. "That means something to you, doesn't it?"

"It's my name," Eduardo says quickly, neglecting to add more.

Lucy lets it go.

"And this Lamar was Johnny's cellmate?"

Eduardo nods. "He saved your husband's life; he got stabbed for his troubles."

"He did?"

"He did. Both men were transported to the hospital."

"But went to the infirmary first?"

"Where your attorney met with your husband."

"My husband's attorney," Lucy says, correcting him, although she doesn't think he accidentally made the slip.

Eduardo uncrosses his legs and recrosses them, a different configuration this time. "Both men went to the hospital."

"And that's where Johnny is now?"

"It was touch and go there for a little while. I hear Johnny's going to be okay. He should be going back to prison soon to recover in the infirmary. Doctors say he was lucky."

"Where whoever attacked him can try again?"

"Not if we can prevent it, but as I said, it isn't my concern."

"No, I guess it's not," Lucy says, then guesses at his concern and why he's sitting on her sofa. "Your concern is Lamar."

Eduardo confirms. "My concern is Lamar—he escaped."

"Escaped? How?"

"Picked the lock on his handcuffs. Used a paperclip. Not sure where he got it, maybe from one of the nurses, by accident, no reason to think any one of them helped."

"Wasn't he being watched?"

Eduardo blushes and glances to the side momentarily, considering how he wants to answer her question. "The marshal responsible for watching him was in gastrointestinal distress."

Johnny used fancy words to confuse her and anyone else who read his reports: *He assisted the perpetrator to the ground with a carefully controlled lower limb maneuver, knocking the perpetrator off balance. Gravity assisted the perpetrator's fall to the pavement, not the grass. Once on the ground, he gently secured and detained him in handcuffs...* just gibberish. He knocked the guy's feet out from under him and then put him in cuffs.

Lucy cuts to it with plain language. "He was in the shitter."

"It was unfortunate timing," Eduardo says.

"Why are you here?"

"To see you," Eduardo says, "and to see if your husband, anyone from his old life, I mean his co-defendants or this Lamar, has tried to contact you."

CHAPTER 8:

MORRIS WOODFORD RINGS THE DOOR-bell with a finger push. The chime ding dongs and then ding a lings. Woody leans to the side and peeks through the front window, which is frosted. Two shapes are sitting on the sofa; he can't make either out. Neither shape moves. Behind them is a lamp. He can make out the bright back windows. He rings the doorbell again, and one of the shapes, a female, tears herself away from the sofa and comes to the door, materializing slowly in the glass into the shape of Lucy Hudson. Woody would know her and that shape anywhere. She's always been a beauty; she's petite but has some shape. He once told Johnny, "Don't screw this one up—she's what dreams are made of."

As he waits for her to shuffle her way to the door, Woody reaches into his jacket pocket and withdraws a comb. He quickly runs the comb through his hair, sweeping it back and ensuring nothing's out of place. Everything is as it should be. He sways on his feet and slips the comb back into his jacket pocket as Lucy opens the door, sees it's him, and seemingly searches her mind for something to say, surprised to find him standing there.

Woody helps her out.

"Hello, Morris," he suggests, laying it on thick. "Long time, no see." He waits for a beat, smiles a big toothy grin, and finishes the next bit. "Hello Lucy, you look wonderful. How you doing?"

Lucy says nothing. She stands there frozen, like she can't believe he's standing on her front porch. She blocks his view of the inside of the house with the door.

Although entirely appropriate for a stranger, he's not a stranger. As an unanticipated guest, the move annoys him. Who's in the house, and why doesn't she want him to see?

Woody glances to the side and notices the car in the drive; it looks government. Woody wonders if it's a cop. That'd make sense, but then why would the guy be here? To tell her about Johnny being stabbed? Do they know who did it?

Woody pushes the thoughts out of his brain. There's no way anyone would know he's responsible, asking the guy who did it, little spic Marcos, through his wife Lorena, to take care of Woody's problem, Johnny. No way the cops knew it was Marcos, and they could not connect Marcos to Woody, so Woody showing up here, if that car belonged to a cop, would not cause anyone any concern.

Woody, wearing gray slacks with a black belt, a white t-shirt, and a black leather jacket, says, "Maybe I came at the wrong time. Maybe you got a man in there, explains the car in the driveway."

Maybe it also explains why Lucy's wearing a white shirt where he can see her nipples poking out at him through the shirt. Tell them their color, too. Maybe that's why she's dressed this way. She threw something on to answer the door like they'd just finished lovemaking. But that can't be it because it seemed like whoever she had inside was just talking before he came along.

Dressed like this, who is she talking to?

Lucy still says nothing.

Woody asks, "Did I come at a bad time?"

"Morris," Lucy says, laying on the same fake sweetness he injected into his voice just a moment ago, almost parroting him. "What are you doing here?"

"I was in the neighborhood..." he starts, shrugging his shoulders. He glances over his shoulder at the Impala parked in the driveway. Something about it seems so familiar, but he doesn't know why. Still, it looks like a government car, so maybe that's it. "You know what, that's a lie. I'm not going to lie to you off the bat. I wasn't in the neighborhood. I mean, I am now... now that I'm standing here. No, the reason I'm here is we need to talk."

Lucy stands frozen at the door. "What do we have to talk about?"

Oh, she's tough, challenging him like that. Doesn't bother Woody much. Okay. Maybe it does a little bit. He doesn't like people standing up to him, but he'll chalk it up to catching her flat-footed and unawares.

Woody lifts his index finger. "Oh, I think you know," he says, edging forward. "A whole lot of things. Johnny. Dickie handing you a key. Telling you something about what Johnny said. Said Johnny hid some money somewhere."

Lucy stares at Woody and doesn't move from the doorway. She grins like she knows exactly what he's talking about, and how couldn't she? But all she says is, "What key?"

Woody is unfazed. He says, "You made a mistake, puss; you said that too quickly and not convincingly enough, almost like you're trying to brush over the fact Dickie, and by extension, Johnny gave you anything. Especially anything that could lead to the money Johnny hid from everyone."

She doesn't move, but the grin disappears. Good enough.

"You going to let me in?" Woody steps forward and wedges himself between the door frame and the door to keep Lucy from shutting him out. "Offer me some coffee or something. That's coffee I smell, right?"

Lucy retains her grip on the door, trying to form a wall against his intrusion. "Morris, I have company."

Woody places a hand on her shoulder. He's taller than her, so now he's looking down at her. "Is your company drinking coffee?"

Lucy lifts his hand from her shoulder. "I can't talk with you right now. Why don't you come back later?"

Woody stretches that arm over the doorframe and leans into the solid core door, opening it wider. "But I'm here now, and it won't take long."

Scrunching her lips and nose like a bunny rabbit, Lucy lets the door go and allows Woody access to the house, but she blocks his way to the living room, and the wall blocks him from seeing who is sitting on her sofa. Lucy directs him to the dining room and tells him to sit down. "I'll be right back. Let me finish up with … my company, and then I'll come talk with you."

"Don't forget the coffee," Woody tells her before she leaves. He could watch her walk away all day. Her jeans highlight her tight can.

Lucy leaving the dining room allows Woody time to think through what he's going to say. He could play it slick and come at her sideways, but that's not his style. He's more of a go-getter, an iron fist type.

So, he stands and strolls around the room, with his hands clasped behind his back, hand in hand, peering at all the knickknacks and bullshit stacked in the cabinets among the suitable dishes and flatware, straining his ears to hear what's going on in the other room. He hears some muffled voices but can't determine what's being said. Then, someone mentions something about a phone call. Then, a door opens and shuts. The cabinets he's looking at are on one side of the room, with a window to his left. He glances out the window again at the Impala and can't help but notice the police lights in the eyebrow shining in the sun. Woody returns to the cabinet and studies a ceramic hummingbird, mainly green with yellow trim and a blue underbelly, with masterful brushstrokes. It reminds him of something his mother would have.

He hears a cabinet shut in the archway behind him and figures Lucy's in the kitchen, now getting him the coffee he asked for, and she didn't offer.

Woody says, loud enough for Lucy to hear him in the kitchen, "You know, I'm thankful your doorbell isn't one of those video doorbells. I'm not too fond of not being able to ring a guy's doorbell and then surprise him. Course, I surprised him with a wooden bat in my day, but it was a flaming pile of dog shit when I was a kid. Put it in a paper bag, light it on fire, ring the bell, and run away. Watch from the bushes as the guy yelled and stomped all over the bag to find out what was waiting for him inside. One time I did it with a chip bag filled with piss, but it didn't have the same effect. Still funny, though. The best times were when we had this perp, and we knew he was good for some of the crimes in the area, but we couldn't prove it. Johnny and I, those were good times; we'd show up, ring the bell, the guy come to the door, we'd ask his name, and then we'd commence to beating the snot out of the guy, so he'd get the picture, crime wasn't welcomed here. Did the same thing with domestic abusers—sad little guys who'd hit women and get called on. We'd go back to the house, ring the bell, and leave him curled up on the porch, moaning in pain.

Lucy steps back into the space from the kitchen, holding a mug. She furrows her eyebrows. "Are you threatening me?"

There's a moment where they both stare at each other, sizing the other up, before she extends the mug toward Woody.

Woody laughs, accepting the mug. "Why... what would make you think I'm doing that?"

He sips the coffee and makes a disgusted face, twisting his lip and running his tongue across his top teeth.

The coffee is bitter and cold.

"You could have heated it some?"

"You didn't ask for hot coffee." Lucy stands firm, head cocked to the side, hands on her hips like what she didn't just say was her rechallenging him. He needs to put her in her place. She says, "Why are you here?"

Woody sips the coffee again and inspects the mug, careful not to check her out more than he already has. "What would make you think I'm threatening you?"

"You're talking about beating someone with a baseball bat."

Woody points at her with the mug. "No, I'm reminiscing with you about what your Johnny and I used to do. I'm not threatening you. I've not even told you why

I'm here to talk to you, other than mentioning I know about the key. If I'd come here to threaten you, I'd at least give you the chance to give me the key and find out what I want first."

"What do you want?"

But Woody doesn't answer her. He says, "Where'd your company go?"

"He stepped out back to make a phone call," Lucy says. "You can't be here."

Woody steps around her and investigates the kitchen, trying to see whoever she has in the back windows. He asks, "Who do you have here?"

"A US Marshal."

Woody whistles. "Really?"

"Yes, and he's checking in on me because someone stabbed Johnny."

"The marshal's here because someone stabbed Johnny. That seems strange. Why would the marshal be here doing that? Isn't that something for, like, the FBI or someone?"

"Johnny's cellmate escaped," Lucy says.

"So, the marshal's checking on you because Johnny's cellmate escaped?" Woody shakes his head. "I don't understand what you have to do with the cellmate escaping."

"Me either," Lucy half-whispers. "He was just getting around to explaining that to me when you rang the doorbell."

"Well, I can't believe I'm here either," Woody says. "I voted for the good lawyer to come here, Dickie. At least he has a relationship with you. Other than a brief flirtation back in the day before everything went to shit, you and I haven't talked."

"We weren't flirting."

Woody goes on like she didn't speak.

"Johnny always found a way for him to be a part of our conversation. We'd talk about what we did over the weekend, all friendly-like, and Johnny would mention how you said you ran into me at the store or would comment about seeing me at Mass or before, during confession."

"I always thought you were following me."

"That's what Johnny said to me. Are you following her? Which is just crazy," Woody says. "No, I'd smile and say that's just a coincidence."

"But it wasn't a coincidence," Lucy says. "You were following me."

"No woman has ever chosen Johnny over me, not when presented with the two choices," he says. "You just never got to see me for who I was, that's all. But I always felt that Johnny spoke negatively about me to you. I could never put my finger on it. It was just how you looked at me when we ran into each other, kind of like you're looking at me now."

"What do you want, Morris?" Lucy steps to the side behind a dining room chair. Her hands grip the top of the chair. "You said something about Dickie. What's he have to do with all this?"

"Dickie came to the guy I work for," Woody says. "You remember Thomas Cooper? He's always been like a mentor to Johnny and me. He was on before we were on, showed us how to do the job, and then retired not long before Johnny met you."

Lucy nods. "I know who you are talking about."

"Cooper and Dickie are friends; see Johnny, before he got arrested, had something, money if you must know, that belonged to all of us, but he hid it. We'd like to find it."

"I don't know where your money is."

"Oh, I know that because, if you did, you would have spent it."

"So, what are you saying?"

"Dickie was hired a long time ago to represent members of the Brass, who might have found themselves in trouble. Do you know what that is?"

"No," Lucy says, and a quick read of her face tells Woody that's the truth.

"A fraternal organization, so to say," Woody says. "Johnny was a member of the Brass. It's why Johnny wanted to work with Dickie during his trial. We all worked with attorneys close to Dickie who are a part of this organization."

Lucy seems to accept his answer, or she doesn't question it. "Dickie told you about the key Johnny left for me."

"Yes, Dickie told us about the key."

"So, why are you here?"

"I'm here to see if you'd give me the key and tell me what bank it goes to."

Lucy starts to say something but then thinks better of it, snapping her mouth shut. She shuts her eyes and gulps. "No, Morris, why are you here? It's strange for you to be here. I've never liked you. Why'd they think sending you would get me to tell you where the key goes?"

"That's what I told Cooper. I said it's strange for me to just show up out of the blue. She's not that kind of girl. It'd be weird. Get Dickie to do it. But Cooper insisted I do it. He said, 'You have to be the one to do it. You're the only one I trust.' I asked him why me. He said, 'Because I don't trust Dickie. He's too close to everything but sees nothing. The guy didn't even know Bob made that tape with Johnny.' He said he needed to know exactly what's on that tape, and I need to know what Johnny did with my money. Which is why I figured I'd come right out and tell you what's happening, so you know where we stand and don't waste each other's time.

"I told Cooper, 'Isn't the Wrench in town? He and Lucy always got along; send him over.' But Cooper wasn't having it. He said, 'The Wrench is off doing his own thing, and he doesn't want to be a part of what we got going on any longer. He's afraid it will affect his retirement.' I argued for Dickie to do it one more time. 'I'm not sending Dickie,' Cooper said. 'I'm sending you. Now, either you accept that as a fact or you don't, but if you don't do what I'm asking you to do, then I'm going to have to make some phone calls.' I told him I'd come over this evening and asked, 'Does that work for you?'"

Lucy steps from behind the chair and sits in it. She puts her head in her hands. "Why does the tape matter?"

Woody says, "Some of the things we did don't just go away. Statute of limitations and all. It's always going to be around. I need to find it. Find out what's on it."

Lucy looks up at him. "And get the money back?"

"Of course," Woody says.

CHAPTER 9:

ERIN MOORCOCK EXITS THE ELEVATOR of her building on the top floor. She is upset because she woke up late and ran behind. Rushing out of the elevator with the doors still closing on her as if she waited too long to leap, mind lost in the business for the day and upset about being late, she bumps her shoulder on the golden tarnished door, feels a brief tug, and hears the zipper stretch of fabric ripping. Erin doesn't know where the fabric ripped on her person, but she can't focus on that now. She's late. She knows with the blow, she'll bruise, guaranteed, and with being so far behind, she'll have to live with whatever damage she's done to her clothing. She can't afford a wardrobe malfunction in the courtroom, so once she's in her office, she can inspect the damage and change into one of the backup outfits she keeps in the closet if she needs to change.

But Erin was supposed to be in court at nine. It's nine-thirty. Even with the costume change, she might make it before the judge finishes his morning docket and notices she's not there if she hurries. Not that it matters. Her client's a goner as soon as court is in session. Maybe being late is the best thing for him and her.

Surging into the main office space, Erin ignores the front desk lady, Carrie, who is on the phone, with the phone up to her ear, talking and chewing gum simultaneously. Carrie is a young, trained paralegal who doubles as the office gatekeeper and Dickie's current conquest. She's pretty in a redheaded sort of way, but Erin doubts it's natural.

Carrie covers the phone with her hand and says, "Ms. Moorcock—"

But Erin's in such a hurry that she ignores the woman, lifting a hand to silence her, and slides by Carrie's desk. From the corner of her eye, Erin watches as Carrie snaps shut her mouth and continues chewing some more. She goes back to the phone, uttering something unheard under her breath.

None of the other attorneys are in the office; the others have already left for their early morning court appearances. Vacant offices and closed doors signal this much. Erin glances at her wristwatch, a gift from her father upon graduating from law school, a gold ring with a black leather band with an inlaid design that looks like a tortoise shell. She checks the time against what she remembers of the judge's docket and figures she still might be able to make it. He moves slowly and is prone to starting late himself. She just has to hurry.

Erin shoves open her office door and glides over to her desk, dropping her bag on the keyboard. It is only when she's looking down at her desk, noticing her desk calendar turned the other way, and briefly wondering why it's like that, that she realizes someone's in her office. Erin glances up from the calendar to the man sitting in the chair in front of her desk. He must be what Carrie was trying to tell her, warn her.

The bitch could have tried harder.

Staring at him, his eyes on her, for whatever reason, Erin is reminded of that scene in *All the President's Men*, the movie, not the book—although she's sure it's in the book, she's never read it—where Dustin Hoffman is waiting at the attorney's office. This man is like that. Except in this case, instead of the magazines Hoffman's character was reading, this man was reading her files, which she left on her desk. This morning's client.

Also on the desk is a coffee cup, a white mug on a white saucer, perched on the edge of her desk next to this morning's paper, which also looks read and used.

Both signal he's been here a while. This man doesn't look like Dustin Hoffman or Robert Redford. No, he has a sly Caribbean feel to his look—handsome but relaxed. He clasps a Panama hat in his lap, with a closed file resting on his thigh. He uncrosses a leg, shifts the file to the armrest, and balances it there. His clothing is crisp but loose. No wrinkles, but not appropriate for a business setting. Which might account for the reporter's vibes she felt. She doesn't know what he is, who he is, why he's sitting at her desk, or why Carrie let him back here. She'll have to address that later.

"Morning," the man says, intruding into her thoughts. He flaps the hat's brim toward her.

Erin tilts her head to the side. "Is that my file?" she says, adjusting her clothing, running a hand down her side, and checking herself. Trying to discover what damage she and the tussle with the elevator did to her clothing. Maybe she just stretched the fabric. Maybe it didn't rip. Maybe it did, and the man's smiling because her ass is hanging out, and he can see the black thong.

The man glances down at his lap, the file, and then back at her. "I believe it is."

Erin curls her lips. Annoyed, with her hands on her hip, she asks, "Why are you reading my file, and why do you have it? How did you get back here?"

The man says, "I got bored sitting here and finished the paper about an hour ago." He explains. It should cover her query, but it doesn't.

"But that doesn't tell me why you have my files. Who do you think you are?"

He scrunches his face and nose like a rabbit, which is proportional to his face. "Who I am...?"

"Yes, who are you, and why are you sitting in my office?"

"This is your office?" He says it like he can't believe it and is checking it against his recollection. He points at her and says slowly, "You're Erin Moorcock? Your daddy was Bob Moorcock, that right? That's some name, an unforgettable name."

Erin sighs and relaxes her stance. "I've heard it before," she says. "You want to make fun of my last name? His name? You think I haven't heard it before, grown up listening to people commenting about it."

The man says, "No, that's not it." He says, "When I heard Bob's name, I thought about the case he had a few years ago, those cops."

"Yeah, what of it?"

"And then I heard his kid took over his business. They said, Aaron Moorcock. I didn't think Aaron was Erin."

"Congratulations, you've learned something new today."

The man doesn't speak.

Erin adds, "Well, now you know I'm a girl." Then, she corrects herself, "Woman."

"Yes, you are."

Erin crosses her arms and taps her foot against the floor. "So, I'll ask you again, why are you here? Who are you?"

The man smiles. He has white teeth. It's a friendly smile, crooked, with a small scar on his chin. "Those are two questions. How about this? Which one do you want answered first?"

"Who you are."

"I am United States Deputy Marshal Eduardo Chavez."

Erin tries her best not to show her surprise. She keeps every muscle in her body as before he spoke. "What can I do for you, Deputy Chavez? That doesn't explain why you are here. Or why you would be here?"

He says, "Eduardo, please."

Erin says, "I don't think I will."

Eduardo grows quiet, his features hardening some, the smile fading to a facade of its former self as he thinks her comment over and her attitude. "I am here because you represent an associate of a fella I'm looking for, and I'd like to talk to him."

Erin sighs. "I'm not going to make it to court today, am I?"

"Remains to be seen."

Erin is quiet.

"If you have an afternoon appearance scheduled—I don't think I'll be here all day. Though, that's up to you."

Erin considers the man and how she, as an attorney, can help him.

"Would you like some more coffee?" she asks, returning to her door. She doesn't give Eduardo a chance to answer. That wasn't the point. She needed to buy time to form an argument. Think things over.

She pokes her head out the door and tells Carrie. "Carrie, call over to the courthouse, tell them something's come up, and I'm not going to make Mr. Smith's hearing, and then, can you bring us some more coffee?"

Carrie nods in response, confirming she heard Erin. Carrie picks up the phone and holds it to her ear. As Erin steps back into her office, she hears Carrie ask for one of the court clerk runners who works for the district attorney's office and will pass messages along to others, including the judge.

Erin shuts the door. "The judge won't be happy I'm not in court today."

"You would have been late."

Erin walks over to her desk and sits down after studying the marshal some more. Amazed at finding herself sitting across from the US Marshal, she tries to understand why he's in her office. She says, "Of course, my client will notice way before the judge, but that doesn't matter. He's a goner and, thinking about it now, maybe coming in late," she pauses to lift a hand toward Eduardo, "or not at all will make the ADA sweat a little bit and offer a better deal, make the government think I'm playing hardball, which of course I am."

She pauses to gauge his reaction.

There is none beyond that crooked smile.

Erin points at her file, which is still in Eduardo's possession. "The ADA thinks—he, a boy fresh out of law school, a novice—it's a slam dunk case. I mean, it is. And the best way to beat it is by playing mind games and getting them to plead it down. Maybe coming in late will make him itchy and make him come to the table on his 'slam dunk' case."

Eduardo waves the file and says, "After reading this, it might benefit the poor sap. They've accused him of several robberies; maybe he's done one of them."

"He didn't do *any* of them, but we can't tell the cops that."

"They seem to think he did."

"Like I said, ADA dipshit thinks it's a slam dunk," she says. "And the poor sap's name is Dante Smith. The guy's a behemoth. I figure the only way the cops got onto him was because of his size. The best thing he did was sit quietly in the interview room—it's an interrogation, no matter what the police say—and not answer their questions. He didn't even invoke his right to counsel. He sat mute."

"Did he?"

"Yes, he did," she says. "You have his file. You were reading it. I assume it's Dante you are interested in."

She puts it to him as a statement of fact. Not a question. Eduardo nods.

"Look, Dante's sweet. He spent almost a year in jail on this bullshit. He didn't do it, but I don't think we can prove that. I think he knows who did, not that it matters. He doesn't say but five words every time we talk. One of them is goodbye. Every time." She drops her voice to mimic Dante, "*Goodbye*. I don't know if the guy is dumb as a box of rocks, but I will tell you he has a great smile; it lights up the room. And I'm late; Dante deserves better."

"I don't think he can do better than you."

"That may be so," she says.

"So, why are you late?"

"You want me to get into my personal life with you? I don't even know you."

"Isn't that how you get to know someone?"

Erin hesitates before speaking. He thinks he's sly, giving her these witty comebacks to see if he can shake her. He can't.

"Why are you late?"

So, she tells him, "Look, Ed—"

"Eduardo," he corrects.

"Ed," she says again. She knows. She did it on purpose. "Being late is my business, not yours."

"I'm just curious, late night?"

"That's none of your business."

Eduardo waves the file again. "I'm sure Dante would like to know."

"You going to tell him?"

"I'm going to see him later."

"So that's a maybe."

"Well, that depends on you, doesn't it?"

"I don't... you know what? I don't like being late. I like to get in the office around seven-thirty and kick off for the day after the afternoon docket call. Being late bothers me. It means I'm behind, and I can't stand being behind. In my mind, the whole point of ligation is anticipating the other person's argument, laying a foundation against it in my argument, without letting on that's what's happening before it's too late, and strike hard, fast, and first."

"Is that what you are doing with me?"

Erin doesn't answer right away. She scoots her chair back and stands, straightening the skirt. She rounds the desk, saying, "My father called it 3-D chess and compared it to the game Spock and Kirk played in *Star Trek*. My father told me to offer no quarter and to operate in the courtroom with no mercy. 'Take the queen, kill the pawns, clear the board,' he'd say while reminding me that my job wasn't to be nice; it was to be ruthless because a client's freedom, fuck his innocence, was on the line and I must perform at peak efficiency."

She plucks Dante's file out of Eduardo's hands and leans against her desk as she says, "Some days I work harder, later into the night than I like, because I am meticulous and good at what I do. But the way my father worked and the way I work, seeing he trained me, I structure my court appearances in the morning and fuck off the last half of the day, leaving it for whatever I want. If it's work, I work. If it's a date, I go on the date."

If it's meeting Craig at a shithole, then it's that too, but she doesn't tell Eduardo that.

He nods like he comprehends.

"The whole point is I don't want to be doing anything I have to be doing after eight hours of solid labor. My father told me to treat law school like a job, work eight hours studying, and go to school the rest of the time. I studied in the morning, spent my afternoons attending class and sleeping through class breaks, and then worked at a bar at night. I was a shitty bartender, but a pretty decent lawyer. Still am better than most. The bar I worked at, a cowboy honky tonk, only required me to open bottles and mix soda with alcohol. I've continued the tradition, minus the school, so my afternoons are my own."

One time, while working the bar—after she finished school just a few years ago—a guy walked in and ordered a martini. She asked what that was. "The one that I shake?"

The Richard Gere-looking guy said, "Yeah, that one."

Erin said, "You look around at where you're at?" Guy just looked at her, wearing a suit like an accountant, while everyone else wore cowboy hats, blue jeans, and boots. "Let's put it this way: the last fifty orders were beer buckets. Beers differ for each bucket; we have five to choose from, but all the same thing, you know?" But the guy said he didn't want beer; he wanted a martini. Told her he had just come from court and got beat up there. He didn't look beat up. She said, "How about this? You return with a cowboy hat, and I'll make you a martini," issuing the challenge because he wasn't the type the bar catered to. The guy looked at her crookedly and then pushed himself away from the bar.

Twenty minutes later, he came back, getting Erin's attention. He tossed a cowboy hat on the bar. It had blood on the rim; he sat down and ordered a martini. He said, "There, now the drink."

Erin looked at the hat and then at the guy, knuckles bruised, suit torn, commotion in the background. "How about this? You walk me through how to make one, and I'll get it to you." The guy agreed. "But I don't shake for anyone," she said.

The guy said, "Well, tonight, you'll shake for me."

That was the first time she met Craig Jentsch. Erin may have liked the brawler attitude then, the independence, the charisma, and charming personality, that damn crooked smile, but today she's annoyed that Craig didn't wake her up. Last night, she drank too much, made him drive her home, and told him since he was already there, he might as well stay; she got undressed to underline her point, dropping the dress right there, having already, expertly and secretly, removed her underwear which was shoved in her bag, and spent the night with him. "For old time's sake," she said when she crawled into bed.

When she crawled out of bed this morning, Craig was gone. He left a note stating that Thomas Cooper had called. When Cooper calls, it's like a dog whistle. Craig will go running.

But here in the office now, and after a moment of consideration, all Eduardo says is, "So you're saying, in your lawyer way, you don't appreciate me being here?"

Erin nods, grinning. He can listen. "I'm saying, who the fuck do you think you are, coming in here, reading my files, and making me late to court?"

Eduardo stares up at her. Both feet are flat on the floor, hands on his knees.

"I'm me."

"That's not an answer."

"No, you are wrong. It is an answer. Maybe not the one you want, but it is one."

"So, what is it you want?"

"A meeting with Dante. He's not in trouble."

"Why?"

"Because I'm looking for a fella he's friends with, and I'm wondering if this fella's going to see Dante."

She hugs the file to her chest. "Explain more and hurry up."

Eduardo considers her body language, eyes dressing her up and down, quietly noting the annoyance. Then he says, "The fella I'm looking for escaped prison. You might know him; he's cellmates with a friend of one of your old clients." Eduardo stands. "A guy named Johnny."

"Hudson? He's escaped?"

"No," Eduardo says. "His cellmate."

Erin crosses her hands, making a T. "Time out," she says. "One thing at a time. Where does Dante come in?"

"Seems the fella I'm looking for and Dante were in Tulsa County jail, probably when your boy was in on those robberies." He points to the file secured in Erin's arms. "I thought he might come to town and get in touch with Dante. I wanted to know if you, his attorney trying to keep him out of prison, could impress upon Dante the importance of cooperation with the government and how that could benefit a man—looking at a *slam dunk* case."

Eduardo's done his homework.

Erin says, "Which is why you are here in my office and not knocking on his door."

"Yes, ma'am. I figured what I heard about Bob Moorcock's offspring was correct."

"What'd you hear? "

"That you could be persuasive."

CHAPTER 10:

LAMAR HENRY KNOCKS ON THE DOOR and glances left and then right. The street is quiet. Not too early to move about and attract unwanted attention from bored patrol police officers, but late enough, those same officers are bogged down taking reports about stolen bicycles and credit card fraud and not thinking about people moving on the street. After all, it's well after rush hour, and this is the edge of the suburbs at about noon—a no-man's-land between the central metropolitan and the no-nonsense bedroom community.

Lamar—dressed in cheap blue jeans and a black t-shirt he shoplifted from a Walmart, shoes too—will have to be careful not to dally. If he sticks around too long, someone will call on him and tell the police a black man is walking on the sidewalk. It's happened more than once, but usually when he hasn't done anything wrong. When he's out casing a joint or committing a crime, the pressure and worry are there, not the unwanted attention. The last time he was on the run, the paranoia was ever-present. This time, it is barely there.

The lawn in front of the one-story house is well-manicured, with straight-edged lines running along the concrete. The whole house looks small and perfectly placed, about 1,500 square feet if Lamar had to guess. Maybe three beds, one bath. One and a half? A single car sits in the driveway, backed into the spot, rear-end against the single-car garage door, nearly touching it. The car is a black, well-polished 70s model Chevy Chevelle. The whole scene, everything, it's all bright and shiny, from the grass to the concrete to the car.

The front door flings inward, revealing a chest wrapped tightly in a white wife-beater, thick biceps, pecks, and a neck almost as thick as Lamar's waist, all glistening mahogany. When Lamar knew the man, he worked out multiple times daily, the same way most people watch TV.

Lamar looks up at the giant man on the other side of the screen door and smiles wide.

The enormous man, Dante Smith, stares down at Lamar. His face is like concrete, unmoving and pockmarked, rough in some places and smooth in others. Clean lines are defined and distinguished. His head is shaved cleanly for a trim, thin-line goatee squared around the right corners of Dante's thin-lipped mouth.

"Man, am I happy to see you," Lamar says, and he is. Lamar knew Dante when they were in Tulsa County jail together, bunked next to each other, and ate nearly every meal together in comfortable silence. Lamar was there on a writ, the government bringing him back to testify against a guy he pulled a small job with way back when, and Dante was in jail because the police thought he robbed some businesses and some people around town. There is something about the man, a calm. The only time Lamar's ever felt this way around anyone or anything else was when he talked a cute little zoo docent with trimmed tone legs, long and smooth, into letting him pet some elephants.

But right now, Dante doesn't look happy to see Lamar. From what Lamar can remember about him, Dante doesn't usually look happy until he smiles. He has a great smile and straight teeth, bright and white, like The Rock or Tom Cruise.

Remembering their time together in jail, this is what Dante does. He doesn't talk unless he needs to, doesn't move unless necessary, or even twitch when a fly lands on him.

Lamar guesses he doesn't need to talk, but Dante doesn't move either. He doesn't open the screen door, step to the side to let Lamar inside, or step inside to shut the door in Lamar's face. Any of these reactions would be fine, but this eye-fucking each other on his front porch through a screen increases the uncomfortableness seeping into the muscles between Lamar's shoulders.

All Dante does is stand there mute, staring down at Lamar. Face unmoving. Resolute.

Lamar leans to the side and peers around Dante to see more of the house from the front door. From what he can see, the inside of the house is as sparse and well cared for as the outside, much like how Dante was in jail. He's an institutional man. That much is clear. Limited means. Limited aspirations. The body is a temple. In Lamar's mind, all of this means that Dante may be the only one in the house. Dante's not stupid, though. Then again, he might not be alone; Lamar hears a shout from inside the house, asking Dante who it is at the door. The voice is male, whiny, and unfamiliar to Lamar.

Lamar rocks on his heels and asks, "You the only one that lives here?"

But Dante doesn't answer. He continues to stare down at Lamar.

A smell wafts through the door. The inside of the house smells good.

"It smells like baked beans," Lamar says. "You making beans? I bet you are. They're your favorite, right?" Lamar taps his temple with his finger. "See, I remember. I don't forget shit like that, not when it's about a friend. I remember how much you like them."

The only time Dante opened up to Lamar in jail was on Dante's year anniversary of being incarcerated. Then the guy wouldn't shut up. He told Lamar about how his mother, dead now, made the best baked beans and made them for Dante on his birthday, making them with smoked baloney, the heel nearly burned black from the heat, the inside a tender pink.

"I only ask about you being alone 'cause, with a car like that, you'd think you'd park it in the garage. Maybe you got a girl... boy... someone living here who wants to park in the garage. Someone who might not like someone like me dropping by, coming to see you, seeing you're fighting a case and where we met."

Dante glances at the car and the side of the house, the garage, hidden from the front door, almost even with the porch. Dante grunts a response and pushes the screen door open.

Lamar steps back, allowing the door to open while yanking the door open the rest of the way, and steps forward nearly into Dante's chest. He flops his hand against Dante's chest, flicking him to get him to move.

"Like I said, you going to invite me inside, or do we have to reminisce out here?"

Dante steps away from the door, pushing it open wider.

Lamar steps past Dante into a tiny square living room with cream-colored, bare walls, a gray couch, and a black rectangle TV on the wall to the left. No decoration. No knickknacks. No indication of who lives here. Couple of windows to the front yard and the side yard, which means the siding of the neighboring house.

Once Lamar is clear of the front door, the screen door snaps shut behind him.

Dante follows Lamar a few steps as he scans the room and leaves the front door open.

Coming from the kitchen, another man, slightly smaller than Dante, skinnier, with slim arms and spindly legs, enters the living room, wearing an oversized white t-shirt and baggie black basketball shorts, hair long and in corn rows, saying, "Who the fuck is this?"

The guy's eating a cheese stick.

Lamar mutters, "Hard to take a guy seriously when he's chewing on mozzarella."

The man grimaces. "I axe you again, who the fuck are you?"

"Who the fuck are you?" Lamar snaps back, circling the couch and checking the place out. Lamar learned a long time ago to confront aggression with aggression. That way, the aggressive person knows Lamar isn't a bitch. Aggression acts as a roadblock that stops the person cold and makes them decide how they want to handle the situation. If it's going to be a fight, Lamar can handle it. Partly why he boxes, something his father taught him when he was little. His father said, "If you're going to pop off, be a smartass, then you need to be able to back up your words when communication fails." If the guy backs down, Lamar can handle it and see how the other guy goes about backing down. But some guys do, some don't. Some act like pussies. Some handle it well. Mostly, the aggression is misplaced posturing.

Lamar waits for the next step, his honed *flight or fight* response.

The man, facial hair shading his chin like a chinstrap, turns toward Dante and points at Lamar. He says, "D, who the fuck is this?" The aggressive tone still shades his words.

But, like with Lamar at the door, Dante doesn't move. Doesn't speak. Doesn't answer.

Glancing from Dante to the man, Lamar dials back the aggression. He showed he wasn't a bitch or pushover. "I'm a friend."

But the guy pushes harder, the hostility adding a bite to his words. "A friend of who? Of D's? D don't have no friends."

This reveals much about him, and Lamar judges the man in seconds. If the man were to step into the ring with Lamar, he'd be KO'd in two seconds flat.

All bark, no bite.

The man adds, "You sure as hell ain't a friend of mine."

"I'm friends with Dante."

The man's dark, beady eyes dart over toward Dante. Dante stays quiet. The man says, "If you're his friend," pointing at Dante with half the cheese stick, "where you been? I've never seen you before. Dante doesn't have any friends. None like you. Not any that come over. Not any as ugly as you either. So let me axe two crucial questions to the strange fuck in my house, who the fuck are you, and what the fuck are you doing here?"

Lamar sighs and says in a patient voice, "I already told you who I was. If you don't accept it as an answer, that's your problem."

The man moves closer. He walks loose with a slide, mocking him. "*I already tole you*–no, the fuck you didn't. You said you a friend of D's, but I tole you, D don't have no friends. So, who are you? And why the fuck are you here? I'm not going to ask again."

"Are *you* dumb?" Lamar asks.

"What?"

"I asked," Lamar raises his voice, ensuring he can hear him, "are you dumb? If you were dumb, then maybe I would understand your inability to understand the words coming out of my mouth."

The man scrunches his nose, trying to figure out what Lamar said. "*What*? Speak English."

"I am, and I told you I'm a friend of Dante's. We go back a couple of years."

"This true?" The man turns to Dante. "You friends with this bitch?" He hikes the cheese stump toward Lamar.

"You get one pass, don't say that again," Lamar says.

The man glances at Lamar and then at Dante, who nods once.

"Well, why didn't you say so? Why did you let me go on barking at him if he's a friend of yours?"

Dante shrugs.

The man offers his name to Lamar, calling himself Cecil Reyes. His tone shifts to friendly and pleasant, salesman sly, saying, "Call me Cece; I'm Dante's cousin."

"Cousin?"

Cece munches on the rest of the cheese stick. "We look like brothers, don't we?" Cece smiles wide, putting on a show, showing how much they look alike and how innocent he is. But they don't look anything like each other. Not when Cece smiles. His smile is nothing like Dante's.

Dante's more intelligent.

"If you're cousins, then you must be the runt," Lamar says.

Cece does a double-take and stalks over to the front door, choosing to ignore Lamar. He glances out the screen door, saying, "But you see the family resemblance, don't you? It's quite striking. My whole life, people kept thinking we the same person, 'cuz we look the same. Got that all the time. Thing is, I'm me, a high school graduate, and he's a bit … *slow*. Don't know if you've noticed. His mom's afraid he can't live on his own, live a normal life on his own, axed me to look after him. If you friends, then you know what happened to him couple years back; people saying he robbed some places. Mom wanted me to make sure he was all right. Make it so nothing happening to him that shouldn't."

Lamar turns to Dante again. "He doesn't strike me as someone who would need anyone looking after him."

With a flat voice, Cece says, "He's a big teddy bear; people take advantage of him if we ain't careful."

"People like you," Lamar mutters.

Cece tenses again. "What was that?"

"Nothing," Lamar adds.

"So, if you're a friend of Dante's, why are you here, and why haven't I heard of you before?"

"I've been away."

"Where?"

"You going to ask me twenty questions? Want me to start taking clothes off if I won't answer?"

"That's a game?"

"It's a game."

"I've never played it."

"I bet you played pick-up sticks," Lamar says. "With your ass cheeks."

Cece puffs up. "You have a problem with me?"

"I have a problem with most people, but loudmouths who don't know when to shut up—yeah, I have a problem."

Cece fake laughs and jams his fist onto his hip. "Well, aren't we all hard? You ain't hard. I know hard. Why you here, Mr. Hard man, what you want with D?"

Lamar grins. "I wanted to see if he ... and you ... wanted to make money. I need another hand, someone I can trust. Muscle too. And location was the key, made me think of only one man who fit the bill."

Nodding and showing he understands what Lamar needs Dante for, Cece checks with Dante, who doesn't move, and then says, showing some interest, but barely, "What you have in mind?"

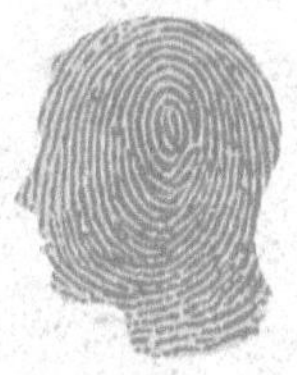

CHAPTER 11:

MORRIS WOODFORD SITS IN HIS BLACK Lincoln Continental passenger seat, dressed in a white T-shirt, jeans, and a black leather jacket. He rests his head against the glass while telling Craig Jentsch, who's in the driver's seat, about the marshal at Johnny's wife's house.

"He comes into the room, although come isn't the word I'd choose that best describes him 'cause when I think of something coming, I think of something else. Like how I want to cum inside Lucy. No, he glided—glided, glides, whatever the fuck he did—he came in like he doesn't have a fucking care in the world. The balls on this motherfucker. They have to be like this fucking big." Woody holds his hands out about a foot apart. "This fucking big, I couldn't believe it. Says, 'Hello, Morris,' like we're fucking friends, on a first-name basis. Doesn't offer his name, doesn't act aggressive or nothing. Voice syrup-like, acting like he isn't surprised to see me. Sure, as shit makes it known, he knows my name, knows who I am. Smiling the whole time like a fucking rat—the fucking balls."

Craig, dressed in a cream-colored polo and stylish blue jeans, looking like he's about to go out on the town for the night, smelling like it too, nods along, listening or, in Woody's educated assessment, playing along like he's listening. For all Woody knows, the guy could be daydreaming about that lawyer pussy he's always going on about, which probably means he is. The same woman he said he was with when Cooper called and told him, no demanded, he come to the office and then shack up with Woody for the day; Woody, who in turn said or demanded himself, "If I'm stuck with that moob, then he's driving." Woody can't stand it. Craig used to be all right. But now that he's become semi-famous and started shacking up with that bitch, he won't shut up about her. He's always going on about how he likes her, her feistiness, and her attitude. Woody's been in the same room with her. By his estimate, she's nothing special. That and that scar. How does Craig kiss a woman with a wrinkle on her lip?

But Woody will give it to the man; she's got it where it counts. She does have a smoking body. One Woody wouldn't mind touching. So, if she's got Craig wrapped around her finger or her thighs—more like fucking pussy whipped. This reminds Woody he needs to talk to Craig about it and tell him how a man should handle it—then so be it. Woody understands, but doing the shit they did— still do—Craig still has responsibilities that need to be tended to from time to time. Tell the man, sure, he joined the Brass, and now he's—Well, Woody doesn't know what he is, a cop, not a cop, fast-tracked to retirement, whatever the fuck Craig's doing these days—he needs to remember that someone who once carried brass constantly fucking carries brass.

Craig asks, "How long should we wait here for her?"

Woody lifts his head from the window and looks over at him.

"We wait as long as we have to."

What the fuck does he not understand about this? Woody considers letting it go, but then doesn't.

He says, "What don't you understand? You got wax in there?" Pointing to Craig's ears. "That hundred-dollar haircut fucking with your hearing? Making it to where your brain don't work no more? Cooper was really freaking clear; he said he wanted that tape, so we could find the money Johnny stashed away, and if Lucy isn't going to tell me when I asked nicely, then we have to deploy other, less than savory, means to get what we want, which at this moment means sitting here, waiting for this bitch to leave and following her to where she goes with the idea we'll take it from her or make her see the error of her ways."

Craig yawns and stretches his right leg, pressing against the space next to the brake pedal. The car smells like cleaner and car wax, and Woody is nauseated. It reminds him of his father.

Craig says, "You were here yesterday. How do you know she didn't go last night, wherever she's going?

"I sat up on her, not the way I want her to sit up on me, and I followed her."

"She see you?"

Woody shakes his head. "No way she saw me. I'm too good at this shit."

This shit consisted of Woody sitting in his Lincoln in the dark, sipping—and then spitting dip into—coffee from some flea-ridden gas station that tasted like it'd been sitting on the burner all day, ducking every time a car drove by, watching her move throughout the restaurant in her proper yellow and white uniform, pouring freshly made coffee in other people's cup. He thinks to himself constantly; she's just giving it away to everyone but Woody. Then, he thought, considered, and further meditated on what she would do if he walked into the restaurant, imagining it. If he sat down at one of her tables—he'd watched so long, he knew what her section was—and ordered a fresh cup of coffee. What would she say? Would she give him some? Would she act all defensive and shit like she did at the house? Would that dipshit marshal show up? Which made Woody wonder why that marshal was in her house. Was he there for Johnny's cellmate? Maybe Woody needs to find the slippery fuck and turn him over to the government to get rid of Mr. Rico Suave so he can have Lucy Hudson to himself.

Woody says, "You know—she talked about how she used to catch me following her around, but I don't know. I don't think she did as much as she thinks she did 'cause I'm freaking good at this shit, and I don't think she knew. No, I think Johnny told her, but I don't know why he would do that."

Craig drums his fingers against the wheel and, at the mention of Johnny, snaps out of whatever funk he's in and asks, "How's he doing, Johnny? Doctors say he going to make it?"

Woody just stares at him. "What the fuck do you care?"

Craig shrugs. "He was my friend, too, you know."

"You don't have any fucking friends. You're famous now. Famous people don't have fucking friends. They, you, have," he snaps his fingers to think of the word "whatcha fucking call it, an entourage. They have that. Like those shits on that show with the immortal Jeremy Piven, aging backward like Benjamin Button. You see him in *Seinfeld, Heat*? The guy looks totally different now. Has hair, and not the hair he had on his head, body hair. Makes me wonder if those plugs came from his back. I have great fucking hair. Famous people, though, they don't have friends; just look at that poor schmuck; no one likes him."

"That doesn't mean I don't have friends."

"Oh, it doesn't? When's the last time someone took you out for a beer that wasn't that lawyer slut you're sleeping with?"

Craig bristles at Woody's slight insult toward his little piece of snarled snatch and thinks the question over. Craig doesn't have the balls to challenge Woody. Never has. It's amazing. A guy like him, he could be the first one through the door on an entry arrest team, but can't confront nobody. Least of all, Woody.

Craig confirms, "It's been a while."

"That's what I thought," Woody says. "How long exactly? What's a while? Three days, three weeks? Couple of years, what are we talking about here? Help me out." Woody uses his hands like scales.

Craig shifts some in the seat; he looks uncomfortable.

"I'm not asking what the fuck your girl likes shoved up her ass. I'm asking what time frame a while means to you. It's not a hard question."

Craig hesitates before speaking. "I don't know. A while." Then Craig asks, "Why the fuck do you care?"

"Why do I care?" Woody runs a hand through his hair, smoothing back the silver portion of his wings. "Why do I care? I'll tell you why I fucking care because there's a couple million dollars that ain't in my fucking pocket thanks to that shiv sheath mother fucker sitting in prison far outside of our reach. Cooper won't let us go after him and even said Johnny's off-limits. Said we'd find the money, stones, whatever, sooner than later. Not that he isn't just as pissed off at this as I am, but now it's later, and we got no moola to show for nothing. When I got out, I expected that money, counted on it. But it's not there. So, you want me to cry tears of sadness 'cause that stupid fuck gets stabbed? Boo-fucking-hoo. There, those are my tears. He cost me, and I personally think nothing better could've happened to the dumb, stinking mook."

"Jesus," Craig says, shifting in the seat.

"Jesus, what?" Woody questions, staring at him. "You don't like the truth? We should have hammered that guy, get him to tell us where he hid the shit. But, Cooper says, Johnny's standing up. He don't like it, but Johnny didn't rat us out, and we cut him loose. Says that means something. Means Cooper's willing to play the fuck's game. Cooper didn't have to go to prison and wasn't depending on that score like the rest of us. He says the worst we can do is try to accelerate things and kill the guy and not get no money to show for it. That's not the worst thing. The worst thing is no money ever, you think—you think Johnny's going to get out and say, 'Hey guys, thanks for trusting me. Let me take you to what's yours?' I'd be freaking surprised he hasn't spent all the money or even forgets where he hid it after doing his time. Come out all degenerate laden and shit."

Craig twists his head to the side, scrunching his nose. "What?"

"Degenerate laden," Woody repeats. "What's with you? You don't understand? I'm not speaking clearly enough?"

Craig doesn't say anything.

"Cat got your tongue? You leave it inside your girl-friend? She bite it off? Shove it up her who-ha. Degenerate laden—can't remember shit—Alzheimer's."

Craig offers, "Dementia?"

Woody slaps Craig's shoulder with the back of his hand. "That's what I said."

Craig shrugs. "I'm just saying I liked the guy. We always got along. If he dies, I'll miss him. I mean, I won't cry or nothing. But it'll make me pause and say, that sucks."

"Yeah, well, everyone fucking dies, and it don't matter if it is sad or not. You could walk out your fucking door, and boom, take a fucking bullet to the noggin or get hit by a bus. Hell, you might even take a shank in the fucking side half a dozen times."

Woody can't suppress the smile cresting his lips.

He says, "We all die. Get over it."

Craig turns his head away from Woody. "You have issues."

"No, no, I don't have issues. What I have is financial responsibilities. You think I got into doing what we were doing because I'm a bully, some psychopath with no feel-ings? That I like hurtin' people? Do ya?"

"I don't know."

"That's right. You. Don't. Fucking. Know. You know nothing. We could write a book with all the shit you don't know, dedicate it to Rumsfeld and say there's even unknown-don't-knows. Say that's going to be the sequel. The *Known Unknowns* followed up with the *Unknown Unknowns*, and then complete the tri-fucking-fecta and release the third book of your stupid ass saga, put out *The Unthought of Unknown Unknowns*, the shit we don't even know we don't know or even ever thought of. Go around doing book tours and shit, except when you get to the stores, they're going to ask you why you're there, but because you don't know, you won't be able to tell them nothing.

"No, let me tell you why I did it—my ma. My ma needs the money, needed the money. You think a home's cheap? You think I'm made of fucking money that working as a *po*-lice man paid all my fucking bills? Gave me a comfortable fucking life? Before we started doing what we were doing, I was working three part-time jobs and another full-time job. Now why the fuck do I want to kill myself, run myself ragged so that I can put my ma someplace that's going to hold her while we wait for her to fucking keel over? You think that's living? That's not a life. No. I'll tell you what's a life—what *you* got? That's a fucking life, banging pop stars and being on TV. Hell, even what I fucking got right now is a life, but what I don't have, especially right now, is fucking money. Money, I deserve. Money that stupid shit stick said we couldn't have and hid."

"Cooper doesn't seem that upset."

"You think Cooper's hurting for money? You know how the kick-ups go? We ain't the only crew he's got around. Everyone gives a percentage. He just don't like us mingling with the others, with clean, goodie two-shoe shits who aren't any cleaner than the massive weight that drops out of your asshole when you sit on the throne of all men. Good cops, he says, shouldn't be seen with fuckups." Woody touches his chest. "You think I'm a fuckup? I ain't no fuck up, and neither are you."

"You think he means 'cause you went to prison?"

"Of course, that's what he means. Damn, you are dense. Why aren't you paying attention?"

"I am paying attention, but I don't know why we are sitting here and why we've been sitting here all freaking morning if she could have gone to the bank yesterday evening."

"I followed her. She went to work. Then she went home."

"So, no bank?"

"No bank. And it didn't sound like she went yesterday because the marshal busted in on her while she was getting ready for work, or so she said, but I think she just enjoyed looking how she looked—teasing him and me."

"How did she look?"

"Nipples poking through her white t-shirt like she's just waiting for the bucket of water to come splashing down." Woody demonstrates with his pinkies, placing them over his nipples. "And you know what? She's got small tits, not like your girl. She's got some nice knockers—great rack. Lucy's got those itty-bitty perky things, but they're nice. Proof gravity's been kind to her. 'Course not having a kid helps there too."

"She talked to a marshal dressed like that?" Craig says, talking it out loud. "Maybe she didn't know he was coming over."

"Oh, the fuck knew. Probably watching us right now." Woody swipes a hand across the dashboard. "Somewhere out there, just sittin'."

Craig considers the idea, nodding. "That's also what I don't get. Don't you think it might be a little…"

"Dangerous?" Woody suggests.

"No, I was going to say risky, to be sitting here like this. What if he's watching her, too, trying to see who you say he's looking for? Johnny's cellmate? See if the cellmate's going to make contact with her. He could be down the street or at one of these houses, and we wouldn't know it. Not just him, he's got a whole office and resources he could draw from and use to wait for this guy."

"You want the bullshit answer or the real answer?"

"What you going to tell me? You know where he is?"

Woody nods. "I know exactly where he is."

"You going to tell me?"

"Not if you're going to ask all sarcastically like that."

"Where is he?"

"You don't know?"

Craig shakes his head.

"Dickie texted and said the marshal's sitting in your girlfriend's office." Woody pauses, acting like he's checking his watch against his mental calculations. "Said he was in the office when he left for court this morning, and I bet by now he's screwing your girl's brains out on her desk, a handsome-looking man like him—those fucking balls."

CHAPTER 12:

ERIN MOORCOCK POUNDS A FIST ON THE screen door, muttering and cursing Dante for not picking up his phone. Through the mesh screen, browned by the sun, she can see inside. The living room's just how she remembered it. Sparse, with a couple of chairs, a TV, and a few lamps. The lamps and TV are on, showing an NBA game. The sounds are loud and on; she can hear the announcers giving introductions and recapping whatever series it is. She doesn't care, and the anger coursing through her temples drowns out whatever they say.

"Dante!" she shouts to overcome the TV. "We need to talk. It's important. You didn't pick up your phone. You're supposed to pick up your phone!"

Erin pounds her fist against the door again, the wood grain rough against the outside pad of her hand. The frame bounces against the hinges as she pounds out a rhythm. The trim around the door is scuffed in some places and chipped in others.

"Any time I call, you pick up. That's the deal. That's what you agreed to. I call; you pick up! You don't pick up; I show up here!"

Erin hits the frame around the screen door harder. Twice. Three times. It's no use. She figures his car isn't in the drive; he isn't here. She kicks the door. He's probably gone, but she wouldn't think he's someone who would leave the screen door open. So maybe he'll be back soon? Or someone's here? Like his damn cousin, what's his name?

Erin tries it softer now, "Dante—open up. I'm sorry I didn't make it this morning, but something came up."

Other than the TV, she is met with silence.

"Dante."

It's no use. No one is here.

Then, coming from the kitchen, holding a beer under his armpit, carrying a bag of chips, Dante's cousin appears. Erin searches her memory for his name. What was it? Something with repetitive syllables.

"*Cece!*" Erin exclaims, remembering his name, putting too much inference in the syllables. "Where's your cousin?"

Pausing mid-step, Cece coolly regards her, lifting an eyebrow, and then pops a chip in his mouth before continuing the trek from the kitchen to the front door. He crunches the chip with his teeth, lips open, chewing slowly and deliberately as he walks. He stops within reach of the screen door. He calmly eats another chip and wiggles his bare toes against the wood floor, looking at and speaking to her through the screen door while making no offer to open it. With apprehension in his voice. Cece says, "He not here."

"I know he's not here," Erin says, hating having to speak through the screen.

"Well, then, why'd you ask?"

"Cece, where is he—"

"Why axe a question you know the answer to? I guess that's what attorney bitches do, axe questions they know the answer to. They teach that in school? How to be an annoying twat? People don't want to be patronized. You know that's how you make people like me feel. Like you're better than me. You think you're better than me? I bet you—"

"It's important."

Cece tilts his head to the side, abandoning his diatribe. "Important?"—testing the word, repeating it—"Important. Important, like his court date this morning? Important like that? Important like our time and money, that sort of important? You know when you—you remember how you made such a big damn deal about money before *representation*, went on and on and on about how you'd got to get paid before you could do anything on his case—you said since you were paid, D was important to you? You remember that? We talkin' that type of important?"

Erin places both hands on the screen door. "Yes," she says. "Where is he?"

"You said—this is what you said—you said," he pretends to sound like Erin, taking on a high nasally pitch, but really sounding like a mother or schoolteacher because there is no way she sounds like that, "*'Now, Dante, when I call you, you need to pick up the phone. And when you call me, I'll call you right back. We have to work together.'* You remember that shit? You remember how we're supposedly in this shit together? You remember saying that, Ms. White Lady Attorney? I remember. D remembers. But something tells me, no, I know you don't remember after this morning." Cece holds up a hand with a chip, presenting it to her to signal she needs to stay silent. The chip looks like a tortilla chip. "And if you do remember, then I'd have to think that means you just don't care. Do you care?"

"I care," she says, dropping her forehead against the coarse mesh. "Where is your cousin?"

"I tole you, he's not here." Cece throws the chip in his mouth. "But then, you tole me you knew he wasn't here. Are we doing that shit again? You askin' questions you know the answer to? 'Cause if we are, then I'm shutting the door. We been through this once. No inclination to go round again."

"When's he going to be back?"

Cece grips the opening of the chip bag with one hand, dropping the bag to his side as he reaches into his armpit to retrieve the open beer. The bag crinkles as it shifts down to his side. He takes a swig from the beer and then a longer pull before storing the beer back in the crook of his armpit. He takes up the bag again. Swallows what beer's in his mouth and then reaches into the bag, slow about it, withdrawing a chip and popping it in his mouth. Crunch, crunch, crunch.

Then he says, "Oh, so *now* you care? Where were you this morning? That wasn't important enough to grace us with your presence, but now all of a sudden, whatever the fuck it is you got goin' on is important?"

"Something came up."

"What came up?" he asks. "Was that important? Did that pay more than we could? Was it something you couldn't avoid?"

Erin drops her shoulders. "I don't have time for this."

"And I didn't have time to waste my life driving D to his court dates every other goddamn month, but here we are. And I sure as hell don't want to waste my time waitin' around some damn courthouse for some white bitch who ain't comin' because something more important came up."

"It's not like that," she says.

Cece pops another chip in his mouth. "Then tell me how it's like."

"Can I come in?"

"Can you?"

"I don't know, that's why I'm asking you. You okay with it?"

"I'm okay with the concept of it, but as far as an answer to your question, axe it *the right* way."

"What the hell? What is the right way? You know what? I don't have time for this. I need to talk to your cousin."

"I tole you; he's out. Now, if you want to come in and wait for him, axe me the right way."

"Fine, whatever," she says, sighing. "*May* I come inside?"

Cece smiles. "No, you may not." His arm blinks into the space and slams shut the wooden door.

Shit.

"Cece, open the door."

Nothing.

Erin rips open the screen door and pounds on the wooden door. The screen door protests on its hinges with a squeal. Then closes on her arm.

"I really don't have the time for this. Where's your cousin? Open the door!"

Nothing.

She knuckles the door. The skin on her fingers rips some like a paper cut but jagged.

"Cece, open the door."

When there is still nothing, Erin resigns herself to the fact he may not open the door. She places both hands on the frame and knocks her forehead against the door.

She says in a small voice, "Cece, just open the door."

Nothing.

Then, he says, through the door, "Why?"

"Why?"

"Yeah; why? Why open it up? I want you to go away; I want to watch my game in peace, eat some chips with some cheese dip—*queso*," he pulls the o out in a long slur, "but if I don't open the door, I got this funny feelin' you ain't going to go away, and if you don't go away, then I can't go enjoy my chips the way I want."

"I'm here to help."

He laughs. "That's fuckin' rich, girl. You want to help. Help like you showing up this morning?"

"Someone came to visit me."

"Someone? Who?" He waits for a beat, but not long enough for Erin to tell him. "You know what? Don't tell me. Let me tell you. I bet it was a cop. People always get vague and shit when cops come around, not wanting to come right out and say, hey, the cops were here, talking about you. Sure, the hood will tell you. But not those closest to you, cuz they don't want people knowing the cops came around. Don't want you thinking differently about them, so they keep it light and misunderstood."

"Whatever," she says. "I need to tell Dante about the visit."

Cece asks through the door, "Why?"

"'Cuz he might be coming here."

The door rips open. Erin nearly stumbles into the house; she had been supporting her weight against the door. She catches herself and stands up, straightening her clothing.

Standing holding the bag and beer, Cece demands to know, "Who?"

"The cop," she says, regaining her composure fully. "A US Marshal."

"What's a marshal want with D?"

"I can't tell you."

Cece twists his face. "You can't?"

"I have to tell Dante."

Cece regards her some more. "This a lawyer thing?"

"Yes, a lawyer-client thing. So where is he?"

But Cece doesn't answer. He steps away from the doorway and says, "You might as well come in; you are already halfway in the house as it is."

Erin enters the house. "Thank you."

"Don't thank me, I ain't Dante," Cece says. "I tole D, 'specially after today, to dump your ass; get himself a man attorney, someone who knows how to keep appointments."

"The marshal surprised me in my office."

"You say that, but that don't tell me nothing. What's a marshal got to do with Dante?"

"Again, I—"

"Have to tell D, I got that."

"Where is he?"

"You want a beer?"

"No, thank you," she says, but then thinks better. "What do you have?"

Cece holds his beer up. "Pacifico."

"Anything darker?"

Cece smiles, eyes dressing her up and down. "You like darker, huh?"

"Amber," she quickly corrects.

"I got some Modelo Negros, you like Negros?"

It pains her to say yes, not at his implication, but because he is flirting with her, and the last thing she needs is Cece chasing after her. "Yes, now tell me, where is he?"

Cece throws the chip bag over the couch and enters the kitchen, holding his beer and leaving her in the living room.

If he comes out holding anything but a beer, she's out of here. She halfway expects him to come out undressed.

From the other room, Cece says, "He's with a friend."

"A friend? Dante doesn't have any friends."

"That's what *I* said," Cece says, returning to the room with a beer for her. "You want a glass or something?"

Erin nods and says she does.

Cece doesn't stop talking the whole time as he processes her answer. He disappears into the kitchen, where Erin hears the opening and closing of a cabinet, the sink, water running, and another cabinet. Cece says, "I don't like those cuz the little gold foil gets everywhere. Sometimes in my mouth. Usually on the floor. D loves those things but hates it when I drink them; he says I make a mess. He hates messy things. Makes him uncomfortable. Big guy like him, hard to believe, right? But he doesn't like a mess. The guy should be a maid, and he's sweeping, dusting, and cleaning all the time. Might as well be like my mom, complain' about how she has to pick up after me all the damn time."

He comes back into the living room with a glass.

"Is he supposed to be back soon?"

Cece glances over at the TV. "I think so," he says. "He and his *friend* were going to do something with some girl; I don't know. He didn't make a lot of sense." Cece pauses to scan the television. "You know, he won't let me eat chips?

Says they leave too many crumbs. When he returns, I bet you ten dollars—naw, you a lawyer—I bet you one hundred dollars. One of the first things he does is pull out a vacuum and go to town."

"Because of the chips?"

Cece nods. "He won't say nothing out loud. He's either too polite or stupid to complain about the chips, but it'll bother him so much that he'll get downright compulsive about it. Funny how them cops think he's the one that was out there robbing people. D wouldn't hurt a fly. Sure, he's capable of it, watched him play enough football to know he can hold off three linemen with his size—I'm exaggerating—but D don't hurt no one. He likes to keep house, do what little work he can find, work harder now that we have been fighting his case, and work out. He'd make a great wife to someone. Maybe that's what the bitch boy came by, saying he was D's friend. Maybe they had something going on—on the down-low."

"Who? Someone he had been locked up with?"

"Yeah, some handsome mother, who has dreams of grander, coming in here, telling D he owes him one, axing us if we want to make some money, saying something about some shit—I got bored listening to him, but D said he'd go with if the fucker would drive. Guy said, sure, suits him; he might need D—tried to get me to go along." Cece holds up his hands, showing innocence. "But I don't want none of what he's peddling. Wanted one of us to go in a bank, maybe cuz he couldn't or something. I ain't never met no one allergic to money, but that's what he said... I just figure it's the cameras he don't like."

CHAPTER 13:

LAMAR HENRY AND DANTE SMITH WATCH Johnny's wife exiting her car as they pass her. She is in the nearby paid parking lot because meter parking lines the curb outside the bank and requires skilled parallel parking. So, the wife parked in the paid lot and will have to walk to the bank.

Lamar drives by, saying, "I've always liked downtown Tulsa, large buildings with wide streets, never busy like in other cities."

The wife walks to an electronic kiosk in the parking lot to pay for the spot, even though the lot has an attendant. The kiosk is for electronic transactions. Cash is king in Lamar's world and the reason for the attendant.

Lamar says, "Like in the old Dillinger days, how he'd stay in places like Chicago to lay low, I'd come here to lay low—no one looks for someone like me here. So many people, but so spread out, you know."

Dante, in the passenger seat of the Chevy, doesn't say anything, as usual.

"You know Dillinger?"

Dante doesn't move. He doesn't indicate whether he knows the infamous outlaw or not.

Lamar says, "How about Pretty Boy? He was from Oklahoma."

Dante nods.

"Those guys knew what they were doing. Had style. But they died. You know why they died; they were violent. Carried guns. Shot up the place. I don't carry. I don't like to hurt people, you know, not like them, machine guns going rat-a-tat-tat-tat, standing on the sideboards of some old clunker, souped up to beat the cops. I've never been like that. Punch people, yes. Shoot them, no. I don't like guns, carrying them or using them. Good way to end up dead. I prefer my dashing persona; go up to some *mamacita* behind the counter—that's the key—find some attractive teller, tell her what's happening, but do it with a smile and a lift in your voice. Be kind. No one has to get hurt. I'd act like I might have a gun. Remind her it's not her money or the banks. Not her problem. Tell her let's get on with the day. No reason to frown; make a scene. Tell her how to give me the money, do it cool, smile, put it all right here on the counter. I'll take care of it. I'd stuff the cash in an envelope so no one thinks anything's happening. Then I'd walk out of the bank and dump the envelope as soon as possible after moving the money to a backpack with a lock in case I got stopped. Cops wouldn't be able to search it without papers."

This time of day, downtown, the buildings act as blinds to the sun and send streaming lanes of light in intermittent bands. Only a scattering of people move about, an eclectic mix; many of them are wearing business attire, dark suits, both men and women, lawyers and accountants, while the post-yuppie generation of adult children differentiate themselves from the homeless through a devotion to cleanliness and by wearing clothing designed to be distressed and frayed and not ravaged from time and life on the street. Everyone else that works down here is tucked securely in their building, their office, enjoying lunch and a view.

"I always liked this city, liked it down here with the homeless," Lamar says. "Made it easy to move around without attracting a lot of attention. Wear some ratty clothes, holes and dirt, old t-shirts, and sweatpants found at Goodwill. Opposite what people would be looking for. Amazing what slapping some dirt on your cheek and smelling like piss will do to other people's memory. But man, do I like this city. These buildings have character and life. I used to just spend days walking around dressed like that, gazing up, going around, looking around. I like how Art Déco's still in vogue here, never going completely out of style, like in Miami, and still very much a part of this place's aesthetic, unlike Miami, and how even though time's necessitated the evolution of the block to something bigger, better, and newer, many of these buildings sport some sort of homage to the city's past as much as promise a future. Miami, as nice as it is in trim, is a white-washed hellhole that cashes in on neon lights—my second favorite city."

Lamar pauses as he drives down the street a little ways and turns around at the first opportunity. He brings the Chevy next to the curb, just down from the bank's front door.

He parks, saying, "Tulsa's my favorite, but it's a shame about the city's past. In my experience, this could have been a great city. People say that, but I've always found the place kinda racist. I hear it's getting better. People trying and shit. See in the papers how the city's trying to right old wrongs, investigate cemeteries for mass graves, about a hundred years too late, which means they're only opening old wounds. See how excited everyone gets when they find some bodies, but it's a cemetery—there's bound to be someone there. What was it, two people dead? No mass graves. I been thinking about it, talking to my cell-mate Johnny about it, telling him how I feel like the city's like an old boxer; you see the guys in the gyms, broken down, look like shit, still in shape, but dumb as a fucking box of rocks, trying to right family wrongs but not doing too good of a job because the only thing they, the boxer, in this case the city, knows how to do is punch; not talk. I think talking's what's needed. But I guess maybe that's what needs to be done, some sorta painful surgery. Break down the scar tissue. Clean up the area. You know, they say scar tissue carries pain receptors. Maybe once the scars are reopened and properly sutured, then maybe true healing will come. Maybe then the talking happens, but I doubt it."

Dante nods in agreement.

Lamar sits there, window down, the breeze cooling his forehead and shoulder, and watches the wife, done with putting the little parking tag in the dash of her car, stroll down the sidewalk and open the bank's front door, tugging it open with some effort. "That's the wife," he says, tossing an arm against Dante's to get the big man's attention. "Lot of door for such a small woman."

Dante looks at him and slowly rotates his head back to the window. He sees the wife, but he remains quiet.

Lamar says, "I would go in there, but with my history, that might not be such a good idea. Plus, I'm not dressed right. Don't worry; you're not going in there, either. You're too memorable for this place. Cece should have come with us, but I can't stand him, so maybe this is better. He wouldn't fit in in there either."

Dante lifts an eyebrow.

The wife holds the door open for an older couple. The man is wearing some kind of veteran hat, walking with a cane, and looking ninety years old. The woman may be a few years younger, wearing a Pepto Bismol pantsuit and a teal blouse to match the jewelry. Her hair is something like brunette, not natural, and borders on red—goes with the suit. She'd fit right in in Miami.

"Don't know who's about," Lamar continues. "Never know who might be watching. Watchin' her or lookin' out for me."

Almost on cue, Lamar spots the black Lincoln creeping down the street behind the wife, not doing too good of a job at looking inconspicuous. Two older-looking white dudes in the front, a GQ driver with the sunglasses and the haircut, good square looks, looks like someone he knows, but he can't place the face. The passenger looks like Paulie from *The Sopranos*, even with wings and sun-beat-to-shit skin. Both men, eyes locked on the wife's perfect rear end, are tracking the wife's movements as she slips inside the bank. Once the bank's doors close behind her, they return to the road and drive past.

"Speak of the devils," Lamar says, pointing them out to Dante with a chin jerk.

Dante either doesn't notice them or doesn't care. He says nothing.

Lamar says, "I was looking for someone like them, two cop-looking dudes. I spotted them before at her house, but I wasn't sure then; now, I'm sure."

The black Lincoln passes Dante's Chevy, and neither man pays Lamar or Dante any attention.

"Would you look at that? It's like neither of us are even here. Which, I guess, sadly, is more common than I think most Americans want to admit, or it should be, burying their heads in the sand about all the racist shit out there, but in this situation, it might be an advantage for us, them not looking for us, so they don't see us, but we see them."

Lamar tracks their movement in the side mirror, reaching out the window and adjusting it to watch the Lincoln go down and then turn around, coming back his way.

"Think they're going to pull in behind us?" Lamar asks Dante, but the big man doesn't offer an answer, not that Lamar thought he would. So, he says, "Wouldn't that be a look? Two cars with two dudes, one car with white guys and one black, waiting for this little good-looking lady to come out of the bank? That's a sight."

The two dudes in the Lincoln pass them again, going the other way, still not looking around, not noticing or seeing the Chevy. Lamar watches their back-end bounce as they pull into the paid lot, pausing at the entrance to slip the attendant, a skinny black dude with legs like dowel rods dressed in fluorescent blue and red, a couple of dollars. From where Lamar's sitting, they disappear for a bit, but their front end reappears, pulling into a space with the correct sight angle on the bank's front door.

Almost an hour passes before the wife appears again, storming out of the bank, taking a wrong turn, and walking down the sidewalk toward Lamar and Dante, not the parking lot.

"Don't move," Lamar says to Dante. "Don't look at her. Don't say nothing."

Dante does as he's told; Lamar knew he would.

The wife passes them, doesn't glance their way, and digs in her purse. She looks upset, as if she heard bad news and doesn't know how to take it.

Lamar turns in the seat, eyes tracking the perky rear-end stomping down the sidewalk in the side mirror. "You got your phone?" he asks Dante.

Dante turns his big head on Lamar's way. He nods once.

"You can drive, right? Do you have your license and know how to do it? You just don't like it, right?"

Dante nods again.

"Okay, stay with the car." Lamar points two fingers at the black Lincoln's nose. "When those two pull past, I want you to drive back to the house, get Cece and his cell phone, and come back here."

Dante just blinks.

Lamar pops open the driver's door and unfolds his hand out flat. "Phone."

Dante digs the phone from his back pocket and slaps it in Lamar's hand.

"Any password or something?"

Dante shakes his head.

"Okay, you clear on what I want you to do?"

Dante nods, but his eyes show that he doesn't understand why.

"Look, I'm going to follow that woman on foot. She's on foot. If I lose her, then we just start again tomorrow, but I don't have a phone. You have a phone. Cece has your number. Now, I have Cece's number. This way, I can hook up with you when we are done. But she's going somewhere. See how she didn't go back to her car? I want to see where she's going."

Dante blinks once.

"So, when that car," He points to the space where the Lincoln, now gone, was, "goes by, get out, get in the driver's seat, and go home."

Lamar exits the car, slamming the door behind him.

Through the down window, Lamar, bends over and checks again, "Do you understand what you're to do?"

Dante nods. He opens his passenger door and steps out of the car.

Lamar lightly jogs across the street as the black Lincoln creeps down the street behind him. He resists the urge to look back. Once Lamar jumps the curb with his last step, and the Lincoln is down the street some, Dante's Chevy pulls away from the curb and heads in the opposite direction.

On the sidewalk, Lamar parallels the wife from across the street. He watches as the wife gets on the phone, talking to someone. She keeps glancing back over her shoulder. He stays almost a half block behind her and on the other side of the street. She's good-looking and won't be hard to miss. He can keep an eye on her unless she jumps in someone's car or he can't get to a corner in time to ensure she doesn't slip into some building.

Dante's phone rings.

No way Dante could be home already.

Reluctantly, Lamar takes his eyes off the woman and answers the phone.

It's Cece. "D, where you all at?"

"It's not D," Lamar says, snapping his eyes back to the wife. Talking on the phone slows him down some, but the wife's also on the phone, so she's slowed too.

Cece half-whispers into the phone. "Why the fuck do you have D's phone?"

"Don't worry about it," Lamar says. "Are you trying to keep your voice down? Why are you whispering?"

Cece ignores Lamar's question. He didn't think Cece would tell him anyways.

"Where the fuck is D?"

"He's not here," Lamar says.

"Where is he? It's important."

"We just went through this. He's not here."

"Then where?"

"Don't you worry about it? You didn't want to come anyways."

Still struggling to keep his voice low, Cece says, "Don't worry about it. Don't worry. I'll decide what I need to worry about. You don't tell me what to worry about. Who the hell are you to do that? Put D on the phone."

"I can't."

Loud. "Why the hell not?"

"He's coming to pick you up."

"Pick me up? Why's he coming to pick me up? He's supposed to be with you... tell me D isn't driving; he's driving, isn't he? He doesn't drive. I tole you that. I said, don't let D drive; he doesn't drive. Why is D driving?"

"Look, I don't have time for this," Lamar says.

"You don't have time? I don't have time. Why is D driving?"

"I need you all to come pick me up."

"Why—what are you doing?"

"I don't want to get into it on the phone. This isn't the time, and I don't have the inclination."

"You don't want to get into it; who the fuck are you? Where do you get the gonads to tell me what you want to get into or not?"

"It's too much to explain," Lamar says, slowing his voice down so Cece can understand like he's stupid. He is. "Look, come back here with D, pick me up, and I'll explain everything to you."

Cece doesn't sound convinced. "No, you won't."

"Yeah, I won't; you're right," Lamar says sarcastically. "I'll tell you we had to separate. I need a ride when I'm done. I have D's phone, so you could call me and hook back up when I'm done."

"When you're done? Tell me what you're doin'," Cece says. "Tell me what's happenin' now, not later. Why you separate?"

Lamar doesn't tell him. Instead, he asks, "Were you calling for a reason?"

"Yeah, I was callin' for a fucking reason. I don't just call people for no reason, 'specially D. Anything I have to say to him, normally, I just yell at him from the other room or wait until one of us gets home. I don't just call nobody. When I call, I got a reason, and I've got a reason."

"You going to tell me what that might be? Or are we at an impasse?"

"At an in—what?"

"Impasse," Lamar repeats. "You know what, never mind. What do you want?"

"Oh, so now you want to be all hypocritical and shit, axe me what I want. 'Speckin' me to tell you what you want to know, and you not say nothing to me about what you doing. 'Speck me not to ask what you want. Keep quiet when you act like you. I don't know you. We just met, far as I'm concerned, fuck you. But I'll tell you anyways. What I want is to know what the fuck you are doing with my cousin. Why you here? But seeing how you like to play mother fucking games, I guess I won't get that. What I want is for you to get fucking lost. Tell me why you have D's phone and haven't hit the road."

"I'll tell you later. Why were you calling?"

Cece is quiet for a moment.

"I'm going to hang up," Lamar says, challenging him.

Cece says, "I was going to tell D there's a lady here to see him."

"Who is it?"

"Don't matter to you, none. D knows this lady, and I wanted to see what he wanted me to do with her."

"What does she want?"

"She says it's important—won't tell me nothing. Wants to tell D, but she's axing all these questions, doin' it in her way—I don't trust her."

"What type of questions?"

"She axin' about anyone, old *friends*," he sneers the word, "who might've come round to see my dear old stupid ass cousin. Things like that, like she needs to know if some-one's reached out to D or will reach out. She talking about you? I think she's talking about you."

"Again, who is she?"

The wife stops in front of a building with mirrored glass

Lamar sits down at a bus stop bench, careful to keep eyes on her, but also looks like he's waiting for a bus. He won't admit it, but Cece's calling helps with the cover. He's just a man on the phone waiting for a bus.

Cece sucks in the air and tries to turn it around on Lamar, adopting his hard-ass persona, bubbling with false anger. "Man—why you want to know?"

"If she's asking that question, I need to know who she is."

"I'm not your secretary or your bitch; I'm not here to answer questions for you."

"Cece, shut the fuck up and focus," Lamar says.

"*Man*, fuck you," is all Lamar hears before Cece ends the phone call.

Lamar slips the phone in his front pocket. He leans back on the bench, throwing an arm over the back. He glances the wife's way when a man appears at the wife's side, someone Lamar's seen before.

CHAPTER 14:

EDUARDO CHAVEZ WATCHES THE WHITE Toyota Corolla pull up to the curb outside the motel, John Rafferty driving, all the windows down.

With his hands in his pockets, Eduardo says, "This is the best they had?"

Rafferty removes the mangled straw he had been chewing on from his mouth, a particularly annoying habit, leans across the passenger seat, and unlocks the door. "You said rent a car. I rented a car. What's the deal?"

"This is the best thing you could come up with?"

"It's the cheapest thing I could come up with in the time allowed. Remember, we're here on our dime," Rafferty says, stressing his point. "You don't like the car, then you can go rent your own. You said you wanted something that doesn't stick out and that we can use for surveillance. This is what I chose. You don't like it? You can go get one. You said take care of it. I took care of it.

"And you know what, while we are on the subject, we're barely three days into this little jaunt, and I'm getting tired of your attitude. Remember. You came to me. Reclaim our reputation, you said. This will help us, you said. Come along with me, you said. Yada yada, a whole helluva lot more bullshit you said. All of it begging me for my help. But now you're complaining. That's all you do. Done. You stand there; you sit there; hell, you even scoot your ass across the damn carpet like a dog over there; the whole time, you're mute as a fucking church mouse. All introspective and shit, thinking. You're typical you. But then the first thing you say is some sorta bitching. I don't get it."

"I'm not bitching. I asked a question."

"It's bitching. Asking questions to those doing you a favor is a form of bitching. You don't believe me? Go ask Miranda, tell her what we're doing. I'm sure she'd love to hear all about how we're trying to salvage our reputation by tracking down the guy we lost. We're suspended. I'm sure that will go over real fucking well. Now, mind you, I'm all for this little vacation of ours, going off the reservation, this time away from the house—"

"So, you can now take a shit in peace."

Rafferty holds up a hand as his eyes flick away, and his voice adopts the dad tone of someone with multiple kids: patient, stern, and bored. "Don't, just don't." He rights himself in the driver's seat, flicking the straw to the passenger floorboard. He picks a fresh dip packet from the can in his left hand and shoves the packet into the corner of his mouth, saying, "Get in. We're running behind. We don't have much time to get back. She went to the bank. I don't know how long she will be there, but she parked in a paid lot, so it should be easy to figure out if she's still there or not when we get back."

Eduardo nods. He had asked Rafferty to follow Johnny's wife this morning while he visited the attorney and ran down an old contact from his Fugitive Task Force days. Asked him to pick up a car that wasn't like theirs so they could move around the city without raising suspicion.

Eduardo opens the door and sits in the passenger seat. He shuts the door. "How did the morning go?"

Rafferty picks up his dip cup, a used coffee cup with a cheap plastic lid that has to be torn to be used. Folding the lid mouth flap back, Rafferty holds it up to his lips, carefully placing his lips on the rim of the cup and ejecting the dark tobacco waste into the cup. He then places the cup back in the cup holder.

Then he checks his mirrors to pull away from the curb. "Well, it went well," he says, navigating the Corolla away from the curb. "I stuck with her all morning. No real problems. Nice day. The temperature was fine, which made it easy. But I'll say, she's a looker, that one. Certainly, don't mind following *her* around."

Eduardo stays quiet because he agrees, but he doesn't want to admit that to Rafferty because he doesn't want to hear Rafferty complain and question Eduardo's thinking on this, not that it stops Rafferty from doing just that.

Rafferty says, "Look, we have to talk. The way I see this, we're way out on a limb here. Not that it hasn't stopped us from getting out there on that branch, crawling all the fucking way, but I need to know."

Eduardo knows what he's about to say and doesn't want to hear it.

"I have to know, are we following this broad because of her husband's celly? Or are we doing it because you got a hard-on for her?"

"To be honest, I'm not sure," Eduardo says.

He didn't plan on admitting his feelings to Rafferty, but he is a confederate in this off-the-books operation where, essentially, they've formed "some sorta half-ass posse," Rafferty's words, to go after Lamar. The man, his partner, is owed something of an explanation. No matter how light on details it might be.

Eduardo admits, "I've been asking myself that same question."

Rafferty considers the confession, humming to himself, sucking on the bottom portion of his lip where he's stuffed the dip packet, a giant bulge deforming his jawline. "Well, now I'm the one asking it. I need to know, *one way or the other*," he nearly sings the phrase, "'cause it's my ass on the line here too. Now, I get it." He chuckles. "My ass is the reason we're even doing this, and I'm sympathetic, even apologetic, about that. No reason you should be suspended, too, but heavy is the head that wears the crown, and that's what you get for wanting to make that supervisor money. So, what's the play here? 'Cause from what I'm hearing from Susan back at the office, they think Lamar's in *New Orleans*," he pronounces it with an accent, "not in Tulsa. So, what do you know that I don't? Are we just here so you can play patty cake with Sweet Cheeks waitress? All alone in that big house of hers, with no husband around, waiting for a big, strong, dark-skinned man to come along and use his charm? Or do you really think he's here, and why would he be here? What's the point?"

Before Eduardo can respond, Rafferty continues, "Now, as far as the wife goes, vacations, for that matter, I don't mind following her around," Rafferty says. "This isn't a bad gig. It's quiet. I get some time to myself. Get to hear myself think. Read, relax, enjoy some nice weather, all while holding up inside a car."

Eduardo doesn't miss the sarcasm.

"The wife's got a fine ass for sure. Talk about a round. She's attractive, and from what you told me last night, I'm pretty sure she likes you. She was coming to see you at the house yesterday. Remember, that's all from what *you* said, so it could all be bullshit. Who am I to say differently? But what I don't understand is your interest. If you said, 'John, I fucked her.' I'd get it. Or even just admit you would like to fuck her. I'd get that, too. But no, you're Mr. Gentleman. Mr. I don't know if this is purely a professional curiosity or something more—more emotional, more basic—and it's fine if you don't know, but I need to know. The only way this works out for us is if we find Lamar Henry. I still don't know the plan for when that happens, but I'm willing to go along with you until we figure that out. What I'm *not* willing to do is waste my time."

"You're not wasting your time."

"Then what do you know that I don't because I'm questioning our intent here? No one seems to think this guy would come to Tulsa, and now I am starting to wonder why we are here. And I don't think it's 'cause Lamar is here.'"

Eduardo tells him. "She's the key. The wife. Whatever is going on, she's the key. Whatever happened in the prison—Lamar's escape from the hospital—she's the key."

"How do you know that? You can't possibly know that."

"I feel it."

"Deep inside your gut?" Rafferty asks. "Is that where you feel it?" Grabbing his stomach flab. "Right here? That where? 'Cause if it is, I got to ask if what you're feeling, is that instinct, or is it just those butterflies encouraged to take flight by looking *at*, and now, *being* in the presence of the pretty girl who was in the picture we found in Johnny's cell?"

Eduardo sighs. "I don't know."

Rafferty makes a noise. "That's what I'm saying. You don't know." He jerks the wheel to the left to turn left. "I need to know. I need to know what we are doing here."

Eduardo braces himself in the seat as Rafferty finishes the sharp turn.

"What'd the attorney say?"

"Not much," Eduardo says. "I got the address for that Dante Smith, Lamar's cellmate, from when he came back on the writ. I think we should pay him a visit."

Rafferty looks at Eduardo. "You can visit him. Only way for me to come along was for me to stay in the car. My wife doesn't like this idea. Didn't like that I was suspended. Didn't like Miranda not knowing what we were doing. Told me to stay safe, stay in the car. Asked me what would happen if something happens to me. What would my girls do? What would she do? I'm not protected here; neither are you. That is why I told you to see the wife on your own, which you did. But you came back different."

"I'm not different."

"Yes. You are. You seem happier. Relaxed. You like this hotdog bullshit. You like that we're chasing this guy you know so much about. You never told me why, you know, but you know. And all that's hunky dory. I'm good with it. Just cause I'm not doing anything other than staying in the car, don't mean I want to be left out of the loop."

He has a point.

"Don't leave me out of the loop. So, tell me about what you got from the attorney."

"I dropped the idea that Lamar would come find Dante," Eduardo says. "The attorney didn't like that. She seems actually to care about her clients. That what she was doing isn't a show. But I don't know. That care could just be her competitive nature. She doesn't like to lose. Them, her clients, going to prison for what the state says they did, is her losing. If she gets to dictate the terms, I think that's a win for her."

"That's what you think?" Rafferty says. Eduardo nods. Rafferty adjusts in the seat and adds, "You really think what the wife said is true? That there's some pot of gold out there at the end of the rainbow?"

"It doesn't matter if it's true. Lamar thinks it's true. I'm sure Johnny told him about it."

"How do you know that?"

Because Johnny told him, Eduardo knows, but he says, "I don't. That's why we are here—low key."

"Low key, right." Rafferty grows quiet as they pass the bank entrance and the paid parking lot. "But you didn't know about this money before we came here, right?"

Eduardo doesn't answer him. Eduardo told Rafferty what the wife told him last night when she told him about her interaction with Morris Woodford. Instead, he says, "So tell me what you saw this morning. Our boy shows up?"

"Maybe," Rafferty says, reluctantly allowing the change in conversation. "I saw a Chevy lurking around; it might have been him if what you're saying was right. I think he's going to approach the girl, too; I concur. But whoever it was in the Chevy was staying too far away for me to get a good look at them. I didn't want to give up what I had. I had a great spot. Backed in across the street, a couple of houses down. The old lady who lives there didn't have an issue with me, saw the badge and said I could borrow her driveway. She's working. What's she doing with it during the day? I didn't tell her the badge means jack about what's

going on with you and me. I set myself up in the backseat. No one would've known I was there."

"But you saw this Chevy?"

"I saw a Chevy but couldn't see who was driving. Also, I saw a Lincoln."

"A Lincoln, what Lincoln?"

"I'm not sure."

"You're not sure what Lincoln you saw?"

"No, I'm sure what I saw. It was black. Reminded me of that Big Black Lincoln song, you know it? That's all I could hear, watching the two dipshits inside of it. Know what, it doesn't matter. I don't know who was in the Lincoln either. But these two idiots didn't know how to do surveillance too well. Which kinda leads me to believe they might've been cops."

Eduardo confirms. "They might be cops. Ex-cops, at least."

"No shit? You think?"

Eduardo does. He says, "My bet, it's that Woodford guy."

"The guy who tried to measure dick sizes with you?"

"The same. He was in a Lincoln. Could be his Lincoln."

"Then it probably was him," Rafferty says. "They weren't too good about staying far back and out of the way. Not like the Chevy. Not like me."

"It's why I wanted you."

"Why's that?"

"Because you're good at staying in the car."

Pulling in front of the bank and going around the corner, Rafferty says, "Fuck you." Then he asks, "You went to see Bill Ruth, didn't you?"

"I figured a guy like Lamar was in town; maybe he'd heard something."

"I don't know what you see in that guy. He's a snake. No, know what, he's a shark. That's what he is. Loan shark and fucking squirmy."

"He has a better network in this part of the world than anyone around."

"So does Mazzios. But you don't see me ordering pizzas to some guy's house and him ending up in the hospital with a broken leg."

"If it matters, he thinks Lamar is in town, too."

"Mark my words, Romeo. By the end of this, somehow, someway, that shark's going to be involved in all this."

Eduardo is quiet for a long time before he responds.

"Why do you think I paid him a visit?"

CHAPTER 15:

LUCILLE HUDSON THROWS OPEN THE door, exiting the bank, thankful to be free and out in the open. In the fresh air, she can breathe and process. God, she needs to process. Process what she just learned. Process what she knew about her husband—what she *thought* she knew. Process her next move. And Lucy worries she might be in danger after Woody's visit and what she knows now. How could she not—all that money?

She walks as fast as she can without breaking into a run, shouldering her purse with a heft of her arm, confused, a little hurt—probably would have been more hurt two years ago—and she is convinced someone is following her. She can't shake the feeling. Someone's out there. She's sure. And after what Johnny said, she's doubly sure.

All that money.

Lucy digs her cell phone out of her purse. She doesn't have to enter or even try to remember his number. She pre-programmed the number into her phone before he left last night. With a couple of clicks of her nails on the glass, she navigates the screen to his contact, selects his name, and calls him.

Eduardo Chavez picks up on the first ring as if he had been expecting her phone call.

"Good morning," he says, his voice calm, smooth, and exactly what she needs right now. "To what I owe the pleasure?"

He sounds like he is outside. She can hear the blur of the wind against the speaker. Is he following her? She'd be okay with that. At least, that would explain this feeling. Maybe he isn't following her; that's just wishful thinking; maybe he's sitting on an outdoor cafe patio having a late breakfast. Maybe he's in the car with the windows down. Maybe he's working, maybe he's not working, maybe at home, sitting on his back porch or something.

But again, if he were following her, she'd be okay with that.

"I wanted to hear your voice," she says, not thinking about the implications.

"My *voice*?"

"Yes, to feel safe," she says. She pauses to look around. "You handled yourself well with Woody yesterday. You weren't nervous. I liked that. It helped me feel better. You weren't mean or rude. You just handled him with strength. I need that right now. I feel like someone is following me."

"You do?"

Lucy continues walking. She doesn't acknowledge his question. She whispers, "I just left the bank."

"What bank?"

"I guess you wouldn't know what I'm talking about," she says. "You don't know what I'm doing or where I am— what I'm thinking. And last night—after Woody left—I unloaded on you about why he was there, his little *visit*, what he wanted, the divorce, what Dickie told me. And you know, you were so nice. You just sipped your coffee the whole time and listened politely, nodding and interjecting at appropriate times, but I didn't miss it. I saw the look you were giving me." The look in his dark eyes. "You might've been listening intensely, but you were completely lost to the context of the conversation."

An old, black car passes slowly, the engine purring, catching her eye.

The phone is silent for a moment as Lucy glances left and right, tracking the car with her eyes until it turns left. She then tucks her chin to her chest and forces herself to breathe evenly. It's in her head. She doesn't see anyone following her, but that doesn't mean someone isn't there.

Lucy detects the upturn in Eduardo's tone as he puts it together. "Ah—the *one* that belongs to the key? You did say something about something last night."

"The same. I just finished watching Johnny's recording." She hesitates before continuing. "And now—I... I feel like I'm being followed and watched. It's not like the feeling wasn't there before entering the bank, but I thought I was overreacting, but now, after watching what Johnny left me—I used the manager's computer to do it." Not knowing why she was telling an almost-all-but-stranger, Lucy tries to reassure herself and him, the words spilling out of her mouth. "I'm not overreacting because now, knowing what I know, God, I wish I didn't know—it's overwhelming, the feeling. I'm being followed—Where are you?"

"I'm working."

"That is a non-answer," Lucy says bluntly. "Johnny used to do that to me, giving me an answer that isn't really an answer. Doesn't tell me anything. Doesn't answer the question the way it should be answered. I didn't like it then and don't like it now."

Eduardo responds, "I'm not Johnny." Then Lucy hears Eduardo say something to someone and the dinging of a car door. Eduardo says, "What if I told you I was close?"

"Close to me?"

He half laughs. "It might explain why you feel like you are being watched."

"Are you watching me?"

"No, not watching per se, not officially—not creepily either," he quickly adds. "Also, we're... I'm not following you—shadowing maybe is the word you'd choose—maybe not." He pauses. "I guess that doesn't sound any better. But I'm close."

It sounds excellent to her. She asks, "How close?"

"Close enough. Where are you right now?"

Lucy tells him her location, glancing at the street sign and reading the numbers on a building beside her. She says, "I'd feel better knowing it was you—being the one following me, watching me."

Then her mind plays out the scene in her imagination, glancing out the dining room window, seeing him sitting in his assigned vehicle, sweating—she bet he looks good, sweaty—and she making up and bringing out some lemonade, asking him to come inside, saying it's too hot out here. Telling him he can keep tabs on her inside.

Sounds like a bad movie.

Lucy jostles the thought away, and Eduardo's voice brings her back. He says, "What was on the tape? Was it that bad?"

"A confession," Lucy says. "And yeah, it's so much worse than what came out in court. I had no idea. How could he?"

"What do they always say? The money, it's always about the money."

"Who's they?"

"Those that do bad things for themselves."

"He called it a gift," Lucy says, agreeing, nodding her head so that he can see her. "Said he left it for me so we could build a new life together when he got out. But if something happened to him, he wanted me to have it. His gift to me for being such a shitty husband. A gift, my ass. If he really loved me, he would've told me about it sooner, so I didn't have to spend two years busting my ass to make ends meet."

"Reduced to living in Johnny's grandmother's house," Eduardo quips.

"Right," she says. "Jesus. Someone is following me. Has to be. I don't know who, but it's probably Woody like he used to. He's probably greasing his hair back out there looking at me. He came by yesterday telling me about the money he wanted, but I had no idea it was so much, no idea what Johnny and his friends had really done, were capable of."

A block away from the bank, Lucy realizes she's holding her breath and lets out some air, releasing a tiny amount of tension from her chest like a pressure valve releasing steam.

"But it could be someone else out there. I guess it could be Johnny's cellmate. Maybe he stabbed Johnny, knowing about the money, and did it in some half-witted plan to get to the money. Make a new life."

"Sounds like life-altering money."

Lucy thinks about it. Maybe his cellmate knew about the money, and that's why Eduardo is in her life.

Does he want the money?

He doesn't strike her as someone who cares about money.

She says, "How could I not have known? Seen what they were doing?"

Eduardo doesn't provide her with an answer.

"I knew something wasn't right, but I never guessed ... *this*. When Johnny went to Costa Rica the last time and insisted I go with him, I knew then that something was happening, not the legal issues, but that he was keeping something from me. I should have known. I should have... I'm hurting, you get that? Maybe you do. I probably would have been more hurt two years ago, but time's hardened me, and I've learned not to trust Johnny; the latest knowledge, some bitch in Costa Rica, just cements I'm doing the right thing in divorcing him—"

She cuts herself off suddenly after thinking about her current affairs, and she is two blocks from the bank; the pressure is too much.

"Someone is watching me," she says. Glancing over her shoulder, she sees nothing and no one, but that doesn't mean whoever, whatever, is out there isn't there.

"I felt like that last night, but I brushed it off, choosing to bury myself in my work. But occasionally, I caught a glimmer in the reflection of the diner's windows and thought I saw someone lurking there, outside. Thought I saw Woody, hovering just out of the corner of my vision, smiling that stupid toothy smile of his, that hair, the silver and black. The smell of his cologne. I couldn't shake it. Thank God you happened to be at the house when Woody came by. What would have happened if you hadn't been there?"

Lucy stops abruptly.

"How did Woody know about the recording?" she says, the realization she hadn't asked this question before dawning on her. She doesn't give Eduardo a chance to answer; she knows the answer. "Had to be Dickie. Damn him."

Lucy stops in front of a building with high windows from the sidewalk to the top of the second story. The glass is dense with a reflective coating that blocks her view of the inside but gives her a perfect representation of herself.

Digging in her purse and withdrawing her sunglasses, she slips the dark sunglasses over her eyes, turning to check her reflection in a mirror and to catch anyone following her. That's what they do in spy movies, right? Turn suddenly, check reflective surfaces, and scan the area and people around them.

Her eyes scan the reflection, looking beyond her frame in the simple black blouse, tight blue jeans, and black boots to the street around her. She tracks cars as they pass, not seeing anything that looks out of place, but how would she know? It's just a feeling.

Maybe she should trust her feelings.

But her plan doesn't work because all she sees is herself; no matter how often she is forced to look beyond herself, her eyes bounce back, and how much of a mess she is right now. Her blonde hair is up, but a few strands have come loose. She tucks them away, behind her hair and off her forehead, and wipes her fingertips with both hands across the crests of her cheeks, just under the sunglass frame, clearing away any remnants of tears.

Stepping into the frame behind her, wearing a primarily taxi-cab yellow bowling shirt with a broad blue stripe down the middle, khaki pants—not quite slacks—and his

Panama hat, US Marshal Eduardo Chavez appears over her right shoulder, slipping his phone in his pocket.

"Mrs. Hudson," Eduardo, not Ed or Eddie, says, tipping his chin as he slides the hat off his head and down his chest gentlemanly.

Lucy glances at him in the reflection, refusing to turn to address him. "What are you doing here?"

He's not wearing sunglasses, so he's squinting, adding the right amount of crease and shading to his olive complexion to give him a youthful look.

"I'm talking to you," he says, offering a slight grin, lightening the mood.

Lucy turns around and pulls the frames down her face to reveal her puffy and red eyes from the crying, but she hopes he can't see them. "I know that," she says, looking over the frame at him. "What are *you* doing *here*?"

"I wanted a cup of coffee," he says. "Do you want a cup of coffee?"

Without missing a beat, she retorts, "Does it just have to be coffee?"

"For you or me?"

"Can it not be both?"

"'Fraid not," he says, slipping the hat back on his head. "I'm sorta on duty, so just coffee for me."

"Damn," she says. "I was hoping to get you drunk."

"To take advantage of me?"

"Do you want me to take advantage of you?"

He doesn't answer.

Lucy likes that, the verbal tussling. She can't help but feel a lightness in his presence or keep a smile from caressing her lips.

"You couldn't have appeared more opportune," she says. "Must be your police sense, or maybe just a normal sixth sense. Johnny never had it, and he was the police. But then again, him being where he is, in prison, not the hospital, for doing all those things he and the others did, maybe he never was the police. Maybe he lost it. You don't strike me as someone who loses it. You seem like you're always in control."

And she could handle someone taking control of her life.

Lucy wraps her arm around his, intertwining limbs, her other hand lying over his, like when Johnny would walk his grandmother into a restaurant. Except where that was chaste and familiar, his grandmother patting Johnny's hand, telling him how happy he makes her, this is anything but, exotic and thrilling. Eduardo allows her to take his hand, assuming the expected male escort position as if he's an usher walking down an aisle or they're a couple that's been together forever. Immediately, she feels comfortable and safe in his presence. Comfortable doing this, being with him. The pressure of someone watching her evaporates away with just the merest contact of her skin against his and sends electricity up her arm. Her heart stutters and beats faster. She's grateful the sunglasses conceal the flush in her cheeks.

Lucy says, "I can always get drunk. Walk with me. I know a place. Has both—in case you change your mind. Good coffee and even better bourbon."

CHAPTER 16:

MORRIS WOODFORD STARES OUT THE window and breaks the silence for the first time in an hour. He says, "I swear to God, you can't miss this freaking guy. It's like he picks the brightest, loudest shirts to wear just for the fucking fun of it. He dresses like a fucking clown; look at him."

With his right arm supporting his head, he leans against the window and watches the two love birds framed in the bar's window. Woody motions to the windshield, the couple beyond, before he checks his watch against mental calculations.

They've been in there for two hours.

"The *balls* on him," Craig says, thick with sarcasm, fiddling with the driver's side mirror.

Woody snaps his head toward Craig. "What the fuck did you say?"

Craig turns to give him a look. "I'm messing with you, relax."

"Relax?"

"Yeah, chill out, lighten up. We've been sitting here for, like, what? Two hours? While they yuck it up in there. I'm bored, and it's hot. It's stuffy in here. You smell like a mobster's underwear drawer. And you bitching all the time's not helping anything."

Woody leans his head back against the window and grumbles to himself. "Oh, forgive me, Mr. Shit Stick. I'm sorry I decided to speak the first fucking word for the first time in one fucking hour, and here I was thinking I was doing you a fucking favor by not mentioning nothing about our past because for some reason you, Mr. Hollywood, although you go to New York for some freaking reason to film your stupid fucking show, doesn't like thinking about all the big bad boogie man shit he's done. What the fuck do you know? Nothing. That's right. We already covered this. You know *fucking* nothing."

Craig takes a deep breath. "That's right, *nothing*, because I can't tell you what we don't know," he says.

Craig starts flipping his phone end over end on his right thigh while he ignores Woody's digs about his career. He used to do this shit back in the day, too. Sit quietly while probably internally counting to ten or counting sheep or whatever the fuck he does to keep his temper in check, fucking fiddle with shit. The thing was then, like now, the redness would creep up from his chest, first at the base of his neck, going all the way up like one of those color-changing cups, until the little vein in his forehead, a translucent blue, started swelling and throbbing.

Craig says, "We don't know what they are talking about." He says, "We don't know what was in the bank."

"Like I need to be told."

Craig goes on, "We don't know where Johnny hid the money or even how to find it. And we don't know what he said in the recording he left."

Woody lifts an eyebrow. "What's the recording matter if we can get the money? The recording ain't nothing. The shit he took is everything. It should be everything. All I care about."

"The recording isn't nothing. It's *everything,* but you're too freaking stupid to figure that out."

All Woody says is, "I ain't stupid. Don't say that. Don't call me stupid." He says, "Teachers used to call me stupid. I was never stupid. Slow, maybe, not retard slow, but not up with the sprinters in the class either. But I understood, *understand,* everything. I just get there on my own time. And what I understand right now is *you* have a guilty conscience."

Craig pauses the flipping phone, swipes a finger against the screen, and checks the time. Then he mumbles, "The recording *matters,* or it should—at least to you—it matters to me."

"Why—you afraid someone will find out you been a bad boy? That's what you are afraid of, isn't it? You have a lot more things to be afraid of. Afraid people might find out how you were a cooperating witness? A fucking rat?"

Craig quickly says, "I'm not a rat."

At the same time, Woody mocks him, mouthing the words almost in rhythm, although slightly delayed, like he's singing to his favorite song, *"I'm not a rat."* Woody slaps the dashboard and says, "Then what the fuck are you if not a rat, cause you sure as shit ain't a TV star. No, I don't see you on *Letterman,* or whatever the fuck they have now, doing the talk show circuit, making Jimmy Fallon laugh at his stupid jokes. 'Member on *Saturday Night Live* how the motherfucker couldn't ever stay in the moment? That's you, not able to keep a straight fucking face. You crack the fuck up. You're the first one to break, first one to talk. That's fucking you. That's why you're a reality star, worse, a reality TV host. I bet people say to themselves, 'What's worse than a cop, a rat cop at that?' Nah, it's you, a whole new fucking category, a rat dick, a fucking reality TV host rat dick, the big cheese, nothing lower. Some guy spilling all our secrets like that magician in the fake fucking kabuki mask, telling people how cops do their jobs. People don't care how cops do their jobs. They care when cops get caught doing their jobs, and you're out there putting on a show about it. Saying what a cop show is, showing people what the media thinks a cop should be, but not putting it out there like it is. It's like those fucking ride-alongs we used to do, people sitting in the seat, like writers and shit. Like that fuck, Michael Connelly, sitting there, seeing what we do but not what we do, 'cause they don't get to go inside, deal with the shit we deal with, see the shit we see. The dead kids, the gruesome crime scenes, the abusive fucks. Sitting there thinking because they took a couple of nights out of their busy shitty lives, they know fuck all about our lives. That's what *you* are doing. That's what rats do. Package it up and sell it to the public. And here I thought the ride-along is bad, but this shit, this shit makes you a fucking rat king, tied up and intertwined with the masses who'd just assume eat your ass as soon as you stop being entertaining. 'Cause no one wants to see the truth—that's why you aren't on the air right now."

"I'm not a rat," Craig says again, although not with confidence.

"Then tell me what you are. A princess? A pirate? A fuck-nugget? No, princess is about right. I bet you are. You sure as fuck dated that pop princess. Let her jerk you around, dress you up like the dancing monkey you are, put some cymbals in your hands. Tell you when to smash them together like you're clapping. Dressed you in a tuxedo, to parade you around just like you let that twisted-lip attorney of yours that you're supposedly fucking—methinks it's the other way around. Her with a big massive dildo, strap-on, giving it to you up the ass. Your ass should have gone to prison, you'd fit right in. But how you let her boss you around? If you aren't that, a rat, what are you, then? A bitch? Tell me—what are you?"

Craig hesitates a moment. "I'm in love," he says. "Yeah, I'd classify it as being in love."

"In love? What the hell is that? I don't know what that is. What is love? What is being in love? What does that mean?"

Craig closes his eyes for a moment. "It means I want to be done with you, with Cooper, with all this, and live my life—"

"With her? That's a stupid fucking idea."

Craig shrugs. "Yeah, with her, I love her. I want to be done with all this to be with her—if she'll have me."

Woody laughs, really putting himself into it. "She don't love you back, does she?"

Craig shrugs. "I don't know. She's not the easiest person to read or get along with—kind of like you."

"You know they got a word for what you are," Woody says. "You know that right."

Craig says, "What's that?"

"Pussy whipped."

"I'm not pussy whipped."

"How you know?" Woody says. "Most men don't know when they are. That's the thing about pussy, good pussy, at least. Although all pussy could be considered good pussy, 'cause most men, the ones I know, aren't the most discerning of men, and anything is always better than *nothing*."

Woody pauses, thinking about why he had Johnny stabbed. *Anger* about that thought right there: something's better than nothing, and right now, he's got nothing. How it got what he wanted, in a way. Not exactly, but close enough.

Woody pushes the thoughts to the side. He says, "Being whipped's like waking from a dream that's just like your everyday and going, 'Oh shit, I was asleep.' Like you're sitting there awake one moment watching football or something—I bet with you it's figure skating, admiring those dicks squished in those tight ass leotards—and the next thing you know, but don't know, you're asleep and in this dream that are you still sitting there. But then weird shit starts happening, and your brain doesn't know what's true and what ain't like an illusion of your shitty life. And then you wake up—maybe even in the dream without actually waking—but you do, and you know what it all was. A dream. Men don't know they're whipped until they wake up."

Woody reaches over and flicks Craig's temple.

"Wake up," Woody tells him. "Before it's too late."

Craig bats Woody's hand away. "I am awake."

"Because you feel love for this bitch? Because you're—"

"In love," Craig says again.

"Fat fucking chance, you fucking rat," Woody says, reading Craig's face, looking for the vein.

There it is, just above his eye, not too far from where Woody flicked him.

"*Good*, motherfucker, get angry. I want you to be angry. I want the old Wrench back. The guy who earned that name dispensing justice with a plumber's tool, because that's the only thing these shits on the street understand. That's what your viewers don't get. What they refuse to see, all tucked up in their homes, safe from the big bad world, worried about their cholesterol and sun exposure. Not knowing they can walk out their door and take a bus up the ass or a bullet to the skull. Not because there's some grand fucking plan or a higher power, or even that life's shit, but because it can happen and does, regularly. Bad shit happens. And I want *that* Craig back, the guy who made bad shit happen to the bad people."

"I only did what Cooper—and you—asked me to do."

"You did what you wanted. Don't lie to yourself. Don't be sanctimonious. No one wants to hear that shit. You enjoyed it. I saw the smile. I know you benefited. We all did. So, what? You worried about some bodies turning up? Oh fucking well. Don't be. It won't happen. Cooper will see to that. What you think we don't all think about that? I don't fear it, but you do. So we went down for some shit, boo-fucking-who. But you, my friend, were, and still are, a rat. Because when the heat got turned up on the stove, you stepped on others to get out of the pot."

"I'm not a rat," Craig says. "I did what I was told."

"No one asked you to do nothing."

"It doesn't change the fact that it happened," Craig says.

"Oh, so you feel bad about it?"

Craig turns in the seat. "Do I feel bad about it? Yeah, I do. You don't?"

"What's there to feel bad about? First, there was this one thing," Woody used his outstretched hands to demonstrate. "And then there was this other thing."

"You went to prison for being corrupt. Not murder."

"You think that's a distinction anyone else makes? Anyone else fucking cares?"

Craig says, "I think if you were found guilty of murder, they wouldn't have let you go. So yeah, I do."

"Fuck 'em," Woody says. "Fuck them all, my life motto. You want to be out there making money? Then you have to reach out and take it when it's there."

Craig is silent for a full minute, which Woody uses to allow his eyes to wander back to the bar. The couple is still there, smiling and chatting in the window.

Craig says, "You don't feel bad about the shit we've done?"

Woody considers the question. "Feel bad…" He pauses. "Feel bad? No, I don't feel bad. The way I see it, the way you should show your viewers and tell the fucking world, we did a public service. You don't know what it was like. You have street gangs airing grievances out in public, bodies hitting the pavement, women getting shot, taking kids in a stroller, little ones getting shot jumping rope, and for what? Something legal here anyways, or close enough? People want to talk about the failed war on drugs. Well, I'm here to tell you, if you want to fight that war truly, you have to do what we did: take the fight to them, make them understand in the only language they know. Fuck 'em, every last one of them. Life's too short. Cops should go out there and take back the streets, make some money doing it too, and show them the government, i.e., society isn't to be fucked with."

"Hate to break it to you," Craig says, "but you aren't a cop anymore."

CHAPTER 17:

LUCILLE HUDSON REMOVES THE SLICK-looking business card from the folds of her purse; the card face is a baby blue sky with a green palm tree over what's supposed to be sand, and white writing is in bold font. She slaps it on the table and slides the card across the table. Eduardo retrieves the card, fingers pinching it to pick it up. He holds it before his face and studies it as Lucy says, "This is the other woman. Johnny left her card in the box with the DVD."

"This was in the box?" Eduardo turns the card over a couple of times, unsure what to say, reading the font and processing the information; the back side has a little photo next to the girl's name.

They are sitting at a three-person high top, framed in the large window of the coffee/bourbon bar a few blocks from the bank. Eduardo's hat rests on the seat between them as if it were at the table. Lucy keeps glancing at it, then at him, and then out the window, the feeling some-one's still out there resting on her shoulders, but not as strong now, not as concerning.

Lucy studies Eduardo as he studies the card. She can see by the look on his face that he doesn't know how to respond to the sudden transition from what they had been talking about to what they both really want to talk about but haven't yet gotten to beyond the discussion on the street, where the feelings of betrayal were still fresh. It catches him off guard.

Eduardo looks up from the card and fills the silence. "This is her; this is his mistress? That's what he said in the video? Just came right out and spilled the beans?"

Lucy nods. "He told me she didn't mean anything to him, not when he made the recording, but when he wanted me to know about her. 'Course watching the tape, I wonder if he wanted me to know so bad, supposedly feeling so bad about it, then why didn't he say anything back then? Why wait for a video no one knows about until he dies?"

Lucy pauses and adjusts in her seat, scooting back some to put her spine against the seatback and straightening.

"Johnny confessing his sins as if he's in confession; it hurt me," Lucy admits to Eduardo, unsure why she admits it other than he makes her feel comfortable. But maybe it's the alcohol, maybe it's the comfortable atmosphere, or maybe it's just Eduardo. But finally talking about the business card and, by extension, Johnny's video, the real world begins to intrude upon her. Once again dousing the previously growing warmth that filled her limbs. It brings a chill back to her and the scene. "He should have told me."

For the last hour, she avoided talking about what was in the safe deposit box, instead choosing to learn more about Eduardo. For example, he was married once, has a thing for poodles, and had always wanted to be a marshal since he was a little kid. They talked about things, large and small, getting a feel for each other, getting to know each other.

But after a while, the card in her purse grew too heavy. She could feel it. The pull of it. Even if she didn't have her purse at hand, it was hanging on the back of her seat. She could feel the weight of the thing pulling on her. A change of gravitational forces, what went up, went back down.

The talking was lovely, and she was even welcomed. If she's honest with herself, she wanted this when she opened the door and saw Eduardo standing there yesterday. And if she's *candid* with herself, she wants more—imagines more—and can see how this would work. Take him home, Johnny's grandmother's house, to her bed. Strip that shirt off him. Be careful with the buttons. See what he looks like underneath. See if he's as muscular as he appears. She bets he is. Wonders if he has chest hair. Would it be a lot, or just a little bit, curly pieces twisting up at her, tickling her chest as she rides him? Maybe he doesn't have hair. That wouldn't upset her, either. It would be fun. Nice. Relaxed.

Lucy says, "The new revelations make me sick to my stomach. How could I have been so stupid? So blind? How didn't I know? How could I not know what he was capable of? Maybe I did—but like always, anytime I had those negative thoughts and emotions, those pesky annoying things that threatened my happiness, tried to reveal the truth, I pushed them down into that tiny internal box where I keep all my feelings." She pauses. "I've gotten good at doing that over the last two years, like with those job interviews, the dirty looks, and such, and the questions. I tried not to let those things affect me.

"My mother taught me about the box," she says. "Showed me how to use it. When I was a kid, my mother warned me about letting negativity control my emotions. She'd say it would start a fire—burn down the whole town if I didn't get a handle on it, learn to save it, store it away, and forget about it."

Eduardo says, "What she was saying is don't let things control you. You control you…"

"Maybe," she says, seeing it that way and agreeing. "She said the box is more like a cage. That's what it feels like, for sure. Never letting anyone inside. Never getting out of it. Never letting anyone see the real me. My mother, she would say, that's where a *proper* woman puts her feelings because the world doesn't deserve to see them."

"My mother called that *poise*."

"Poise, I like that," Lucy says. "When my mother talked about the cage, I didn't know what she meant. I do now. Maybe that's getting older. Maybe that's being an adult. It's the same cage, my mother said, where a person keeps the wolf they choose to feed."

"My mother called that free will."

Lucy is quiet, thinking it over, then talks about what Johnny said on the tape and points at the card. She says, "He said the other woman knew about me but that he didn't think they were that serious. Said she wanted to marry him. Said it was a cultural thing. He said he wasn't going to do that."

"Marry her?"

"Yeah, but guess he'd just fuck her instead. That's alright in his cultural understanding."

"In this DVD video message, he explained all this, that? He explained how they met?"

"No, just said they had."

Eduardo reads the other woman's name on the card out loud. "Violeta."

"He called her Violet," Lucy says. "In the video, he kept referring to her as Violet. I didn't know what he meant at first. Who he's talking about? Mind you, all I had from that box was this card. There was the DVD and this card. And I was thinking about who this Violet woman was; this woman's name was Violeta. I kept expecting him to say that—her name Violeta, but he never did, and then it struck me that he was talking about her." She points at the card, to the smiling, dark-haired, dark-skinned woman in the little photo—looking like a sorority sister from hell—an angel in disguise. "He's saying Violet as in her."

Eduardo glances up from the card to her. "The A's silent?"

"Something like that."

Eduardo also reads the last name and number on the card out loud. Then he flips the card and says, "Says EcoTours. What's that? They have that sort of thing here? Or is that just a Costa Rica thing?"

Lucy smiles and admits she doesn't know if Tulsa has anyone doing EcoTours. "I think it's a vacation destination thing."

"I still don't know what that is. I know where Costa Rica is; there's some rainforest, and Nicaragua is north of the border. Above it. No nice people there. Still, don't know what an EcoTour is, though, much less a Violeta."

Lucy explains what they are. "EcoTours—you go around, look at nature, zip lines, and stuff, walk trails, that type of thing. Take in the *natural* sights of the area, the country."

Eduardo asks, "You need to pay someone to do that?"

"Down there," Lucy says, "you do. You ever been?"

"To Nicaragua?" Eduardo twists his features, making a face and saying it like he's genuinely lost.

Lucy suppresses a chuckle at his misunderstanding. "No, Costa Rica."

Eduardo holds up a finger. "One time."

Lucy waits for him to explain more, but he doesn't. He doesn't say anything.

She asks, "Well, did you ever do one when you were down there?"

"An eco-tour?"

"Yeah," she says.

Eduardo considers the question. "Maybe."

"Maybe?"

"I'm not sure," Eduardo says, "I seem to remember walking through the rainforest to get to an active Volcano—that was a trip. Was that an EcoTour?"

"Could've been," Lucy says. She picks up the glass from the table. She sips the bourbon.

"Johnny and I did that once when we were down there—go to the volcano…"

Lucy's voice fades as a thought intrudes. She sighs and blinks a few times, processing the new revelation. She sets the glass back on the table but leaves her hand around it.

Lucy tips her head toward the card. "I guess she could have been the fine young thing that led our excursion."

"Hey, that's what they called it," Eduardo says, snapping as if it had just come to him. "An excursion."

But now, Lucy's mind's turning. "It must have been."

"You think?" He says it like he can't believe it.

But she can't believe Johnny would have done something like that.

"Yeah, thinking about it," she says. "It makes sense. Johnny set it up. It must have been her. The girl in the little square on the back of the card. That picture by the name, that's her. I knew she looked familiar. She must've been the one leading it. Short shorts. Khaki. The top and shorts looked like they belonged to a twelve-year-old girl except for the ass and tits—not that hers were enormous, just shapely—more meaning how small everything was on her, like it was painted on her body. I remember thinking, how'd she get those shorts on? Did she have to lay down to button them and use pliers to zip up the zipper? Then I was thinking, how did she do anything in that get-up? Who goes walking through the woods dressed like that?"

"Rainforest," Eduardo says. "Bit more than the woods."

Lucy brushes the comment to the side as she leans into the table. "She looked good. I remember thinking that. She was pretty and had this skin—it just glowed. Not that she was pregnant, but just looked healthy."

Eduardo points the card at her. "Sounds like you were envious."

"I was," Lucy says, leaning back again, getting comfortable. "I wished I looked like that."

"So did Johnny, apparently," Eduardo quips before he has time to think about the comment or how it might affect Lucy.

But the comment doesn't hurt Lucy's feelings; it makes things lighter. She chuckles. "I guess so. It does sound like that, doesn't it?"

"I have to say, I don't know why you envy her." Pulling the card back, he pauses to check out the picture again on the back. "You are just as pretty, or prettier, than this woman."

"Just as pretty?"

Eduardo thrusts the card through the air. "It's a small photo. I don't know her. I don't want to talk out of turn. For all I know, she could be Ms. Central America—but probably more so."

Lucy sips the drink. "She's not. She's a whore."

Eduardo points at the card. "Says here, she leads EcoTours. Maybe that's how she finds John's."

Playfully, Lucy snatches the card out of his hand.

"I liked that trip." Lucy stops talking.

"That memory?" Eduardo asks with a soft voice, searching for her.

Lucy nods, thinking she did, and then grows quiet, lost in herself.

Eduardo asks, "What did you do with the DVD?" His eyes flick to her purse. "Is it in there, too?"

Lucy says, "No." She says, "I dropped it in the mail."

"What?"

"I mailed it to myself."

"Why?"

"I'm not sure. It seemed like the right thing to do. I didn't know if someone was outside the bank waiting for me. I had that feeling. So, I asked the manager for an envelope and a stamp, which he provided for a small fee, and I sealed it up and asked him to mail it. I should get it in a day or two."

"Sounds like there's something of worth on the DVD."

Lucy nods but doesn't say what. "I'm not sure why I didn't put it back in the box. Maybe I will need it to find the money or whatever Johnny hid, but that means I'll have to watch the video again. I don't know if I can do that."

Eduardo waits a moment. "You going to tell me about it?" He pauses. "I don't care about the money. Just wondering what all the fuss is about. You said something about murder?"

Lucy says, "You remember the Brinks heist from a few years back?"

She pauses to see if Eduardo confirms if he remembers. He doesn't.

She says, "Remember the truck was parked at one of those cross-country all-night truck stops. It was carrying jewelry and precious gems from a show up in Kansas City, and they, the two guards, armed—the newspaper making a big deal about that—were on their way back to Houston but went inside the gas stop to use the restroom, get some coffee, and stretch their legs. They were inside for like twenty-seven minutes. Paper made a big deal about that, too, at the time. Then the two guards return to the truck and find out someone had burglarized it."

"Not robbed it," Eduardo says, "like in the movies? Cuz that's what they do. Rob it at gunpoint. The guy gets shot. Makes the wrong move. They all get shot. By the end of the movie, everyone is shot."

Lucy shakes her head. "In the tape, Johnny makes sure I get it right. He claims they didn't do the crime. Like that is some important distinction. Anyways, yes. It was burglarized. The paper said they defeated the locking mechanism on the storage area and broke into all the separate containers. Even used some of the containers to haul off the gems."

"Sounds like an inside job."

"Could've been, I don't know. I don't remember the outcome, and Johnny didn't say."

"That type of stuff usually isn't reported."

"Or if it is, it's some little mention shoved in the corner of the page deep inside the paper. It's not news anymore."

"What was the total?" Eduardo asks, skipping ahead like an actual cop. "How much do they get away with?"

"One hundred million," Lucy says. "There's some debate about that. I remember that, and Johnny mentioned it. The company said everything was insured and valued at ten million, but that's a lot of money even then. Johnny said one hundred million, that's what the paper valued it at, but he said there's no way they would get that much."

Eduardo works it out in his head and says, "If they stole gems, then they would've gotten pennies on the dollar trying to dump them right away. They'd be hot. Maybe too hot. Maybe wait. Maybe sit on it for a bit. Maybe they could line something up and get fair value for them after some time has passed."

"That's what Johnny said too, which is why he hid the gems, but he said he didn't hide them where he was supposed to. He said he didn't trust the guys he was working with—you met one yesterday, Woody."

Eduardo processes the information. "What else did Johnny say?"

Lucy hesitates. "They didn't do the heist."

"So, how'd they get the haul?"

"That's the question, isn't it?"

"Not the question I'm thinking of," Eduardo says.

"What question are you thinking of?" Lucy asks.

"Did you know anything about any of this?"

"I got a necklace from him before we left for Costa Rica."

"I see," he says. "You think it was stolen?"

"I do," she says.

"Did you think it came from this … heist?"

"I didn't at the time," Lucy says. "But then I thought I knew my husband. I thought I knew who he was. I had no idea."

"How does this all equal murder? I'm assuming Johnny has the stones, which is why he brings it up in the DVD. But I don't see where he and his boys come into it."

"Johnny was part of a special unit within the Major Crimes Task Force, and they were combating organized crime, gangs, and shit. Anyways, after Siriano's organization stopped being a thing—essentially dismantled from the inside out through petty squabbling—Johnny said they turned their attention to the gangs and drug dealers at the street level. Started rolling the dealers to dissuade them from their life of crime and to disrupt their networks."

"I sense greed became a factor."

Lucy, nodding again, agrees. "That's what Johnny went to prison for, taking payouts, basically protection money, and robbing the dealers, taking their money and drugs, and then turning around and selling the drugs."

Eduardo senses where this is going. "And then the heist happens."

"And then the heist happens," Lucy says.

"Did Johnny say how they got the gems?"

"Yes," Lucy says. "He said they were asked to join the investigation. Johnny thought it was an inside job, but not one of the drivers. They found a GPS tag, and Johnny knew some guys who specialized in this sort of thing. He thought it was someone local who pulled it off. Said the guy lived in an apartment complex on the west side of Tulsa.

So, he and his boys—that's all he said—backtrack the tag and go to this apartment. Except Woody was responsible for kicking the door in. In all their excitement, Woody kicks the wrong apartment door. Johnny said this twenty-something kid was sitting on the couch when the door was kicked. It isn't the right apartment, so they freeze at the doorway. The kid starts yelling and stuff, telling them to leave. Telling them he's going to call the cops. Meanwhile, the guy they were coming to get opened his door to look outside at what was happening. Craig Jentsch sticks a gun in his face and forced his way into his apartment. The guy's roommate and girlfriend who helped are inside. They all put their hands in the air, according to Johnny."

"What happened next?"

"The movies happened."

"What do you mean?"

"Johnny said the first kid is hooting and hollering about them being there. The kid swings on Woody and clocks him. Woody pistol-whips him and drags him over to the right apartment. Throws him on the other people's coffee table. Woody's pissed now. The people who did the heist are cooperative. They know what this is. They know what they've done. The original plan was to go in under the guise of cops. But the kid, his dad's a cop, a trooper, highway patrol. He wants to follow in Dad's footsteps. He knows how things are done and how they aren't. Johnny said he wouldn't shut up. Kept mouthing Woody, who kept hitting him. When Johnny and the boys huddled up to figure out what to do next, the kid got up. Said he didn't need this shit. Said he was leaving, fuck them. According to Johnny, Woody turned from the group, saying he did it before anyone could stop him. Woody shot the kid twice in the chest. Of the people in the apartment, one of them had a gun on the couch. When the kid was shot, he knew what was about to happen. He stuck his hand under the cushion, so the other guys, Bradford, Craig, and Woody, turned their guns on them. Johnny said it was deafening. The roar. Something like forty rounds were fired. Guy died with his hand shoved between two cushions."

"Shit," Eduardo says.

"Johnny laughed about it. Said it like he was joking about that movie with Steve Martin and John Candy, quoted the line about how 'those aren't pillows.' It's sick."

"I take it that's where they recovered the jewels."

"He said they found them behind the water heater and under the washing machine. Johnny said he didn't fire his gun, but I don't know. The guy is making jokes about dead people. Said he couldn't stand being in the apartment. He took the cop's kid's dog for a walk while they figured out what to do with the scene."

"No one called the cops?"

"No, they did, but they radioed in that they were in the area and would respond pronto. Made up some story and cleaned up the scene. Stomped all over the place to mess with forensics. Really fucked it from the beginning. Made it look like a drug deal gone bad and that the cop's kid was an innocent bystander. They made Johnny leave with the stones. Johnny said he had a guy that could flip them. Johnny told them he got the money and hid it to ensure no one would spend it too quickly."

"Yeah? They believed that?"

"No, but what are they going to do? He's got the money. The thing is, two things happened." She holds up two fingers. "The indictments for robbing the drug dealers and..."

"And?"

Lucy lays her hands flat on the table. "Johnny never flipped the stones. He hid them. According to him, the girl is supposed to know something about where they are. I'm supposed to call her, and she's supposed to tell me something that means something to me and no one else to help me find them—Johnny's insurance."

Eduardo is silent for a long time as he works through the revelation. He sips his coffee and then says, "So, where do you think the stones are?"

CHAPTER 18:

ERIN MOORCOCK SITS IN HER CAR DOWN the street, watching the house and waiting. What she's waiting for, she isn't sure. She knows Dante's cousin Cece wasn't honest with her in the house and that he knows something more than he said. She knows he called someone. She overheard part of the conversation. Cece initially thought he was talking to Dante, but it wasn't Dante on the phone. That much was clear. He also thought he was whispering, but the conversation quickly became heated. So, who was it?

Then, after she left—he made her leave—a couple of miles down the road, she passed Dante's car, which was hard to miss, heading in the direction of the house. When she turned around and returned to the house, his car wasn't there, and when she knocked on the front door again, the house was quiet. It seemed like no one was there. Dante must have picked up Cece, but where did they go?

Erin decided to hang around so she could talk to Dante. With the marshal's appearance in her office today and waking up late, her day felt off. Not to mention whatever is going on with Craig. She'll have to figure out how to save him from prison if the video Johnny made with her dad comes out, whatever might be on it. Craig seemed to think there were secrets, and if those secrets indicated complicity in murder and Craig didn't disclose anything about that to the federal government during their deal-making, then he doesn't get a trial. He gets time—hard time. Revocation. No questions asked. They don't want liars. He'd be just as guilty as any of the other guys. That's the agreement. He signed it.

Erin parked down the street to think and wait for Dante's car to return.

It does.

Dante and Cece exit the car and go inside. An hour passes, and no one else gets out of the car or comes to the house.

What was she expecting? The escaped convict?

She's pretty sure the house was empty when she talked to Cece. Later, when she knocked on the door again, the TV was off, and the house was silent. The convict wasn't there. If he was, he was Anne Franking it somewhere.

Erin adjusts in the driver's seat, jams her fist against the window frame, and leans her head against her biceps and the glass. "Why am I here?" she asks herself.

Of course, there's no answer.

She blinks a long blink, shutting her eyes and trying to calm her mind. Feeling the calm that comes with refocusing her mind, the brightness from the day fades to nothing. She opens her eyes, and nothing's changed at the house.

She sighs and says, "The things I do for clients. It's driving me insane. Look at me, I'm talking to myself here, and the crazy thing is I'm expecting answers. Knowing there won't be any, I still expect them. So why am I here?"

Just then, there is a knock at her window.

It scares her.

Erin jumps from the glass, her heart leaping into her throat simultaneously. She cuts her eyes to the widow to find a man standing there, half bent over and smiling a wide, friendly smile, wearing blue jeans and a white shirt. His lips say something, but she can't understand the blood rushing in her ears. It is something like, *who are you talking to*? He motions for her to roll her window down, circling his hand with his extended index finger.

Erin touches her chest with a hand to calm her breathing. She hesitates, pondering what to do. What her next move should be? She should run. She should drive away right now. But she can't. She's not sure why. She's frozen. She doesn't move.

Erin stares at the man and doesn't dare reach for her phone, which is sitting in the cup holder of her center console.

Erin's hearing comes back to her, and she hears what the man is saying. "Roll your window down," the man says, voice muffled by the glass. "Come on. You can do it. Just roll it down." His hand rotates repeatedly, pausing for a few seconds to see if she gets the point before starting to circle again.

With a deep breath, Erin reluctantly complies. Slowly, she reaches forward and flips the keys to complete the circuit to the car battery. With her other hand, she presses the button on the door to drop the glass a few inches. Cooler air rushes into the car. She flips the keys back to kill the battery's use.

"Come on, a little more," he says.

"No, no, thank you," Erin says through the thin slit in the glass. "That's all you get. What do you want?"

Maybe if she is short with him, he will go away. Something tells her he won't.

And it doesn't work.

The man steps back and laughs. "What do I want?" He looks in the window at her and studies her. "Lady, you've been sitting here for the better part of an hour. I've been watching you. What do you want?"

Erin licks her lips, trying to come up with an answer. She chooses defensiveness. "That's none of your business."

Amused, the man smiles. "I think it is. It's my neighborhood. I want to know what you are doing. Why are you sitting here?"

Erin resolves herself to not tell him. "What can I do for you?"

The man scratches the fresh stubble on the crown of his head. It looks like he routinely shaves his head and hasn't in a few days. The hair on his face has a similar appearance but defined lines.

Maybe this is the guy she's been waiting for, maybe not?

Erin chastises herself mentally for not knowing what the escaped convict looks like. Is this him? Or is this some nosey neighbor?

She should have asked the marshal what his escaped convict looked like. She was so preoccupied with him reading her files in her office that it knocked her off her game. She was also thinking about how she could use the information he gave her to trade the convict for Dante's freedom. That distracted her, too.

She gets like that sometimes; it's a form of greed, her father explained to her one time. It was a quality her father warned her about and told her she needed to get a handle on and guard against it, or people would use it against her and take advantage of her. "That's how they will win," he would say, "and you get beat—remember, it's 3-D chess."

Well, she forgot to ask. And it's too late now. She doesn't know what the guy looks like. He could walk up to her, like this guy, and she wouldn't know unless he said, "Ta-da, it's me, Lamar Henry," like he's Mario or something.

It's not an excuse, it's a reason. That's what she would tell Craig when she explains this to him later. She'll tell him she met the man but wasn't sure he was the man. But she knows him, knows Craig would wonder why she was even here, in this position; he'd ask her what she was thinking.

What *is* she thinking?

She wanted to bring the idea to Dante and tell him how he could get out of trouble. Show him her plan where she'd tell the court, "My client cooperated with law enforcement and brought a dangerous criminal to authorities. He is not the man the State is alleging." To see if she can get them to dismiss charges or at least deal with something advantageous to Dante. If Dante went for it, it would help him, but Erin knows how popular culture feels about giving information to the authorities; he'd be seen as a rat in the circles he runs, and the street wouldn't care why he did it, which is why Erin didn't tell Cece.

Of course, if she told Craig all that, he'd just ask her why she thought it was okay for him to do it and not some freebie client she picked up on the street corner that the public defender's office threw her so she could get early lines on the big fish who can pay but don't have a handle on the court system before their first hearing.

Erin loves nothing more than being in the courtroom when the judge asks the kahuna who their lawyer is, and before they can respond, she stands up and tells the lawyer she'll be representing them. Usually, these are things like DUIs and the occasional mismanagement of funds. There's been a few sexual assaults and rapes. Maybe more than a few powerful guys taking advantage of others. The occasional domestic, which is always fun because then she can get Dickie on board, and they can bleed the fish on both sides of the line, civil and criminal—domestics lead to divorces, especially when the attorneys are whispering innocuous encouragement that ends marriages.

All of this is if she hasn't already gotten a chance to visit them in the jail, which she also does, waking the kahunas up early in the morning, four a.m., getting them in the attorney-client room, and telling them she'd like to represent them—more like how it's going to be. Very few decline. They like the attitude. She's also prone to calling the station and offering representation to those in interrogations, but that one turns off the investigating detectives and is more trouble than it's worth, creating an adversarial relationship with the prosecution from the beginning and usually leading to conflict.

The man outside her window motions to Erin. "It's not what you can do for me," he says, "it's what I can do for you." He relaxes in his stance, stretching his back, grins a little. "Who said that? Was that Kennedy?" He puts on his best New England accent. He's quite good. "It's not what you can do for your nation, but what your nation can do for you."

Erin shakes her head, not knowing where he is going with this. "Not quite, but yeah," she says. "What can I do for you? I'm busy. I don't need historical quotes."

The man chuckles; it's loud. "Busy?" He points at her. His nails are longer than she expected. "You don't look busy. You look like you're sitting there watching someone's house. Whose house are you watching? Is it that one?" He points to a few houses as he speaks; Dante's house is one of them—the last one. "Or that one, maybe this one. I know. It's that one right there. That's it, right?"

Erin tracks each finger point with her eyes, struggling to come up with something to say, much less a way out of this conversation. He's right, which means he is exactly who she thinks he is and knows exactly why she is here. He must have been the voice on the other end of Cece's phone call.

"I'm not watching someone's house," she lies.

It's not convincing. She could do better.

The man laughs, a big laugh, the biggest one yet, but it is hollow, devoid of warmth, meaning it's fake. There's too much emphasis; it becomes a mockery of what it should be. Further confirming in Erin's mind this is all an act, and he is the man she was waiting for. What did he do, get out of the car, and wait for an hour, watching her watch Dante's house?

He asks, "Then what are you doing?"

Erin says the first thing that comes to her mind, "I'm thinking."

"Thinking—thinking about what?"

Erin drops her eyes some. "That's none of your business, now, is it?"

The man thinks it over and then says, "No, I suppose it ain't, is it? Well, maybe it is. Depends on what you're thinking about." He pauses to consider his next words, or that's how it appears, gnawing on his tongue and lower lip. He says, "How about we try this a different way? What do you do?"

"Excuse me?"

He adds, "For a living?"

Erin asks, "Why does that matter?"

"It matters," he says. "Humor me. What do you do? You a cop?"

She shakes her head.

"You a process server—you're dressed like one."

"No," she says.

The man juts that finger her direction some more. "But you are an officer of the court, right? I can tell. You have that look."

"What look is that?"

"Arrogant."

"I'm not arrogant."

"Some call it RBF, but you know that. I bet you have a great one—resting bitch face."

Erin bristles in her seat. She knows what he just did. He called her a bitch without calling her a bitch.

He continues, "I bet you're good at what you do. You got that feel to you, that hardness. I see it. You probably damn good at cards. Hard to read your bluff. If I were still doing what I do to make money, I wouldn't visit your station. That's for sure. I'd skip right over you. Go to the next teller. But I tell you this: I'll hire you if I get in trouble again. Just one look makes me confident that I know you know what you are doing. That ruthless look. That lawyer look. That's what you are, right? A lawyer. An attorney. You Dante's attorney? That who you are?"

Erin starts to respond, but she doesn't know what to say. She should have left when she had the chance.

The man smiles, shark-like, while his eyes gain a maniacal slant. The man lifts the bottom of his shirt to reveal the handle of a revolver. She isn't sure what kind of gun it is or its caliber, but that doesn't matter. She's seen enough to know it's a gun, and it's too late.

He tells her in the nicest way possible, "Unlock the door so we can chat."

Erin's eyes stay on the handle of the gun. He lifted the shirt as a threat, and she's taking the threat seriously.

She hesitates. "What do you want?"

The man inhales through his nose, nostrils flaring, before he snorts. "I want you to unlock the door, so I'm not standing out here in the middle of the street with my dick metaphorically in my hands. I want to talk to you. I want to know who you are and what you want."

"That's all?"

"I know you're Dante's lawyer," he says. "I got that much. Which means you should know who I am."

She nods. She does. Through tight lips, she tells him, "The escaped convict."

"That sounds so cold when you say it like that."

"How else should I put it?"

"Well, I do have a name. I like my name. Names mean something, you know. I'm sure you have a name." He scrunches his nose. "You know what? I'm sorry. Let's start over." He touches his chest with his offhand. "I'm Lamar, and you are?"

"Erin," she answers, trying to decide the best play here and choosing the truth. She wishes Craig was here. He'd know how she should play it differently. This isn't like the courtroom. It's the street. She knows there is only so far she can push a man with a gun.

"Nice to meet you, Erin," Lamar says, extending the hand toward her. "Now unlock the door so I can sit down and talk."

Erin doesn't move and is reluctant to comply. "What do we have to talk about?"

"Always the lawyer, asking questions," he says. "How about this? We sit and talk, and maybe we will come to an understanding."

Erin tests his resolve, pushing him a little to get a feel for him. "And If I don't?"

"Well, that would be the wrong answer," he says. "As you so delicately put it, I am the escaped convict and have nothing to lose." He touches the gun handle, tapping his middle finger against it.

Erin dips her chin and her eyes toward the gun. "Where'd you get the gun?"

He steps back. "You're full of questions, aren't you?" He pauses. Erin doesn't move. He withdraws the revolver from his pants. He holds it down by his leg so as not to attract attention.

The gun looks like the one Craig wears on his ankle when he isn't wearing shorts. Erin knows when Craig's wearing shorts, he's got that gun—what was it, a .38 Airweight?—clipped to the inside of his pocket.

The man keeps his tone friendly. "You want to see it up close? That's a question for you, Ms. Attorney. You want to answer that one?"

Erin freezes. Her breath catches in her chest. She squeals a reply that starts the signals from the brain to her lungs, reminding them to breathe. "No, I'm good."

"No, you're in trouble, but don't want to admit it yet. We call that denial. So, let's do this. Unlock the door, and we can figure out how to get out of this mess together. Or we could continue this verbal sparring we doing? 'Cause frankly, I'm getting tired of this…"

His voice falls off as he lets the rest of the threat remain unstated.

Erin unlocks the door. The locks click as the plugger on the door raises.

The man tilts his head to the side. "Good, now was that hard?"

Erin doesn't respond.

The man hums, "Mhm," as he walks around the front of the car, staring at her, never taking his eyes off her. He walks with a swagger, long, languid slides, keeping the gun down next to his leg in his right hand. He pauses in front of her door. Maybe he's looking around before he opens the door. The passenger door opens, and the man climbs inside, rocking the car a bit. Once inside, he shuts the door.

Erin refuses to look at him directly.

She sniffs once.

He smells like sweat. It's not body odor, but she can tell he's been outside doing things for the last few hours.

Lamar adjusts himself in the seat to get comfortable, extending his right leg as far as possible but keeping his left leg bent. He places the revolver on the dashboard and turns in the seat to face her.

Erin doesn't speak. She waits. She won't talk first. This is his show.

Lamar takes a deep breath and says, "I guess we should just start over and then get to it."

Erin turns a little in the seat. "What do you want?"

"You keep asking that question," he says, exasperated. "Tell you *this*, I'll eventually answer you because, well, I'm going to need to, to do this next part, but the more you ask—the more you put that tone in your voice—the less inclined I'm going to be in answering you. Understand?"

Erin doesn't like it, but she gets it. "I understand."

"Good, now that we have that out of the way. I'm Lamar Henry, and, hello, I am the man you are looking for." He pauses for effect. Erin doesn't move. He chuckles again. "Lionel Richie, get it? You get it. I bet you do."

"I get it."

Lamar directs his eyes to the revolver, saying, "I don't like guns. Really. I don't. But that doesn't mean I don't see the value in having them around now and then. I don't use them when I'm doing what I do. No reason to. It'd be like having one with me just to take a piss or breathe."

"I know some people who use them just like that."

Lamar waits for a beat. "Sounds like cops. I bet that's what and who they are. Cops. Cops need guns. It's like a religion for them. Need the feel of something cold and steel touching their legs, fillin' their hands."

Careful to keep her tone friendly, although she knows exactly what she is doing, Erin asks, "I ask again, what do you want?"

"*Girl,*" he starts to say, ending the word with a heavy, delayed breath. "You don't give up, do you? I bet that's what makes you a good lawyer." He raises his hands in surrender. "Okay, I give. What I want is to know what the marshal knows."

"What marshal?"

"Don't play games. I know he's in town. I know he's gotta be looking for me. It's what *he* does, you know? He can't do anything else. Can't help it. I know you are here. Know that you are Dante's attorney. And know that you were asking questions about me—even if those questions were more alluding to me than anything. And when I put all that I know together, that tells me the marshal musta talked to you. I want to know what he said and what you were planning to do if Cece or Dante—seeing you were trying to contact him—confirmed I was here?"

Erin takes a moment to consider the question. Just as she is about to answer, her phone, which is on silent, buzzes in the cup holder. She glances down at the phone.

Lamar says without taking his eyes off her, "You going to answer that?"

"I wasn't, no."

"Thinking this is more important, you and I talking?"

"Something like that."

Lamar glances at the screen. Erin watches his eyes read the name. "Craig Jentsch—you know the *Wrench*?" he asks, amused.

"Yes," Erin confirms. "He's a client."

"A boyfriend?"

"No," she says. It isn't a lie. She doesn't know what Craig is to her.

Lamar squints and looks slightly away as if pulling up a memory. "I think I saw him today."

"Who?"

"The Wrench," Lamar says, eyes flickering back to her. "Yeah, that was him. Mr. GQ, he was driving that car with those white dudes."

"What car? What are you talking about? When was this?"

Lamar doesn't say.

"The marshal hasn't been here yet," Erin says, trying to distract him and get him back on target so he will get out of her car.

"I know that," Lamar says, mind returning to her. "I know where he's been. And I know where your boyfriend's been. And I know why—which is all very *interesting*." He pulls the last word out.

"He's not my boyfriend," she says again, but her tone is less convincing than the first time.

Lamar sucks in on his bottom lip and then asks, "Do all your clients in your phone have hearts and smiley faces at the end of their name?"

CHAPTER 19:

M ORRIS WOODFORD SLIDES INTO THE
other side of the booth. He runs his fingers through
his hair before resting his wrists on the table, palms up, gold
bracelets clinking against the laminated wood. Woody says,
"Nice place. New?"

The man on the other side of the booth doesn't respond.
Doesn't even look up at Woody dropping in the other side
of the booth, rocking the table. The man plucks the pencil
from his ear where it had been resting, a whittled, chewed
number 2, schoolyard yellow, and makes a mark on the
paper's Sudoku puzzle, filling in all the ones, then twos,
making it to five before pausing, placing the pencil back
above his ear, and reaches for the coffee sitting to his right.

As long as Woody has known Bill Ruth—simply Ruth
to anyone that matters—he has never drank alcohol. He's
never seen the man take a drop, but he's always working
out of bars. Woody's had a drink with him, but the guy had
one of those foo-foo fake beers with no alcohol content.

Ruth likes meeting in the middle of the night, sometimes in the early evening, sometimes in the morning. He

always seems to be awake, too. That must be why he doesn't drink. He wants to be ready to go at a moment's notice.

Woody's heard the guy's Mormon, the body's a temple or some shit, but he doesn't know if that's true or not. He drinks caffeine. Or maybe he doesn't. Maybe it's unleaded. Doesn't matter. Ruth's like stone; he doesn't share his thoughts on religion or otherwise unless it's about business, and then, and only then, he shares decisions, but never how he came to a decision.

Before Ruth takes a coffee drink, he glances around at the bar surrounding them: the u-shaped bar top in the middle of the room, the two bodyguards sitting far enough away to not be obtrusive but close enough for trouble, the uncharacteristically beige walls with bright lights, and the dark wood-paneled ceiling.

Ruth says, "By product of a war. Not choice."

Woody considers his answer. He tugs at the lapels of his black leather jacket, taking comfort in his traditional outfit: white shirt, blue jeans, black jacket, and boots. It soothes him. It's like slipping into a hot tub or something. Wearing the suit for Cooper is like dressing up to play make-believe. Woody isn't a rich man's driver. He's the guy more at home, being no man's man, being free than a guy in a monkey suit.

"You know, you're a strange fellow," Woody says, filling the silence. "You and I have had this special relationship for a long time. We've known and worked with each other for a long time. Longer time than I've been with Cooper, that's for sure. And in all that time, you've never been much for conversation. You never talk. You always sit there. You aren't rude. You listen. That's for damn sure. You listen but don't say nothing—it's disconcerting."

Ruth doesn't move. Doesn't say nothing. Sits there like he can't be disturbed.

But in this situation, Woody's been here before, so he can handle the silence. He says, "So I got to know, for conversation sake, you know, so sitting here with you ain't weird, but I've been in this bar before. It was different back then. I mean, this place used to be an okay place to work out of, running CIs and the like, sometimes come for a drink—I don't know why but women were always here, maybe it was all the Irish bullshit, greens, and clovers like the tramp stamp most of them had—not that a guy like you would've come here for that so how would you know? But I'm saying this bar used to be owned by an outfit out east, from Boston, true believers, who treated this place, their place in Tulsa, like it was the Alamo, and we were all the Mexicans surrounding it."

Woody pauses, picking up Ruth's spoon, the one that comes with the coffee for sugar and milk, to check his hair out in its reflection, holding the spoon up with his right hand while licking his index and middle finger of the other hand and running the fingers through his hair, slicking stray strands back. This is more for show, just him taking his time to answer Ruth's actual question, more to mess with the guy and talk about how he processes the world around him.

Then Woody drops the spoon, placing it on the table, and asks, "So if I'm not mistaken, and I'm usually not, this used to be Mikey Collins's place, right? He still around, or did you take it from him? From his people?"

Ruth's eyes flick up in Woody's direction, that cold, rocklike stare. All he says is, "It's my place now."

But Woody doesn't let it go. He can't. No one gets the last word with him, not if he can help it, especially a guy who calls him up—well, not him, one of his minions—and tells him to heel like a fucking dog. Woody isn't a dog. He isn't someone's pet. He doesn't jump to it just because someone says so. Doesn't matter what Woody owes the shark fuck.

"Well, Mr. It's-my-place-now, is Mikey still around?" Woody asks, tapping the spoon in cadence with his words. "You didn't say. I'd like to know. I've always liked Mikey. Even if he did come from the stock he came from. I worked with his father for years—this is the first time. You know his father used to be police chief in Tulsa, a real hardass named Crawford Collins. When he came back for that last stint, he wasn't the man I came up with, if you know what I mean. A real self-righteous bastard."

Ruth is quiet, and then all Ruth responds with is, "Mikey's still around."

"That's good, good," Woody says, ingesting the information. "Like a preacher's son, Mikey Collins was. Fell pretty damn far from the tree, if I have to say, getting hooked up with those guys from out east, treating this side of the city like some frontier outpost—fucking father a police chief." Woody holds up two fingers. "*Twice.* Maybe that's why I like the son more than the father. A guy like him coulda had it two ways. He coulda been a prodigal son returned, made something of his life like his little brother. Made dear old dad proud. Brought tears to his eyes. Or he coulda continued being some two-bit gangster."

Woody pauses to read Ruth's body language. Ruth doesn't move much or give Woody much to interpret.

"But with you sitting here and the things I've heard, I guess he's still that two-bit gangster fuck he was pretending to be. So good for him. But that means I got to ask, 'specially with you sitting in this bar since you don't do bars for what they're for, you ain't worried those Irish bastards from out yonder," Woody motions an outstretched arm to the east, pointing the spoon, "won't come to town and try to take over?

"They've been pushing for it for years. They say sweet old Whitey came to town, personally recruited Mikey—might be why he looks the way he does, a little like the dearly departed late fugitive—brought the boy to the table, so to speak, told him how it's going to be.

"You see the movie where Depp plays the man?" Woody asks. "You know what they got right? I saw the movie. Read the book the movie was based on, too. Reading's all you got to do on the inside, and I ain't much of a reader, but I did read that one. Read a few others. It was two years." Woody's making a point of it for a reason. "So I did read. I got to tell you I like nonfiction. Can't stand that made-up bullshit. I liked the book that the movie was based on. I even read some of the others those guys wrote. They were reporters out there when all this went down. They followed it like some mooks who wrote up Friday night football here. I imagine people read the paper like losers here read the sports, eagerly taking in the box scores, tallying up who's still with us, and hanging in the game. But what that movie got right, or at least to me they did, was his eyes. Especially when they were sitting at the table, which really fucking happened; Depp got the eyes right. Eyes like yours. Cold as fucking stone.

"But the reason I bring all that up is to say you don't worry, emissaries from out there will come here and try to take over now that the Ambassador and Siriano are both gone?" Woody makes the sign of the cross. "Those two fucks knew how to keep control. And from what I'm hearing, family Russo doesn't want nothing to do with nothing now, now that their little shit is in the ground, don't want the responsibility. They lost their stomach for it, which is kinda funny seeing how they make their bread working with dead people. If no one steps up, then it's going to be a free-for-all, not that it isn't already."

Woody's asking a question without asking Ruth the real question.

Ruth doesn't speak. He keeps his eyes on Woody, probably if Woody had to guess, waiting for him to shut up.

Ruth sips the coffee from the mug. He doesn't look amused.

Woody quiets down and looks around the place, soaking it in. Thinking, okay, if the guy doesn't want to talk, Woody won't. He didn't ask to be here. That was this guy. He called him here. Woody can wait.

It doesn't take a scientist to know why Ruth wanted to meet with him. A Shylock wants his money. A Shylock on a deal gone sideways still wants his money. Ruth's a street moneylender. He was supposed to wash the money from Woody's last job. Johnny was going to flip the stones; he said he had a guy, and then Woody was going to shuffle it over to Ruth to wash through his various cutouts and legitimate—or legitimate-ish, seeing they're used to clean money—businesses so Woody and gang weren't linked back to the heist. Hard to hide where a couple million dollars came from.

Ruth would get a cut of the whole, his ten percent. Like his moneylending business, Ruth gets his money no matter what. So even though the deal didn't go down—Johnny absconding with the stones, never flipping them—Ruth still wants his cut and is willing to hold Woody responsible. And has.

Ruth's a patient man, a helluva lot more patient than Woody and more patient than a lot of other people Woody knows—Coop included—but Ruth, despite laying off Woody during the trial and his two years away in the penitentiary, wants his money.

That's what this meeting is about.

After a few moments, Ruth drops the stare, places the mug on the table, retrieves the pencil, and fills out the rest of the puzzle in short order.

Woody leans in and sees the paper saying the puzzle's classified hard, supposed to be a brain scratcher. Supposed to take some time. Ruth did it all in his head and completed it in seconds. Not that he might not have been staring at it for a while, seeing how everything worked, following each path like it was a maze to come to a solution. Woody wasn't here. It could be his morning thing, spending hours looking at it, maybe even scratching it out on another piece of paper, but then again, maybe he sat here, stared at it, and knocked it out. Woody doesn't know.

Not that it matters. He couldn't ever get into those damn number puzzles. Tried in prison a few times when he was by himself. Spent a frustrating trio of days going insane and couldn't complete one that was supposed to be easy, labeled that way. Punched the wall after throwing the book at it. Then he proceeded to rip it up and piss on it in the toilet. But then again, he and numbers don't always get along. They do funny things in his mind, come in one way, get twisted, and come out differently. Been that way his whole life. He often said he became a cop, so he didn't have to do math or things like add.

Ruth's a numbers guy. Always has been. Can still recite his first cell phone number, his first dog's birthday, and combinations of locks that rusted years ago. Those locks are being used to house some of his darker secrets, like the one tied to the rock and chain holding a man named Stevens to the bottom of Grand Lake.

Now that he's finished, Ruth places the pencil on top of the paper. He scoots the paper to the side. He brings his hands together in front of him, tight, fingers interlaced into a ball. He doesn't look up right away before speaking. He says, "I've been patient with you."

"I know you have," Woody says. "Coop's working on some things. As soon as I know something, you will know something."

"I've heard *some things*," Ruth says, returning Woody's words to him. "I know things, too. Like you're impatient. So why did you have Johnny stabbed?"

Woody opens his mouth and starts to respond but then shuts it, which is a kind of response.

Ruth points at him. "I don't have evidence tying you to it, but I figured it was you when I heard about his unfortunate change in circumstance."

Woody could deny it, but he figured out what the point was. So, he says, "I don't know what you've heard."

"Funny you should say that," Ruth says. "I've heard Johnny told his wife where the stones are. But you know how rumors are—"

"He didn't tell her where the stones are."

"He didn't?"

"No, he left some breadcrumbs for her to follow to take her to the stones."

"So, she doesn't know where they are?" Ruth picks up the coffee and sips it. "Doesn't have them?"

Woody shakes his head. "No, she doesn't." Then he adds, "Yet."

Ruth sits the coffee down. "Interesting."

"I'm working on it," Woody says after a moment. "She'll tell me where they are, and I'll get you your money. I'm working on it."

"I hope so, for your sake," Ruth says. "It's a lot of money."

"Yeah, well, we didn't get any either. No one did. So, you can bitch and complain about how you're owed your cut no matter what, but no one is holding out on you, 'cept Johnny and he's holding out on everyone."

Ruth nods. "I see," he says. "I heard some people died, so you all could get those stones? Makes me wonder," he pauses between words, "if you can't pay me what I'm owed, then I wonder if this information is valuable to anyone else. Do you understand what I'm saying, or do I need to write it down for you to take back to Cooper? I don't want to wait any longer for my money, and if Johnny dies without anyone finding the stones, then the odds of me getting paid are slim. I always get paid."

CHAPTER 20:

LAMAR HENRY STARES AT THE WOMAN HE found in the car, now in the house with Cece and Dante, studying her, trying to figure out how she ticks. Getting her from the car to inside the house wasn't hard. He just had to flash Cece's dinky little pistol around and give her some vague threats, which could be misconstrued, later, of course, minus the fact of the gun, as a misunderstanding if anyone makes a stink about it. Not that he thinks she will.

"No, you're here for a reason," he says, making his thoughts audible. "I know that reason is me; that's obvious enough with what you said to Cece earlier and to me in the car, but that doesn't tell me why you're really here. What's the angle?"

The woman looks at Dante but stays quiet. She doesn't say, and he didn't expect her to right off the bat. With how she was in the car, Lamar knows he will have to finesse her into speaking or telling the truth. After all, she's an attorney, and she's not going to give it up on the first at-bat, but her attitude is something he can get behind. Her looks are so-so for a white woman, certainly not like Johnny's wife, but with that wit and attitude, Lamar can't help but like her. She's what he would describe as spicy and feisty.

The woman wasn't too happy about being ushered into the house when he brought her inside, yanking her from the car out the passenger side as he got out and pulling her toward the house. She whispered because she was smart enough not to yell, not that it would have made a difference; that's what he was doing, using the gun and threats and dragging her to the house; this, what he was doing, was a kidnapping. He kidnapped her. She said she was being kidnapped, said it like she couldn't believe it. Even went on and on about how this couldn't be real, repeating it like a mantra as they walked toward the house. But it is real. Real for him and real for her. This is real for Dante and Cece, who are surprised to see Lamar bring the woman into the house and force her down on the couch to sit. Shoving her down into the seat by her shoulders.

Now Lamar says, "So, you're Dante's attorney?"

The woman, who said her name was Erin, sits across from Lamar on the couch; Lamar's sitting in a kitchen chair in front of the TV, back toward the TV. She looks over at Dante and then back to Lamar. "I'm his attorney."

"And you are here looking for me, I take it?"

Erin repeats the process. She looks at Dante again and then back to Lamar. "I can't answer that question. I'll have to consult further with my client."

Lamar turns to Dante. "Tell her to answer my questions."

Dante nods but stays mute by the front entryway.

Lamar turns his attention back to the attorney. "You going to look at your client every time I ask you a question?"

Erin glances at her client. Then says, "Yes, I am."

Lamar flashes Dante an annoyed look. All the bug guy has to do is talk, but he never talks. Not really. Unless Lamar's trying to go to sleep, and then the fucker won't shut up. It was that way the entire time he bunked with him when he came back on the writ to testify against that guy.

"This isn't an interview room," he says. "I ain't the cops. This isn't that type of setup. I want to know some specific information from you, like why you are here. What do you know about me? And what you really want."

"We went through that in the car," she says, the body still rigid but composed, posture proper. She doesn't flinch or look away. Her eyes, kinda pretty in their way, stay on him. It's unnerving. She says, "I answered your questions."

Lamar blinks a long blink. "No, we played word games. You didn't answer nothing."

"I answered what you asked. Perhaps you should ask better questions if you don't like the answers."

He points at her. "You think directness is the problem?"

"I think you asked the wrong questions, expecting different answers." Eyes not moving, borrowing into him. It's chilling.

Lamar plays like it doesn't bother him, but it does. He laughs once. "You're calling *me* obtuse." He touches his chest. The stab wound, it hurts right now. "At least that's how you're acting, that a lawyer thing?"

The woman blinks, finally. She says, "I'm not calling you anything. I don't want to insult you. I don't want to talk to you. I don't even want to be here."

"So, what is it you do want?"

"I want what I always want. I want what's best for my clients."

"So, you're after what's best for Dante?"

She nods. "His chances aren't good. If I can use something to help him out, get him out of the trouble he's in, keep him from prison, that's a win."

"You mean give me up so he can cut a deal."

"I mean, anything I can use, I *will*—to cut a deal."

"So, what else you want?"

"You to not be in his life," she says. "He's already got enough problems. His cousin, for one."

"Hey," Cece interjects. "I take exception to that."

They both ignore the outburst.

"I want what is best for Dante. No matter your reason or how I'm going to use it, you being here isn't helping him."

Lamar places both hands on his knees, elbows bent, and leans forward. "Well, I'm here now."

Lamar sneaks a leak at Dante. Does it bother the big man they're talking about him as if he's not here? If it does, he doesn't show it.

But this is a type of courtroom. Different from what the woman's used to, but she's catching up. She relaxes in the seat, some, not much, her body relenting as if she's finally exhaled and taken a breath. "That's what I am wondering. Why are you here?"

Lamar knows what this is. He's been on trial three times. He's seen this before, and she's the best he's seen. She's flipping this around on him.

Interesting.

"What you mean?"

"If Dante's your friend, like you claim, why are *you* here? It's not just to hang out. You are here for a reason. What is it? I want to know."

"Of course you do," Lamar says. "But I still don't understand."

She considers his statement. Her face shows she's rolling it around in her pretty, but scared, head. She puts it to him in a different way. "If he's your friend, then why put him at risk with your presence? You being here could be a lot of trouble for him. Imagine if that marshal came by. Dante's fighting for his freedom."

Lamar motions to Dante. "He looks pretty free now."

"Yeah, on bond, but he's fighting for his freedom. He's lucky he got out at all. They got his car; they got a figure on video. They got the proceeds—coin wrappers, if you must know—from one of the robberies in the car's center console. He's lucky just to be out on that ankle monitor. That is why he doesn't drive and is always here."

Shit, Lamar didn't know that. He directs his eyes to Dante. "This true? You on a monitor?"

Dante nods. Doesn't say anything more. Lamar didn't expect him to, but still, a monitor?

Lamar turns his attention back to the lawyer. "What are the conditions?" His mind runs through all the possible scenarios of how he's fucked.

But the attorney plays it cool, pretending she's not bothered. She's got the upper hand. She knows it, and he knows it.

"He can pretty much do what he wants between the hours of 6 a.m. to 6 p.m. It's nighttime that causes him problems. But what are you going to say when it shows him outside a bank and Cece's here?"

"What you mean?"

"Dante doesn't drive..."

Lamar doesn't need her to finish the rest of the sentence. He directs his attention to Cece. "You drive because of the courts? I thought you said it was 'cause his mom asked you to help him before she went?"

"She did," Cece says. "But yeah, the court don't want him driving either unless he has to, like to the hospital or something. I tole you he don't drive. But you wouldn't listen. You said you would drive. Well, people who live with him drive. I am the only one who lives with him, and Ms. Pretty Bitch there caught me here at home. Not with him."

The attorney says, "Dante and I had an agreement. He has to answer me when I call."

"When you jerk his leash?" Lamar says.

She bats his comment to the side and speaks slowly and calmly. "When I call. If he doesn't answer, I come here. If he doesn't answer the door, I have to call the cops. It's the only way this works. I want the best for my client. And that means avoiding people like you."

"But his shithead cousin's okay?"

The woman licks her lips. "Let me ask you," she says, trying to bring the control back to her side of this verbal tug o' war. "He give you that gun?"

"So, what if I did?" Cece says, cutting in. "No law against having that gun. I'm not a convicted felon."

The attorney grins. She keeps that gaze squarely focused on Lamar. He gets where she's going with this, and she wants him to see the threat in her eyes. Even though he's got the gun, it doesn't bother her being here. "You might not be, but he is, and you gave it to him."

Cece resounds, not understanding, not that Lamar thinks he would. "What you mean? You got a point?"

"Yeah, she's got a point, Poindexter," Lamar says. "Means you committed a major no-no."

"A *crime*?" Cece says, not believing it. "What crime?"

"You gave me a gun," Lamar says. He keeps his eyes on the woman. "It's a crime. I'm the felon. She thinks it's going to matter."

"Well, she not in much of a position to do anything about it, not from where I'm standing."

The attorney doesn't play like any of this bothers her.

"She's got a boyfriend," Lamar announces to the room. "D, we saw him around, too. Mr. GQ is driving that, Lincoln. Don't you?" The question is directed at the attorney.

She nods but says, "I don't know what you would call us."

"But you been intimate with the Wrench," he says. It's not a question, although she answers it with another head nod.

Cece isn't tracking. "The Wrench? Who the fuck is the Wrench?" But then, when the words leave his mouth, he puts them together. "The fucker from the TV, from that show? That cop? You banging that cop? *Shit*, girl."

Lamar holds out a hand. "I got your phone."

The woman says, "You should have left it in the car."

"Why's that?"

"He and his friends will come for me; they aren't the sort you mess with. He'll get concerned that I didn't answer or call him back. He'll use it to find my location."

"That's what I'm counting on," Lamar says. "How's he going to do that? He's not a cop anymore."

The attorney grins, the scar looking as natural as a blue jay in a tree. "Find my iPhone, dipshit."

"Good," Lamar says.

"Good?" Cece questions. "Good? What's fucking good about that? I don't want some cop coming up in here looking for some white side dish bitch. Even if he's

some pretend cop now. We don't need that. D don't need none of that."

"But we do," Lamar says. "We need the Wrench and his friends."

"We do?"

"Oh yeah, because they're in what I'm in, and I'd like to know what they know."

"What are *you* in?" Cece asks, pleading. "What you wrap me and D into?"

Lamar ignores Cece. He withdraws the attorney's phone from his pocket and sits it on the coffee table between them. She looks down at it, barely moving anything but her eyes.

Lamar says, "You're going to make a phone call to your boyfriend."

"I am?" she says.

Lamar nods, scooting the phone a few inches forward. Then he leans back. "You are."

"Why?"

"Because I want to know what sort of figures we're working with. Johnny never told me, but he did say the Wrench was involved."

Even though Johnny only hinted at it.

"And you think Craig will tell you what you want to know?"

"I think Craig will recognize a bargaining piece when he sees one." Lamar points a finger at her and clicks his tongue against the roof of his mouth.

"Me?"

"You said it, kidnapping. I might as well use you to my advantage while I have you. Otherwise, what's the point of *committing no crime*?"

Cece, coming around the couch, far side from the door, says, "I'd find some good mother fucking ways to use a piece o' ass like her."

Both Lamar and the attorney glance at him.

Lamar shuts his eyes and sighs. Cece's going to be a problem. But he has to focus on the now, not the future. He'll deal with Dante's cousin soon enough.

Lamar brings his hands tighter as he opens his eyes and refocuses on what he is saying. He points to the phone with both index fingers together. "Make the call."

Dante shifts in his stance, almost like a bird dog pointing. At the same time, Lamar hears a car door slam close. Lamar looks to Dante, whose attention is directed to the front door, looking beyond the screen door.

"What is it?"

"Company," Dante says. "Man in bright shirt and little hat."

Both Lamar and the attorney mutter, "The marshal."

Lamar throws Cece the gun. "Put that away." As he jumps to his feet and grabs the attorney by the arm. He jerks her off the couch. "D, close the door."

Dante does as he's told.

The wooden door slams shut.

Lamar brings the woman around the couch, crossing next to Cece. "Don't say nothing," Lamar says. "Get rid of him."

"I'm not shooting no marshal," Cece says.

"I'm not asking you to. I'm just making sure if things go sideways, you got your gun back."

But that's precisely what he's asking.

There's a knock at the front door.

Lamar yanks open the coat closet door near the entryway and shoves the attorney inside. When she starts to protest, Lamar slips into the closet beside her and wraps a hand around her mouth to prevent her from speaking, then pulls her close against him. He whispers, "Be quiet. No one wants to hurt you." For good measure, Lamar withdraws a kitchen steak knife he lifted from Dante's kitchen and places it against her back, the tip poking her in the spine.

The attorney nods against his hand, showing she'll be good. She understands.

Cece shuts the closet door as he moves toward the front door.

CHAPTER 21:

E DUARDO CHAVEZ STANDS THERE, AND the door slams in his face. He was almost able to see inside the residence through the screen door.

"That's rude," he mutters under his breath. He looks over his shoulder. The Toyota is parked down the street. Rafferty wiggles in the driver's seat and flips down the sun visor. He refused to come with Eduardo up to the door but said his ethics prevented him from driving away or letting Eduardo come to the house alone. "I'll stay in the car," Rafferty said with a wink, "in case you need to make a quick getaway."

Eduardo knocks on the door. He can hear motion inside, some whispering, scrabbling of feet.

He knocks again.

The door swings open, revealing a tall, slender, black male with pencil-thin facial hair. The man sticks his head out of the door, arms hanging on the door frame, eclipsing and purposefully obstructing most of Eduardo's view into the house. Eduardo's seen this tactic before. There isn't much he hasn't seen.

Peering beyond the man, Eduardo glimpses an inner life. He can make out the form of a large man, who he assumes is Dante, based on the attorney's description of the man. The man stands behind the man, obstructing Eduardo's view near the hall closet.

The guy in the doorway must be the cousin.

The cousin says, "What *you* want?" Slurring the words together in a manner Eduardo is all too familiar with. A false bravado meant to be threatening and "street" but comes off as silly and scared.

Eduardo decides to use the direct approach. No reason not to. It always works best with people caught up in the undercurrents of the criminal underworld who aren't too keen on seeing a marshal come up to their door. But no way for this guy to know who Eduardo is, and Eduardo isn't a marshal, not today, not that he isn't wearing the badge on his hip, gun in a low-profile holster on his right side. The shirt covers it all, which is how Eduardo likes it. He doesn't like to advertise who he is until he needs to; it's saved his life a few times.

As calmly and confidently as Eduardo can, because with people like the cousin, it's a show, he removes his hat, holds it in his left hand, and juts it toward the man. "I'd like to talk to Dante Smith. That him behind you? It's important."

"What's important?"

Eduardo tilts his head to the right. "That I talk with him. It's important."

The cousin eyes Eduardo hard, examining him, eyes squinting, nose wrinkling, as he works out how he wants to play this interaction in his brain. He could say no and slam the door in Eduardo's face, but if Eduardo could help his cousin, or worse, the law, it would ultimately hurt his cousin. That wouldn't be what he wants to do. So, the cousin stands frozen in the moment, switching back to his "street" ways, and challenges Eduardo through obfuscation—again, a tactic Eduardo is all too familiar with. "You have an appointment?"

Eduardo raises an eyebrow. "His attorney told me I could find him here."

"Did she?"

Eduardo nods.

The cousin snarls his lip, doing everything in his power to show he doesn't want Eduardo at the house, at the door, in his life, which in Eduardo's experience is another dead giveaway something going on, and usually means the person he's looking for is right where he thinks he is.

The escaped convict is in the house.

But like playing a game of poker, or better yet, appearing on a 360-degree stage, Eduardo doesn't let on and stays still, calm, exuding a coiled charisma that could strike at any moment so that even though the man's mannerisms continue to be confrontational, Eduardo doesn't back down.

The cousin says, "D, he wants to talk to you?"

Eduardo says, "I would think he doesn't have a reason not to talk to me."

"That don't answer my question," the cousin points out. Then he adds, "D, don't talk to no one. 'Specially people who don't announce themselves or answer simple questions. You feel me?"

"I'm not here to feel you." Eduardo tips the hat toward the big man. "I'm here to talk to him.

Eduardo understands what the cousin meant, but still, he doesn't relent. He steps half a step forward. More leaning in than anything. "I'd like to hear that from D— Dante himself," Eduardo says. "If he doesn't want to talk to me. Is that him back there behind you?" He motions with the hat and makes eye contact with the big guy, "You want to talk to me?" then looks back to the cousin. The question was directed at both. "Who else is inside the house?"

The cousin bobs his head into Eduardo's view. "No one *else* is in the house; what you talking about? Why you axe that? Why would there be anybody else inside this house? Just us."

"Just us mice here," Eduardo mumbles.

"What?"

Eduardo clears his throat and speaks up, tired of this. "Is that your cousin?"

The cousin smiles like the cat from a mathematician's fairytale book. Then, the cousin drops his false "street" persona and adopts a more natural countenance. "Ah, so you know all about me, huh?" He is proud of himself.

"I know nothing about you other than Dante Smith lives with his cousin, so you must be the cousin. You two look like you are related, but you could be his lover for all I know. I would put my money on the cousin, Cecil."

"Cece," the skinny man sneers, correcting. "My name. Is. Cece."

Eduardo brushes the chastisement in Cece's tone aside. "What's wrong with Cecil?"

"Nothing wrong with it; people just don't call me that. I don't want to be called what people don't call me. I like what to be called what I like to be called. People don't use the name Mama gave me. They use Cece."

"And what do you call yourself?"

But the question goes over the man's head. Cece doesn't understand Eduardo's question, and perhaps that's for the best. Eduardo's just playing with him now.

The cousin says. "I just tole you, it's Cece."

"That's what others call you," Eduardo says, agreeing but pushing him some more, figuratively poking the man in the chest to get a reaction. "Right? So, if you're Cecil, that's Dante behind you?"

"Yeah, that's D."

"Took the long way around to get to a short answer."

"What?"

"Cecil," Eduardo deliberately uses his given name. "Are you going to let me in to speak to Dante or move so I can address him properly?"

Cece starts to say something, but Eduardo leaves him nowhere to go. He can't be "street" cause he dropped that act and isn't smart enough to hang with Eduardo in a war of words. So, whatever was running through Cece's mind was probably some half-assed hard-ass response, but he pauses to look back over his shoulder. "D, you want to talk to this guy?" But before Dante can answer, the skinny guy looks at Eduardo. "He don't want to talk to you."

Eduardo steps forward again, nearly nose to nose with Cece in the doorway, adding what Rafferty calls a *pressure of presence*. Rafferty says, "It's like those damn salesman who get all close and shit to you, close talkers, millimeters from your shoulder, damn near sniffing the back of your neck, telling you where to sign, which dotted line, talking fast and shit; that's what they're doing; putting the pressure on, so to speak, invading your bubble, so you can't think things through right; the same way your mommy and daddy use to stand over you demanding to know what happened to the cookies in the cookie jar, it's hard to say no to someone comfortable inside your bubble. They own you at that point."

There's a moment of both men standing at the door, nearly touching, sizing the other one up. Then, predictably, the cousin relents. It's not much, maybe an inch of his head instinctively retracting, but it's enough to signal to Eduardo he's won the staring contest.

Eduardo says, "Let me hear that from him." And steps into the doorway. Eduardo pushes through the gap between the cousin and the door, brushing against and past the cousin, mumbling a sarcastic "excuse me" as he slips inside the house.

Once inside, Eduardo finds himself in the residence's living room.

The big man, Dante, still stands by the hall closet behind his cousin, staring at him.

"Nice place," Eduardo says, surveying the room, carefully keeping his hands near his hips but appearing unthreatening. He turns a few times, getting a layout firm in his mind: Kitchen in the back. Hallway to the bedrooms. One story. The hall closet is on the other side of the couch, far from the TV. The chair in front of the TV must have come from the kitchen. The chair facing the couch, facing the wrong way.

"Man, what's wrong with you?" the cousin asks, letting the screen door shut. It slams against the wood frame.

"Wrong with me?" Eduardo turns back toward him. He's still at the door. "Nothing's wrong."

The cousin points at him. "Yeah, man, you can't just come here like you own the place. Look around. You don't got no warrant. So, I axe you again; what's wrong with you?"

"Nothing is wrong with me," Eduardo says. Then he places a hand on his stomach. "I guess I'm a little gassy. Staying in hotels tends to do that."

The cousin stares at him blankly. "What?"

Eduardo motions toward the chair in front of the TV with his hat. "You got company?"

"No," the cousin says too quickly. Again, another trademark giveaway that Eduardo's picked the correct city and the right house; damn the others who think Lamar Henry went to New Orleans.

But Eduardo has to tread carefully. He's here on his own. There isn't any backup. There isn't a team of heavily armed guys ready to tear the place apart to find the felon. He's not even wearing a vest that says marshals in big white letters. All he has is his gun on his hip, a badge that doesn't mean much now, and Rafferty in the car down the street. At least three men are eyeing the scene here. One hidden. Two in front of him. Eduardo is outnumbered.

"Strange place for a kitchen chair," Eduardo comments.

"D and I had some things to hash out."

"Things?"

"Yeah, he's not pulling his weight with the rent. So, I sat him down and told him how it had to be. He don't like those types of talks. He likes to watch TV—ignore me. So, I sat right there so he couldn't see no TV."

"Really?" Eduardo exclaims, turning his attention to Dante. "That true?"

Dante locks eyes with Eduardo, and just as he nods, the cousin says, "It doesn't matter if it's true or not. It doesn't matter if you are a marshal or not."

"Well, funny thing about that," Eduardo says, returning to the cousin. "I never introduced myself." He puts his hands up. "Rude, I know, or showed you my badge. But you're right, I'm United States Deputy Marshal Eduardo Chavez. But now I got to ask, how did you know?"

The cousin doesn't speak.

Again, another giveaway.

Cece says, "D don't have nothing to explain to you. So, what is it you want?"

Eduardo smiles. "How'd you know I was a marshal?" He sits in the kitchen chair in front of the TV. He settles in the seat and throws a leg over his knee. He examines the hat that he perches on his knee. "I mean, you knew it. You can't go pretending otherwise. You knew."

"Lawyer lady said you might be coming around."

Eduardo will give it to the cousin. He is quick.

"Did she?"

"She said, 'he likes to wear these ugly shirts and act like he own a place.'"

"Really?"

"And with you showing up here, doing just that, I just knew who you were. No need to have you give your name or introduce yourself. You are you. That's clear."

"Crystal."

"So, I axe you one more time before I make you leave, 'cause I don't think you would be here like this if you were official. Yeah, I'm smarter than I look. What the fuck do you want?"

Eduardo holds up his hands in surrender. "I just wanted to see if Dante's talked to an old friend of his, Lamar Henry. He's escaped prison."

"D don't have no friends."

"Be that as it may," Eduardo says. "Dante shared a cell with him a while back, and I wondered if Lamar would reach out to Dante."

"Well, he ain't," Cece says.

"He ain't?"

"Ain't here and ain't reach out."

Eduardo snaps to his feet. He's seen enough. Lamar's in the closet, but Eduardo doesn't want to push this further. He'll pull a Rafferty and sit in the car down the street. Wait for Lamar to make his move. Take him down, then. "Well, if he ain't here, he ain't here."

"That's what I said," Cece says.

Eduardo walks around the couch, kitchen side, so that he will cross in front of the hall closet on his way out of the house. He glances into the kitchen just to make Cece nervous. Sees where the chair is supposed to be. The place is immaculate except for some chips and fixings for nachos on the counter. "You use cheese sticks for your nachos?"

"What?"

"Nothing," Eduardo says. As he moves behind the couch, he notices the door to the closet is cracked open. He glances at it and then crosses between Cece and Dante. Dante looks down at him, and the big guy nods once. The attorney was correct. He's a nice guy. He's got that look. Dollars to donuts, the robber in this family is the cousin. "I'll be going." Eduardo pauses to extend a business card from his pocket to Cece. "If Lamar does show his face, you call me."

Cece snatches the card from Eduardo's hand and, as he crumbles it into a tight ball, says, "I'll do just that."

Eduardo leaves.

CHAPTER 22:

ERIN MOORCOCK SHOVES OPEN THE closest door once the all clear is uttered by Dante's stupid-ass cousin, Cece.

"He gone," Cece says. "I think."

From behind her, Lamar says, "You think? What's that mean?"

"Look like he went out of the house; I don't see him," Cece announces as Erin clears the threshold. He's at the screen door peering outside, but Dante hasn't moved a step. Cece turns back toward the closet. "What was all that about?"

Lamar says, "My dumbass."

"I know you…" But then Cece lets it go as he turns back to the door to continue to stare out the screen, waving his hand demonstratively. "You know what? Forget you, man. You is a dumbass."

Erin doesn't know for sure what the marshal's visit is about and doesn't care. Unless his visit was a tactic the marshal is using to knock the group off balance and let them know he knows where Lamar was. Which is probably correct and the point. That's what Craig and his group would have done. It's what cops do. Drop their pants and measure their dicks. Show everyone in the room how much brighter they are and act all the better than them. It's one of the reasons she does what she does. She likes those kinds. Likes to get them on the stand, let them get comfortable and engorged, and then pop their precious little ego bubbles.

The marshal showing up here shows he already knows where Lamar is, or—she figures—he guessed it because he was in her office just this morning acting like he owned the place. He wouldn't have been like that if he wasn't confident about his abilities, and he seemed supremely confident. This probably means the marshal knows something more than he's letting on, and that's the read she got from him talking to him in her office. There's more at play. Lamar's indicated as much.

Erin looks down at her right side where Lamar held the tip of the knife against her blouse after shifting it from her back. This isn't the week for her and her clothes.

"You ripped it," she says, standing next to the back side of the couch. He had held the knife at just the proper pressure that, if she were to lift her shirt and look, there would be a little red welt, like when she's pricked her finger for blood sugar tests, on her skin.

Closing the closet door, Lamar responds, "I ripped what?" Coming around to see what she's doing, he tosses the knife, spins it, and catches it with his other hand. He does this a few times when he notices her looking dumbfounded. "Fast hands."

Erin blinks a few times and shuts her eyes for a long moment. She sighs and opens her eyes. "My shirt, you ripped it with that damn knife. It's ruined."

Lamar continues tossing and spinning the knife. "You had a knife held on you to keep you quiet, by a convicted criminal nonetheless, and all you are worried about is that I ripped your shirt?"

"Yeah, you ruined it," she says, hands against the back of the couch, gripping the cushion.

Lamar catches the knife in a flourish. He nearly doesn't catch it, almost slicing his hand open, but he doesn't. He stops and stares at her and then uses the knife like a conductor's baton. "Man, I can't figure you out," he says. "Any other person would be pissing all over themselves, having a gun pulled on them, a knife held against their back, but you barely even blink. Your blood's like ice, or you're a cold mother."

Erin circles the couch and plops down. "What's to figure out? You kidnapped me. What? You want me to act scared?"

"You aren't kidnapped," Lamer starts, correcting her while coming around the back side of the couch but thinks better of it. "I just need you here for a bit while we figure out the best play—"

"What's the best play?"

"And yeah, being scared would be nice. Pretend or something. It at least makes me feel like I'm going to get compliance from you." Lamar stops the theatrics with the knife and gnaws on his tongue for a moment, a pink thread caressing his lips. "The best play is the one in which no one gets hurt—in my experience."

"In your experience? What's that? Taking it up the ass?"

Lamar sits down in the kitchen chair in front of the TV. He points the tip of the knife at her; his index finger along the top ridge is the knife. "You say that because I was in prison. You're trying to get a rise out of me. Make me angry. You know why? 'Cause you like emotion. I think you like to make people—men, more, but you're an equal opportunity offender—emotional, angry." He pauses.

Erin stays quiet.

"Am I wrong?"

Erin crosses her arms and legs and jerks her head. He's not wrong.

"See, you ain't too hard to figure out. Now, the only poking that happened to me in prison was when I stabbed myself to get put in the infirmary with Johnny."

Erin's eyes drift as he speaks, but then she reengages with the conversation and cuts them back to Lamar. "You stabbed Johnny?"

Lamar shakes his head. "No, no, I didn't stab no one but myself." He lifts his shirt. He points to the puckered, still-healing flesh that looks red, sore, and wet. "Right here, but I guess I didn't do it right, went too deep, put myself in a world of hurt, but as far as wounds go, once patched up—which I was in an *emergency* surgery—it's like it never happened. A bit hard to catch my breath, but otherwise, I'm on the mend, so to speak. But no, I didn't stab Johnny. I don't hurt people."

"So, who did?"

"Some Mexican, I'd suspect," Lamar says. "Johnny didn't have a lot of respect for 'bean eaters,' his words, not mine. I use them to demonstrate what it was like to be his cellmate. He's not a good cat, and he's pathetic. Didn't have a problem with me, a black man like most cops I know, but when it came to the other dark meat, he had this mean streak."

Erin explains. "One of the guys they robbed was Mexican, and he came forward. Kind of kicked this whole thing off. Guy was a drug dealer, but to the court, that didn't matter."

"Regardless, I didn't stab Johnny," Lamar says, stressing his innocence. "I did use his unfortunate circumstance to my device and devised a way to escape. I don't hurt no one. That's the best way."

Now Erin turns it on and sounds like an attorney, asking rapid-fire questions to probe defenses. "Why were you in prison?"

Lamar relaxes in the chair. "Bank robbery."

"You never hurt anyone during any of your robberies?"

"Never."

"Not once?"

"Never. Threatened it, sure. But hurt someone? No. Not my schtick. Not my cup of tea. Why would I hurt someone for someone else's money? They don't own it. You asked that, like those bosses I had, who think when I get my paycheck, their names are on the check? But just like the bank. That money don't have nothing to do with them. So why hurt them?"

"Why threaten them?"

"Incentive."

"What if you were challenged?"

"I wasn't."

"But if you were? What would you have done?"

Lamar thinks the question over for half a moment. "You know what, *counselor*, you are asking a hypothetical about something that never happened. So, I'm not going to answer your question."

Erin nods approval. He's slick. She asks, "So what's next?" Adds sarcasm for the next bit. "So, what's the best play?"

Lamar says, "You call your boyfriend, and you tell him when he finds what Johnny hid, then he is to hand it over to get you back."

"That simple, huh?"

"That simple."

From the doorway, Cece comes back over. "What are we going to do about the marshal?"

Lamar holds Erin's gaze for a moment longer than necessary, and then he addresses Cece. "You're going to do nothing," Lamar says to him. "The marshal's inching forward using his front foot to drag his back foot instead of driving himself forward with his back foot."

Cece looks at Lamar as lost as Erin is to Lamar's comment. "What?"

Lamar gives in. "He don't have no power," he says, lowering himself to Cece's communication level.

"What's that mean?"

Lamar explains. "You get power from the back foot. He's here alone because he's not here officially. As far as I'm concerned, he can do nothing. So don't pay him any mind."

"How you so sure?"

"'Cause if he were really here as a marshal, there'd be about twenty heavily armored, sweaty, hairy dudes here with him, and we'd all be face down in handcuffs." Lamar holds a look with Cece to act as his punctuation and make sure the man gets it. "That didn't happen. That's why I'm sure."

Cece steps back, mumbling, "Whatever, man."

Lamar points the knife Cece's way and says, "Here's what you're going to do. You go outside and look down the street toward where he went. If you don't know where he went, that's fine. Don't look all around, just the direction he went. You do that until he drives past."

"How do I know if he's driving past?"

"You'll know. He'll make it obvious. Roll down his window or something. Probably salute you."

"Another thing, how you know he's out there? What if he don't drive past? What if he not even there? I don't want to just be staring down the street holding my dick for nothing."

"I know," Lamar says clearly to Erin, frustrated with Cece. "You do that. He'll shift this little stakeout someplace else, whatever—it don't matter—and then he'll come back."

Cece glances at Dante, still standing in the same spot. Then he shoves open the screen door and steps outside.

When he's gone, and the door slaps back, Lamar pulls the phone out of his pocket and sets it on the table. "In the meantime, we have a phone call to make, and I'd prefer it if that marshal don't surprise us again. Dante shut the door and came over here to have a seat. You're stressing me out standing over there lurking in the corner."

Dante does as he is told and joins Erin on the couch. His large frame sinks into the cushions, and his legs are gangly and involving like grasshoppers.

Lamar says, "Now, call him."

"Who?"

"The Wrench," Lamar clarifies. "Pick up the phone—dial him."

"I have a choice?"

"No," he says.

Erin leans forward and retrieves the phone from the table. She navigates the screen to Craig's phone number.

Just as she is about to select the number, finger hovering over the screen, Lamar demands, "On speaker."

Erin selects Craig's number and the speaker option. The call rings once and then goes to voicemail. "Not here. Leave a message."

Erin glances up at Lamar. "Want me to leave a message?"

The call beeps, signaling that it's time to leave a message. Lamar nods and mouths, "Make it short."

"Call me back," Erin says. She adds a pleading, "Please."

She ends the call.

Lamar asks, "Why do you think he didn't pick up?"

"He might be working."

Lamar thinks it over. "You know who for?"

Erin nods. "Yes," she answers. Tom Cooper and company.

"Who else can you call?"

"I'm sorry?"

"Who else can you call that would get the Wrench a message?"

Only one name comes to her mind. "There is one."

"Call him," Lamar demands.

Erin selects Dickie's number.

"On speaker..."

The ringing fills the room until Dickie answers the call.

CHAPTER 23:

LUCILLE HUDSON SITS CROSS-LEGGED ON the rug in her living room in front of the fireplace. A small fire burns inside the framed glass facade, and the light casts long shadows across the floor and walls, accentuating and complementing the twilight of the day outside the windows without adding heat to the room.

Darkness lurks outside the windows, the dying light fading fast, making the shadows of the trees so much taller now. It was like standing on a beach at noon when she was with Eduardo. Everything was so bright and white—no shadows anywhere. A beach where he's holding her, his arms looped around her waist, his eyes looking down into hers. The sounds of the waves lapping the shore in the background. Maybe a seagull or two cawing in the distance and overhead. The smell of salt and sun drifting on the breeze, infusing into their skin. The taste of each other on their lips.

Lucy turns her attention from the windows, the outside, and her imagination to the present. She looks at the fireplace and is reminded it is a suburban lament, a feature taken from somewhere else, commercialized, sold, and used without thought of how it was or how it came to be. The curse of comfort. Leftover industrialization. Fake.

She is wearing a gray t-shirt with blue pajama bottoms, flamingos in sunglasses under a beach umbrella dotting her legs. She called into work this evening. She couldn't go. Didn't have it in her. Samuel, her boss, said he didn't want her there if she couldn't give one hundred percent. He's been a good boss, but it is just a restaurant, and she thinks he's always treated her differently because of her name. Samuel doesn't have a lot of love for cops or their wives—much less dirty cops.

In front of Lucy sits a glass of red wine, standing proudly on the rug next to the remnants of her marriage. Lucy stares down at the accumulated debris of her life: a photo album of her and Johnny's wedding, her name tag from the restaurant, her small purse overturned, the contents a cascade of litter, and the other woman's business card, which lays flat on the rug, the woman's face staring at Lucy. Shifting to the album, Lucy traces a finger along the edge of one of the photos. Johnny is in a tuxedo, a flower clutched in his hand, smiling into the camera, happy. The photo doesn't capture what happened next, but Johnny handed that flower to her before saying the "I dos" as a symbol of their love.

But flowers wilt.

Lucy figured she would make the call tonight and collect the last breadcrumb Johnny had left her, so she was on the phone long past hello.

"The truth is, I don't remember our wedding day," Lucy says. "I don't remember anything about the event. I remember getting ready, drinking champagne, the girls helping me, and the dress. But not the ceremony or the small reception, nothing."

"Tell me," she says after a moment, "do you have a big house? Johnny always said he wanted a big house. Said having one here would be different from the house up there. He said... Well, I guess we can agree that he said a lot of things."

"The house is big," Lucy admits. "Bigger than I need, for sure."

"What do you like best about the house? Tell me about it. Where are you in the house now? What's around you? Describe this house to me?"

Lucy takes a moment to collect her thoughts, wondering why she is talking to this woman and answering these questions. She glances at the fireplace again as a flame of light twinkles brightly before fading. "My favorite thing about the house? Well, remember, this isn't my house. It was his grandmother's, but it has to be the fireplace."

"Isn't it too warm where you are?" the woman asks. "What do you need a fireplace for? You have a fire going now? Is it too hot for a fire? Johnny said winter could get cold there, but not like in other places like Chicago or New York. He always said winter there was mild compared to those places. He said sometimes it snowed. I've only seen snow in the mountains here. I've never seen it snow. But he said it would snow maybe once or twice a year."

"It does snow. Ice is more of an issue."

The woman squeals like a teenage girl. "What I'd give to see a white Christmas. Enjoy a fire inside while watching it snow outside. It sounds so wonderful and pretty." Her accent adds an exotic element to her thoughts, making her sound even more ridiculous. "Johnny said we could go to

Chicago, where his uncle lived, and do just that. Have you been to these places? Visited his uncle? Had a white Christmas?"

"No."

"Johnny said he's been to these places. Said Chicago was okay, at least the suburbs near the lake. A lake as wide as the ocean is here along the shores. I don't think it is the same thing, but he said it looked like it. He said New York was the best. So many people. He told me stories. He told me maybe when he was camping, his family would light a fire, but that was when he was young. He told me he would take me camping. I'd like that. He said... he said his father didn't understand why people needed a fireplace in the city, but nearly everyone had one."

All Lucy says is, "Maybe it's because we take the things we have for granted and forget why they were even there in the first place."

The woman seems to think her words over. "Maybe," she says, adding, "Johnny told me a lot about America. He told me he would take me to Broadway in New York and go to a show. I told you he told me about seeing it snow in Chicago—he didn't seem to want to be in New York when it snowed. He told me he'd take me anywhere I wanted to go. Even said we'd go to Las Vegas. See the desert. See a show. Gamble. He said it's so hot in Vegas in the summer it's like being in an oven."

"He said a lot of things," Lucy says before collapsing into an uncomfortable silence.

What does she say to this woman? How could Johnny have done this to her? Hearing this woman talk makes it sound like Johnny was planning a life with her. So, what was Lucy to him? What was their life to him? Was he just going to leave her? Move her down to Costa Rica and say sayonara? Or would he have ended it just before they moved? Left her here when he left.

That's what he would have done. That sounds like him. Sounds just like the Johnny she knows. Practical. Sell this house, where everything is already packed and in storage, and make a clean break. That way, there's no mess. Here's your half of things: your belongings are already ready to go. See ya.

That is the Johnny she knows, and it sounds awfully like Johnny who made these promises to Violeta and told this woman these stories.

Perhaps the two Johnnys, the one she knows and the one everyone else talks about, aren't separate people but the same person. It's Lucy who's been two people, the Lucy before Johnny and the Lucy left in his wake. Dumb and blind, dedicated and destroyed.

Coolly, Lucy says, "This fireplace... it's more decoration than anything practical... kinda like my marriage, I guess."

The woman sounds shocked. "Don't say these things."

"Why, why not say these things? Is it because he loved me?"

The woman affirms on the phone with a hum. "You wouldn't believe me if I told you," she says. "But yes, in his way, he did—by the way. He did love you."

How would this woman know this? Nothing Johnny did indicates this. If this were true, he'd be here right now. But he's not here. He's in prison. He's in prison because he did the wrong things. Terrible things. Things he wasn't even honest about when it came time for him to stand up for what he did. How can she trust him? He says he loves her now, but...

"But he was going to leave me for you."

"Love is complicated, no?"

Lucy half laughs. "No."

The woman seems taken aback. She reaffirms. "In his way, he loved you. Eventually, he told you the truth—that's a kind of love—a gift, no?"

"Just as he loves you," Lucy spits and then asks, "What do you have that I don't? What did you give him that I couldn't?"

The other woman doesn't answer for a long time. Then she says, "If it matters, I didn't know about you for a long time."

"It doesn't matter. It does *not* make me feel any better knowing this."

"It was just sex," the woman admits. "At first. That's what it was. He came down here for a vacation. We met. It was fun. What do you call this in the States? Friends with benefits?"

"He could have had sex with me."

"He could have had sex with a lot of women. From what I know, it was just the two of us."

"From what you know," Lucy says, "but I didn't know about you." Then she mumbles, "Just the two of us."

She didn't expect the woman to overhear the offhand comment, but she finishes the line, "We can make it if we try..." Then, louder, she said, "If you try, you can make it. Johnny's gone, no?"

This line of reasoning becomes uncomfortable for Lucy. "Yeah, I guess."

"He cares about you, I believe. He left you a house. He told me that. He said he made a deal to keep you from losing everything. He wouldn't have done this if he didn't have feelings for you. So now you have a fireplace. I'm sure its warmth feels good."

"I mean, in the winter, I do turn the heat up to warm the room. It gives me heat, then." Lucy's thoughts turn darker again. "But now, it's more for show. Something pretty. Like me."

The phone is silent.

"But you are wrong, you know, that's the worst part. This house, it's not *my* house. This isn't *my* living room; it's Johnny's grandmother's. Like I said. Like everything else, I do not have anything of my own, but what's tethered me here, to this moment—Johnny, my love for him—was all a lie."

"Like an anchor," the other woman offers understanding. "This feeling, I understand."

Lucy nods. Not that the other women can see her. "Yeah, an anchor keeping me here. Dragging me down."

"So cut it loose. An anchor like that must be cut loose and allowed to sink to the bottom of the sea..."

"I don't know," Lucy says. "I don't know why I even called you. I don't know what I expected."

"I think you calling me means the *anchor* has been cut loose. I think you called me because you needed to know. You knew but didn't know. Now you know."

"What do I know?"

"I know Johnny. I never expected the things he said to come true. But thinking about them made me feel better. Now you can feel better."

"How?"

"By leaving him behind." The way she says it makes it sound like the simplest thing in the world, but Lucy doesn't know how to do that. "That's why you called. I told you; he loves you in his way."

"Sure, he does."

"He called that the weight of love, no? To love someone so strongly, in their way, to love someone so much, it traps them."

Something turns over in Lucy's mind, a memory, specifically a date with Johnny early on in their relationship, during which they visited a place she used to work. "What did you say?"

"That's what Johnny called it, no? That type of love that's so heavy that it hurts the ones we love."

"Why was your business card where Johnny had it?"

The woman is quiet and then says, "He told me that if you were ever to call, I would remind you that he loves you in his own way and how heavy that love can be."

Johnny always loved her, but Johnny would always cut her loose.

She knows where Johnny hid the stones, the gems, or whatever he took from the others. She knows where it is.

From behind her, a familiar voice says, "Hang up the fucking phone."

CHAPTER 24:

EDUARDO CHAVEZ ENTERS THE HOUSE through the back door, hand rotating the knob just so as not to make any noise, pushing the door open slowly, an inch at a time, because he couldn't let it go. Lamar is in this house. He knows it. He can feel it. He slips the hat that he had been holding against his chest on his head. Every instinct inside him tells him Lamar Henry is in the house and was also present when he was in the living room messing with Dante's cousin. He can't ignore the feeling, so it doesn't matter that Eduardo is on his own; he isn't going to ignore his instinct. Not when redemption is just steps away.

That was the thought pinging in his mind as he descended the front step and walked back down the drive, heading toward Rafferty in the car, Rafferty staring at him through the windshield, moving from jovial to dumbstruck, as Eduardo reached the edge of the property, walking along the sidewalk, and suddenly cut to the left at the last moment, disappearing between the houses and some bushes.

Because earlier in the car, before going into the house, Rafferty asked him what he was doing, "What, you think you're just going to bring him back slung over your horse, cowboy? Bring him in warm? That's not how this works." Eduardo told him it would help. Rafferty said, "Help you find yourself without a job." Rafferty urged Eduardo to find Lamar and just call it in. Let others handle it.

But Eduardo can't let it go; he will get his man. The suspension was minor, but the damage to his career was done. Hopefully, if he can recover Lamar, he can undo some of the damage, but he has to recover Lamar—by himself—now.

Now that the door is open, letting the inside greet him, Eduardo releases the knob with a soft shove. The door swings open a few more inches on its own so he can prepare himself or react if necessary. Paused in the doorway, he withdraws his gun from the holster under his shirt but keeps it down below his leg, almost hiding it. Eduardo's heart hammers inside his chest as he steps into the kitchen. His palms start to sweat, moistening the handle of the gun. It shouldn't be a problem. He's shot in the heat, but this is a different kind of sweat, not heat-induced. It's a nervous sweat. He wipes the palm of his free hand on his pant leg and then checks the placement of his hat on his head. Sweat collects at the brim, dampening his hair and forehead.

He leaves the door open as he creeps forward with careful, slow steps, each soft and planned like he did when he used to sneak through the bedroom after getting off work late, not wanting to wake his ex-wife—not an ex then—heel to toe, deliberate and careful. The floor's cheap laminate, and each footfall is quiet.

Except it isn't dark, and this isn't his bedroom. It's not even his house. And Eduardo is supremely aware of how far off the map he's gone. Coming to town to hunt down Lamar is one thing; breaking into someone's house because he thinks the convict is here, on his own, without backup, without a badge, and leaving Rafferty in the car as a get-away driver is something else entirely.

A career in law enforcement has told him that's how people die. That's how they go to prison. It's crossing a line. One he might not be able to cross back. A line that could become a set of bars.

But Eduardo's old supervisor used to say risk brings reward. "No one ever solved nothing sitting behind a desk. Sometimes, you have to get out there and walk."

Something rattles the floor under his feet. He turns his head. Makes out the shuffle of metal struts as the washing machine kicks into a different gear in the walkway between the kitchen and the garage behind him.

Ahead of him, voices sound in the living room. He can't hear everything being said, but he can make out about every other word. The talk is rushed and seems to be mainly between two parties—one female and the other male.

Then, there's a shrill electronic ringing.

Are they calling someone?

Could the dipshit cousin be calling the cops? Will he sneak into a room of people expecting his arrival like a lousy surprise party? Wouldn't that be a surprise?

The ringing stops as Eduardo stops inches from the doorway to the rest of the house.

Now, the voices are talking. Male and female. No, it's two male voices. Hard to tell.

The tone of the conversation tells Eduardo he missed the beginning, but that's okay. He's patient, and he isn't here to eavesdrop.

The female voice asks, "Where is he?"

One of the male voices, maybe on the phone, probably on speaker due to the electronic distortion, says, "Don't you know?"

"No," the female says, almost pleading. "I need him. It's important. Tell me where he's at. He's not answering, and I need him to answer."

"You can't talk to him."

"Why the hell not?"

"He's not available."

"What's that mean?"

"Usually means you can't talk," the male voice says, trying to be funny. However, his comments seem to go over poorly due to the audible reactions, and then he says, "I don't know what it means to you. God knows you aren't available to me."

"Dickie, goddamnit." The woman is frustrated now. Eduardo recognizes the voice as the attorney. "This is important."

Dickie, the voice on the phone, chuckles. "Life or death important?"

"Yes!"

Dickie is silent for a long time.

Eduardo silently shuffles closer to the doorway to peer around the edge to see what the room looks like. He notices the trio's reflection in a mirror hanging on the wall, giving him a room layout. On one side of the room is Lamar Henry, sitting by the TV chair. Eduardo was right. The chair had seemed out of place. On the other side is the attorney, looking frazzled but her usual ball-bustery self with Dante Smith, who seems uncomfortable with the whole setup, seated on the couch beside her.

The problem with mirrors is if he can see someone, they can also see him. He'll have to be careful.

"Dickie," the attorney pleads, leaning forward to put her hand next to the phone on the table. Her voice strains. "I *need* Craig. Where is he? Why isn't he answering me? He usually answers me when I call."

"Why do you need him?"

The attorney glances at Lamar. He shakes his head.

"I can't tell you. I just *need* you to tell me where and what he's doing."

Dickie finally speaks after a forced laugh. The sound coming from the phone. "Alright, I like that, Erin. Do *tell* me how much you need me."

"This isn't the time, Dick," Lamar says, interjecting.

"Who is that?" Dickie asks.

The attorney says, "Not important."

Dickie disagrees. "I would think it is—"

The attorney, cutting through Dickie's continued objections, asks, "Where's Craig? I can't get a hold of him."

Dickie's reply is curt. "He's out, going to the wife's house to get the tape."

The attorney can't believe it. "He's *what*?"

Lamar tilts his head and quietly asks the attorney, "What tape?"

Dickie answers, "From Johnny's wife. He's going to get the tape, Johnny's *supposed* confession. I'm sure the others want to know where the money is, but *Craig* only cares about the tape. Seems you did a competent job of expressing upon him how royally fucked he'd be if it came out."

Lamar just shakes his head.

Then the attorney asks, "What next?"

Lamar says, "Say, Dick, can you get a message to him? Find out where he's at?"

"I know where they are going. I already told you that. The wife's house. You know where that's at?" Dickie pauses, and it sounds like he is shuffling papers. Then he gives the address. "Should be there now. If you hurry, you might catch them."

Eduardo creeps forward. Gun at the ready.

The floor creaks.

Everyone's head cuts toward his direction.

Eduardo decides now is the moment. He wheels around the corner, his gun on Lamar.

"Marshal," Lamar says, revealing his hands and how empty they are.

Dante starts to stand, but the attorney keeps her hand on his knee. The big guy settles, visually uncomfortable with the situation.

"What are you doing here?" the attorney asks.

Dickie asks what's going on. No one pays attention to him or the phone.

"I'm here for him," Eduardo says. He nods toward Lamar.

Lamar says, "Alone?"

"Figured that was the only way. No one believed me that you would be here."

"Well—*here* I am," Lamar says. "What's the move?"

"I'm only here for you," Eduardo tells him. "I don't want any trouble. Just you."

"Just doing your job," Lamar says. "I can respect that."

The attorney processes the situation, glancing at Dante and then back at Eduardo. "Of course, there will be no blowback for my client."

Eduardo grins. "Of course."

The attorney nods. Dante silently agrees and relaxes into the seat. The attorney removes her hand from Dante's knee.

Lamar looks around the room, shaking his head, biting his lip, and looking like Denzel Washington in any realization scene in any of his movies. Finally, he decides to cooperate with a shrug. Standing, Lamar starts to say, "I like your style."

But just as he gets to his feet, Cece enters the house, pulling the screen door open with force, saying without looking, "I did what you said, saw the car go by, the white guy driving, but no one was in the passenger seat—" He stops dead in his tracks when his eyes scan the room taking stock of the situation before settling on Eduardo with the gun pointed at Lamar.

Cece's hand dives for the small of his back for a gun. Eduardo's sure. He's trained this scenario countless times in the mirror, imagining this type of standoff, this type of draw, preparing himself for when things go western. He'll be prepared, be cool.

Lamar yells, "Wait, don't!"

But it's too late. Actions are in motion.

Eduardo transitions from Lamar to Cece, but it's not fast enough. Cece's gun is already out in his hand, approaching Eduardo, who's barely aiming and trusting his thumbs.

There's a blast of gunfire in less than a second and nearly simultaneously.

Both men drop to the floor; Cece with two shots to the chest and one to his forehead—trained a thousand times on the range—Eduardo saw the neck snap back, confirming his placement, before Cece's ill-aimed shot struck him in the chest, cutting through a lung. Laying on the floor, he knows it because suddenly the room's become heavy, weighing on his chest. He knows it's blood filling the cavity, rushing to fill the punctured vacuum. Still, it feels like the air itself has gained density and mass, and he decides to sit on his downed body until blackness encroaches on his vision and his hearing fades to oblivion.

CHAPTER 25:

MORRIS WOODFORD STEPS INTO THE light of the fireplace, revealing himself and the gun in his hand. In addition to his leather jacket, white shirt, and blue jeans, he's added beige pantyhose to hide his face, which pulls upward on his nose, distorting his features to an almost absurd degree, giving his appearance a demonic Bosch-type look, but it blurs his vision. Outside, in the car with Craig before coming in here, when pulling the masks down over his eyes, Woody took a moment to check the effect in the mirror; it was mesmerizing—disconcerting. Itchy and frustrating, too. Now he circles Lucy, sitting on the floor, and stands between her and the fireplace, the light licking at his back and throwing his shadow across the room.

Looking up at him, Lucy says, "How'd you get in here?" Her face twists into a confused grimace. "What's that on your face? What are you doing? What is this?"

Woody leans his head to the side but remains silent, letting her take a complete account of the situation.

Lucy goes on, "You're not fooling anyone. I know that's you. I know who you are."

Her revelation of recognition doesn't faze Woody. It doesn't bother him. That wasn't the point. "Your front door was open," he tells her after a moment when he's had enough of her lip. "You really shouldn't do that. You never know who might just come waltzing in here."

Lucy glances back over her shoulder and then back at him. She takes a moment to study him, calculating her next move. Johnny said she wasn't stupid. Except then she says, "What's that on your face? I know that's you, Woody," which is stupid. So, what did Johnny know? He was always a dumbass, too. "It's kind of hard to cover up all that ugly." That's even stupider considering her current predicament. Lucy waves her hand in front of her face. "And that smell, I'd know it anywhere. That cologne. No one smells like you. That's a good thing. Don't know if we could suffer others smelling so bad."

Woody shakes off the insult. "On my face?" He plays dumb, reaching up and touching the pantyhose. "Oh, this, it's for," he motions toward the front door, "all cameras out there. Your neighbors. Never know who's watching."

"I know it's you."

"Of course you do," he says, pulling the mask up to reveal the lower half of his face, salt and peppered stubble from a long, frustrating day, and his wicked smile. The cool air on his chin feels good. "It wasn't supposed to keep you from knowing it's me. Of course, it's me. I want you to know it's me."

Woody relaxes his stance a bit, drops the gun to his side, and looks around the room.

"You know, I gotta tell you, this feels good. Being here. Feels good being here with you—in your house. Well, Johnny's house, little old grandma's house. Finally, having one up on you, with you thinking you're all high and mighty. Feels good to know I can put you in your place. It's about time."

Lucy frowns and starts to gather her legs under her, rolling to her knees, momentum building, but just as she is about to thrust upward, weight shifting, Woody is on her with a slash of his free hand. The blow is a loud, sharp crack in the empty house as he backhands her across the left side of her face. Lucy drops to the floor, knocking the wine glass over, red liquid spilling onto the light-colored rug.

Tears well in her eyes, caught in the dancing firelight. Lucy's hand snaps to her chin, rubbing the area where Woody's hand connected.

"No, you stay there," Woody says. "You aren't in control here." He pulls the pantyhose up higher, revealing his eyes. The elastic band rests across his forehead. The pantyhose weren't a good idea. He should have gone with the ski mask. But ski masks are hot. Feels good to see.

Lucy stares at him.

Her voice squeaks when she finally speaks.

"What do you want?"

Woody says, "You know what your problem is? You talk too much. Try to talk your way out of too many things. Talk to confuse. Use your looks and feminine wiles to get what you want, mesmerize. I did that the other day. The problem with that is you don't listen. Maybe you should talk less and listen more."

Woody repeats her question a few times, delivering the line differently each time.

"What do I want? What *do* I want? I told you what I wanted when I was here. I told you, but you didn't listen. See, that's your problem. All that talking and no listening.

It must be hard to listen when you entertain some dipshit marshal. But to answer your question, because you deserve an answer when I got a gun on you, I want what Johnny took. It's mine. That's what I want..."

Woody pauses, letting the weight of the situation blanket the conversation. He's done—he's done waiting.

He says, "You know, who do *you* think you are? How did *you* think this was going to play out? *You* think I'm going to play nice with you? I was playing nice with you when I came by and told you what was going on. Told you what I wanted. You didn't listen. You deflected. You played dumb. Like you're doing now. Like *you* don't know what I want, but you ain't dumb, and neither am I, so when I say this, know I know, you know what we did. Maybe you didn't when I was here last; I'm not sure. You shoulda known. But shoulda, woulda, coulda don't help us much now. We are past all that. But you know now. You. Do. Now. The look on your face says it all. The disgust. The fear. I see it. Says a lot more than you want."

Lucy doesn't try to hide her emotions now—the disgust, the fear, the hate. Woody pegged it; he could see all that was going through her brain now. And if he missed it before, the tears breaking the emotional dam and dripping off her cheeks, highlighting the area where he struck her burning bright red now, glistening in the light, tell him everything he needs to know.

Woody says, "Good, everyone's revealing their cards now; that's how I like it. No pretext. No pretendin'. I prefer it this way. So you watched Johnny's little video, did you? What'd he say happened? Nothing? He says he didn't do anything. Say how innocent he was and how terrible I am. That what he says?"

Lucy nods, but otherwise, she stays on the ground, frozen and not moving, her toned legs splayed to the side. Her eyes are upon him.

Woody says, "Good, now we're getting somewhere. You learned your lesson. Must be a quick study."

Woody plants his ass on the brick fireplace, elbows on knees, gun hanging down at an angle. He is quiet for a full thirty seconds, staring at her. Lucy's tears keep falling silently. She wipes tears from her cheek.

Woods says, "I bet Johnny is on that damn tape boohooing into his Cheerios, saying he didn't do nothing, but doing nothing is *doing* something, isn't it? Saying he didn't get his beak wet? Well, he did. We all did. Anything we did, Johnny did. He tell you how he was getting his dick wet? How every Friday night we were working late really meant we were cruising around town looking for a trim? Did he say he had a girlfriend on the side? A hot little Costa Rican number? There were others, but then there were just the two of you; I don't get it, but that was him. He tell you about her in that little fucking confession of his?"

Lucy says, "He did."

Woody laughs. "He did, did he?" The chuckling slows him down, but he gains control again. "Good for him, coming clean. He came a lot, I suspect. She was a hot number." Woody pauses. "Say, that's not who you were on the phone with, was it?" He points to the phone with the gun muzzle.

When Lucy doesn't answer, Woody adds, "It was, wasn't it? What did she have to say? What did you talk about? How big Johnny was?" He waits a beat and then suggests, "How *small*?"

"No," is all Lucy says.

Woody waits for her to say more, but nothing comes.

He says, "You know you can sit there and pout. Let that determination on your face sit in and solidify. Send these signals to me. I see it. That tells me you aren't in a talking mood. That's fine. I don't want you to talk. I don't really want to hear nothing you have to say except for just a few things."

"Like what?"

Woody bounces the gun a few times and then turns it toward her to drive home a point: a hammer. "Where's Johnny's confession?"

She gulps. "It's not here."

"I didn't ask if *it* was here," Woody says, trying to remain patient, but it's hard for him, with blood pumping in his ears as a dull roar. "That would have been my follow-up question. So maybe you can read minds. Can you read minds? No, you can't, good. Now shut the fuck up and do some of that listening I talked to you about. Focus on answering the questions asked. That's all I want from you. This isn't a conversation—not in the true sense of the word."

"It's an interrogation."

Woody chuckles. "Now you sound like a defense attorney," he says, "always telling me it was an interrogation when it was an interview—you can call it what you will. I call it an *interview*... but it's more a reckoning. This shoulda happened years ago."

"A rose by any other name," she mockingly says.

"Is just as sweet," Woody finishes. "Revenge is sweet, isn't it? Cold-blooded revenge. A dish that feels no heat. No one knows what I've done, and no one will know what I will do. Don't see it coming. Revenge ain't justice. It's for the person dispensing it. It's for me. So yes, this should have happened years ago."

"So why didn't it?"

Woody snarls his lip. "*Cooper*," he spits. "That fucker didn't want me coming here putting on the pressure when it needed to be done back when everything first happened because he *needed* Johnny. Who the fuck needs that sad sack? You sure as fuck don't."

"What do you mean?"

"I mean, what I would have done a couple of years ago when all this first happened would show up here in the dead of night, shove a gun in your shitty husband's mouth, and ask him politely before not being polite, asking him where the fucking money is."

Lucy surprises him. She says, "I know it's not money."

"What?"

"It's not money. I know what he kept from you."

Woody considers her words. "So he did confess, shit. I didn't think he had it in him; he had the balls."

"More than you, I would say."

"Ha, your words cut me... oh wait, they don't."

"He told me what you all did—what you did."

"He was just as much a part of it as everyone else. He put that gun on that boy and brought him over to the right apartment. He can say whatever he wants, but that's how it happened. What did he think was going to happen when he did that? They saw our faces. They had the stones. Worth millions. So, he put that problem into play. Don't get me started on the apartment mix-up.

"But that's all in the past, which is where it needs to stay and why I want that tape—why Cooper wants it. The only good thing about Cooper needing Johnny at the time was he went to prison for all the shit we did the longest when he did the least—as far as things went. Sweet satisfaction, if you ask me. Except Johnny was supposed to get those fucking stones turned over as quickly as possible. He had it all set up. Easy as pie. Except when you don't serve the damn pie... or even fucking bake it."

"He didn't."

"No, he didn't."

"He didn't trust you."

"We talking the plural you or just me in general?"

"You, you all, but you. Johnny never trusted you. Whether he sees it now or not, his mistake was he trusted Cooper and Craig."

"Yeah, well neither one of those fucks has the balls to do what needs doing. Neither one of those fucks wants to recognize how we're still on the hook, even these many years later. The only real way to keep a secret is to kill it."

Lucy's eyes widen, proving she isn't dumb. She accuses him. "You had Johnny stabbed."

Woody nods. "Of course I did; it couldn't happen to a better guy. It was supposed to kill him."

"Why?"

"Because fuck him for fucking me over. Isn't that enough? Is there any other reason needed? That should be enough. Is for me."

"But..." She narrows her eyes. "You still owe someone. That's it, isn't it? You owe someone who was supposed to flip the stones. This isn't wholly about the tape. This is about a bill."

"If I did, it's hard to get a secret out of a dead man. Figured death is like a hurricane. An act of God, clear my debts."

"So then, what was all of this?"

"All of this? All of this was because of that tape. Johnny left us all a surprise. One that could really fuck everything up as much as it could fix it. I don't know how, but the guy who was supposed to flip the stones knows they might be out in the open after all these years. Knows about the tape. But if that tape gets out, he can't flip the stones even if he got them. Well, that could ruin a lot of people's plans."

"So you want me to tell you where the stones are?"

"That was going to be my third question," Woody says. "You *sure* you aren't a mind reader? You're doing a shitty job following directions, but wonderful at predicting my questions." Woody stands, groaning some. His knee creaks. "Now, let's try this again, the proper way. Where's the tape?"

"In the mail," she says matter of fact.

"Clever girl."

She explains. "I didn't know who I could trust with it, and I didn't think leaving it in the bank was right."

"You wanted the stones?"

"I thought there might be a clue, yeah."

"And?"

"Was there?" She shakes her head. "No, not really."

"But you know what my fourth question will be, don't you?"

Lucy nods. "Yeah," she says. "I know where the stones are."

Woody smiles. "And here I expected you to lie to me some more and play this out longer."

"Why? What's the point? Seems like a waste of time. Yours and mine."

"You do catch on quick," Woody says. "Where are they?"

Lucy shakes her head a few times. "I'll have to show you. And no, I can't just tell you."

Woody, amused, starts to say, "Mind reader—" but Lucy rolls back off the wine-stained rug and grabs the edges with both hands. She plants her bare feet on the floor, and, in a position that strangely reminds Woody of a frog about to leap, but sorta backward, Lucy yanks with all her might. The cheap rug shifts under him first and then slides out from under his feet, sending Woody stumbling back, falling into the fake fireplace, and knocking a host of picture frames off the mantle. By the time he rights himself, Lucy's up and off the floor, running toward the front door, too far away for him to catch her now without having to run, and he's not going to shoot her; she knows where the stones are.

At the front door, which she collides with at a run, the whole wall shaking, Lucy fumbles with the door handle, trying to open it. Fear does that to a person; Woody's seen it. It clouds judgment and makes what should be simple complex.

The latch releases, and Lucy starts to tug the door open, only to find Craig, wearing pantyhose on his face, standing there.

CHAPTER 26:

LAMAR HENRY STUMBLES BACK HALF A step, stunned at the scene before him, bodies falling, hitting the floor. His voice echoes in his ears, telling Cece to stop. The smell of fired weapons fades into nothing, with the staccato blasts replacing the silence with a soft ringing in his ears.

Leaving Lamar thinking, *Shit, that happened so fast.*

First, the marshal's there with a gun on him, it was all over, end of the game, don't pass go, go to jail, and then Cece's coming in the house talking without looking, and then he was being stupid. Then there was the deafening release of gunfire.

Then silence.

Deafening silence.

It all happened so fast.

He can hardly believe it. He licks his lips as he assesses the situation, the turn of fate. The marshal had him. Gun on him. Intent behind his eyes. That hat cocked to the side like his attitude. Guy out front in the car, Cece said it. He drove by with the passenger seat empty. His last words. Hell of a set of last words.

They were going to capture Lamar and take him back. That was going to happen.

And then it didn't.

Now, it doesn't look like the marshal's going anywhere. He's laying over there bleeding, and Dante's cousin—well, he didn't make it. Hard to play Quick Draw McGraw with someone who carries a gun on his hip for a living. Lamar saw the tight-cop-trained-groupings as the bullets punctured their way into Cece. Lamar knows his law enforcement. That's what guys in prison, jail, and even the street don't get. Cops train to shoot to kill. Guys on the range are looking at targets, pretending it's some guy pointing a gun at them. How fast can they draw their weapon? How Wild West can it be? At the turn of the target, shoot. Go. Bang.

Lamar's eyes drift to the couch. The woman watches the scene with a strange look on her face. Lamar reads it as some sort of detachedness, but Dante doesn't sit still. The big man jumps to his feet and rushes to his cousin. But Erin sits there just as stunned as Lamar was at the whole thing, eyes blinking, mouth open, not comprehending what just happened, muttering to herself, "Shit," she says. "Shit!"

Lamar goes for the Marshal. No reason this guy should die.

Blood is on the guy's loud shirt, staining the yellow and red. The marshal gulps like a fish but gets no air. Wound about where Lamar's stab wound is on his chest. Lamar's hand absently touches the tender spot on his body. Did this guy get a punctured lung out of the deal, too? Doctors say it can be deadly. What do they call it in the movies? A sucking chest wound. But the guy's chest isn't making a sound. He's sucking for air but not getting any.

Lamar drops to his knees next to the marshal, checking on the marshal. He yells back at the woman and Dante, "He's alive."

But they don't get it. They don't get he can't die.

Screw Cece. He's done for. He punched above his weight and went down for the count.

But the marshal...

The attorney turns her body at the waist on the couch to look at Lamar, her eyes empty and unseeing, and then she rotates toward Dante. Her concern and attention are with her client, not the escaped convict. Lamar doesn't take it personally.

Lamar briefly turns his face back to the marshal, who's looking up at him, eyes open but the lights out. Lamar's seen it too many times. Knows the signs. Guys on the mat are not even trying to beat the count. Ref over here, in this case, the grim reaper, counting it out, one, two, three... hand slapping the mat, going to count to ten and then take the Chicano home to the big guy in the sky.

Lamar bunches up the guy's shirt to apply pressure to the wound. He doesn't want to get blood on his hands. He can't be here. He's got something to do.

Or all of this, everything that's happened, will be for nothing.

"Get it together," Lamar yells, talking to himself, too. "I need you to call 911." He does not say it in any way.

But since he's talking to no one specifically, no one pays him any attention. Dante, he figured, wouldn't. Guys said two minutes' worth of words the whole time Lamar's been here, but the woman's not shut up the entire time, thinking she's so tough, thinking she can talk her way out of anything, her, and anyone she's representing.

But this isn't the courtroom. This is life. This is real.

As real as it gets.

Lamar yells again, putting all his weight on his left arm to put more pressure on the wound as he snaps at her with his right hand, "Come on, snap out of it. Look over here."

His words are ignored. The attorney still doesn't come out of her daze.

And Dante...

At his cousin's side, Dante kneels, the big man whimpering softly but staying quiet, grieving, and confirming what Lamar already knew.

"Fuck your cousin," Lamar says, turning his attention back to the marshal. The words are harsh, but he needs Dante to snap out of it. The marshal's hand finds Lamar's wrist. Even dying, the guy's got a grip, eyes roving the ceiling, maybe searching for Lamar's. Lamar says, "What you see? Nothing? Light? Sure, that's it; you see the light, the light of the lights shining down on you. Stay with me. You're not going to die. I got you."

But he doesn't, not really. Having him in this moment is like capturing a river in your hand. Nothing you can do but watch it slip through your fingers.

The marshal utters the wife's name. "Lucy."

"I know," Lamar says. And he does know. "I know. She needs help."

The wavy nature of his consciousness clicks into solidity as the marshal's eyes lock with Lamar's eyes. "Lucy," the marshal says. "Help her."

"Yeah, yeah, save the wife, got it," Lamar says.

There's movement to Lamar's side. The attorney gets to her feet and rounds the back side of the couch, hand trailing along the backside of the couch. Like her eternal actions, her mind has to be numb, her senses dull. She's looking down at Cece, probably seeing the same trail of blood seeping from a hole to the man's forehead at his hairline, a near teardrop. Lamar can see it from here. So small. So insignificant. His eyes are wide open. Mouth open. The body crumpled in on itself.

She closes the distance to the body. Places a hand on Dante's shoulder as Dante cries more now, touching his cousin, his hands roaming over his cousin, searching for life, and then holding his cousin.

Lamar yells again, "D, fuck your cousin, man. This guy's alive. I need you."

Erin rotates from Lamar to Dante.

Lamar repeats himself. "Leave him be. There's nothing we can do for him. But this guy, he can't die. We can save him."

Dante looks over his broad shoulder at Lamar but doesn't move. The look is sharp and raw.

"Come over here; I need you to hold pressure here." Lamar demonstrates what he wants as he presses down on the marshal's chest. "I can't stay here. You have to take care of him. He can't die."

Dante shakes his head defiantly.

"If his ass dies, you go to jail. Do you want that?"

Dante pauses.

But the attorney doesn't; she assesses the situation in an instant. "You have to," she says softly and then stronger. "Dante, you have to. We can't stay here. We have to go. You have to save him. We'll call 911."

"What do you mean we?" Lamar says.

"But Cecil," Dante mutters.

Lamar tells him, "He's dead. We can't help him. But we can help *him*." Jerking his head down toward the Marshal.

Dante stands and looks down at his cousin.

Lamar says, "Come on, we don't have much time."

Dante steps backward once.

The attorney's coming to life more now. "What do you need?"

"Phone and duct tape."

"Duct tape?"

"Sucking chest wound, or whatever they call this. We got to seal it," Lamar says. "Dante, you got tape?"

Dante turns toward Lamar, his eyes wet and red.

Lamar repeats. "Tape, you got it?"

"Yeah," Dante says. "In the kitchen."

"Go get it," Lamar says. The marshal's hand releases Lamar's wrist. "He's still alive, but he's fading."

Dante steps past Lamar. He's moving now, each step faster and surer than the last.

The attorney woman calls 911, yelling into the phone, giving Dante's address, and not worrying about anything the person on the phone says. She's yelling about a man being shot, correcting herself, saying two men. Saying, hurry.

Dante drops to his knees.

"Start taping here," Lamar says, pointing to where he wants him to start, ripping the shirt up and away, the blood delayed in flowing but getting started as soon as Lamar lets up on the pressure, bubbles, pink, and gurgling. Blood at the marshal's mouth. "Hurry, tape there, then I'll hold pressure, and once we get it taped, I have to go."

Dante glances up at Lamar as his hand works the end of the tape and stretches a new piece, ripping it and applying it to the marshal without thought, hesitation, or even looking at what he's doing.

Dante says, "I got this." He directs his gaze down to what he's doing, moving faster now, strips coming every few seconds, taping over the hole

"I'm sorry," Lamar says. Dante stays intent on what he's doing. "D, I'm sorry about your cousin. I'm sorry. None of this shoulda happened."

Dante shrugs it off.

Lamar hates to ask this next part. "I need your keys."

Dante keeps working.

"I need your car keys. I have to take the car."

"You can take mine," the woman says.

"You sure?" Lamar asks, twisting his neck to look at her.

"Yeah, but I'm coming with you."

"Why?"

"Craig's my client too."

"Your boyfriend?"

"He's my client too," she repeats, with that fervor she's so damn proud of. "And if anyone's going to get through to him, it's me. It's the other guy I'm worried about."

"Yeah, well, that's where I come in."

"What are you going to do to him?"

"First thoughts, I'll do what I'm good at."

"Robbing banks?"

"No." Lamar shakes his head. "Hitting people."

CHAPTER 27:

LUCILLE HUDSON KICKS AT WOODY AS Craig pulls her off her front porch, the stairs falling out from her other foot, stealing all her power, body whirling in the air, but Woody slaps her leg down and out of the way. The slap makes her shin sting. Woody laughs, taunting her. "Have spirit in you; I like that in a woman. Keep it up, and I'll show you just how much I like it."

Then he and Craig carry her across her front yard as she struggles to get loose, but she's much smaller than both. The whole time, it doesn't seem real. She can't believe this is happening. She thought these guys were Johnny's friends. Okay, not Woody, but Craig. Yeah, she thought he was always good in Johnny's book. But Craig's got his arms around her waist, pulling on her, tugging on her, dragging her across the front yard. This is just as much as Woody is.

Halfway across the yard, her bare feet touch grass, cool and wet against her toes. Lucy opens her mouth to scream, but Woody anticipates this action and punches her hard in the stomach, doubling her over and driving the air necessary for her to cry out from her midsection. She wheezes, trying to catch her breath, but nothing comes in. She winces.

Then they're at the curb.

Craig throws her tiny body against the side of the car parked out front, a Lincoln or something; go figure, something large and douchey for Woody. The toss sends her colliding into the car. Lucy bounces off the door. She's free. But then she isn't. A body piles into her, causing her to brace herself against the side of the car as Woody's there behind her, his hands groping her, running up her waist, wrapping around her body, pinning her against the side of the car. She pushes back against him, but he pushes into her, his breath hot in her ear.

"Keep struggling, and I'll teach you a lesson right here," Woody threatens, humping her once from behind. "Wouldn't that be a thing to see? All your neighbors, or should I say Johnny's granny's neighbors, are coming out to see how big of a whore you are."

Placing her wrists on the top of the car and working her bare foot up against the door panel, Lucy shoves with all her might, squealing, "You're disgusting!"

But Woody doesn't budge. He laughs harder, ripping the pantyhose from the top of his head with one hand, revealing all his salt and peppered hair, wild and standing on end, going in all directions. "And you're a cunt, but you don't see me going about shouting it for everyone to hear."

He reaches into his pocket and takes out the gun. He jabs it into her side.

"See, this is how this will work," he tells her, half whispering. "You're going to get into the car, and you're going to stop being such a stupid little cunt; I don't know what Johnny saw in you, but I have a feeling it has something to do with what you are, and I'm willing to risk tasting just to see what all the sweet fun's about, you hear me? Straighten up, quiet down, and stop struggling."

Craig rounds the other side of the car, going for the driver's door. He asks over the car roof. "Where'd she say the tape was?"

Woody stops his threats to answer him. "Get this shit— in the mail."

"The what?"

"She says she mailed it to herself."

Craig pauses before opening the driver's door but then shakes his head and doesn't say anything more.

Woody fills in the unstated. "She might use it to figure out where the loot's at, but I think she knows where it's at." He turns his hot breath to her. "Don't ya, you little slut. You know where Johnny stuffed his salami and where he hid what's mine."

"Screw you," she screams.

"Screw me?" Woody says. "Baby, you'd be lucky to fuck me. And if that's what you want, I'll give it to you, but first, before I get those rocks off, I want the stones."

Lucy heel-kicks Woody in the nuts like she's trying to kick her ass, as she does in her warm-ups before she goes running.

He grunts, body tensing behind her, and then he slithers a hand through her hair and slams her face into the roof of the car.

The blow nearly buckles her knees, and things get woozy.

Woody cusses and says something, but Lucy hears none of it. Can barely perceive what's happening.

Next thing she knows, the door opens, and Woody pushes her into the back seat, gripping the gun in one hand and holding his nuts with the other. "I'll make you pay for that. More than I already have, you stupid fucking bitch. I'm going to enjoy it. I'm going to enjoy making you cry out."

Lucy rights herself in the seat. There's a squelch of tires somewhere down the street. Through the windshield, she sees a car taking the curve too fast, the whole thing leaning to one side as if it's too much for it.

Woody asks, "Isn't that your girl's car?"

But before Craig can answer, the car finishes the curve and heads right for them, gaining speed.

"What's she doing?" Woody says, gazing out the window. "Who's that driving?"

Craig doesn't answer. He snakes the seatbelt across his body as fast as he can, snapping the buckle in place just before the other car plows into the front end of theirs; the loud crunch of metal and plastic, rocking them in place, pushing the car back a few inches, crumpling the front of the Lincoln, making the airbags go off in a puff of smoke, knocking Lucy into the floorboard. The airbags smack Craig in the face, stunning him. Woody bangs his face into the headrest in front of him, breaking his nose.

Dazed, Lucy untangles her body from the heap on the floorboard and crawls onto the seat.

This is her moment.

Her eyes land on the gun, right there in the seat, within reach. Woody's forgotten it in the collision.

She reaches for it, but the movement catches Woody's attention. His hand juts forward and grasps for the gun, too, both getting to it at the same time.

Lucy yanks it toward her as Woody pulls it toward him. They struggle over it, and then it goes off, shooting Woody in the thigh and surprising and scaring Lucy. She releases the gun and flings herself back toward the door. Woody howls in pain, grabbing at his leg and dropping the gun to the floorboard. Yelling, "You stupid bitch!"

Lucy inches backward, foot wedged under the driver's seat.

Woody grabs her while trying to hold pressure on his leg.

There's a lot of blood. More than she expected.

And just as she has that thought, kicking Woody's groping hand away with her foot, the driver's seat creaks as Craig shifts in the seat; Craig, with a cut above his eye, blood streaming out as he's turning in the seat, a gun in his hand, Woody dividing his attention, exclaiming, "What the fuck is this—"

But he doesn't get to finish the sentence. Craig shoots Woody in the face, ending him as a threat, just as Lucy screams and her roaming hand finds the door handle. The door gives way, and she spills out of the car into the street.

CHAPTER 28:

EDUARDO CHAVEZ OPENS HIS EYES TO Rafferty standing over him in the hospital bed with the newspaper under his arm. "Morning, sleeping beauty," Rafferty says. "Actually, it's not morning. It's two in the afternoon, but the same principle applies. The nurse said you passed out after breakfast; neither she nor I had the heart to wake you."

"God, don't tell me you'll use the restroom."

Rafferty frowns. "No, that's not what I'm... what's the matter with you? No, that's not it. I'm leaving. Just thought I'd let you know... And just so you know, I went out to the lobby to do my business in the boy's room out there."

"The least you can do," Eduardo mutters.

"Always the critic," Rafferty says. "You have company." He steps to the side, revealing Lucy standing there in tight blue jeans and a white t-shirt, with her hair back, showcasing her features, and teasing him with that slender neck of hers that twists and slides into her petite but well-shaped cleavage.

"Lucy," Eduardo says.

Lucy half-responds to him, still standing in the doorway, before her voice cuts out, "Ed—"

Rafferty says, "Eduardo, he don't like Ed. God knows I've been trying it out on him every couple of months for years, but no more."

"What do you mean?" she asks.

Rafferty pauses, glances at Eduardo, and then back at her. He slaps Eduardo's blanket-covered legs with the paper. "I'll let him explain it. I gotta go. Girls have a choir performance my wife wants me to attend, aka not miss, aka get my ass there if I ever want to have sex again."

Eduardo says, "You ever get to have sex?"

Rafferty fake laughs as he backpedals toward the door. "Always the funny man. How you think I got all them girls? Anyways, you two kids have fun."

Lucy steps to the side to allow Rafferty to leave. Then she shuffles toward the bed, smiling. "How are you feeling?"

"Sore," Eduardo says. "They said I have fluid around my heart. Have to have another surgery today—I guess any time now."

Her smile breaks into concern. "Are you going to be okay?"

"It's not life-threatening, yet, if that's what you are asking. Doctors say it could always go bad, but I think I'm doing all right. I started physical therapy a few days ago. So there's that."

Lucy smiles again. It's a nice thing to see in a hospital room.

"You doing okay?" Eduardo asks. "I heard things got pretty rough."

"Lamar got away."

"Yeah, I heard that too," he says. "Makes me feel pretty stupid to have to go through all this just to end up with him out there somewhere and me losing more than just him. Job too."

"They fire you?"

"Not yet, but like an eight ball, all signs point to yes." Eduardo motions for her to sit. "That's what Rafferty says, pretends to shake one, and then listens to the answer. Why? I don't know."

Lucy sits in the recliner next to the bed where Rafferty had been. "Still warm."

"Pretend it's from his body heat," he tells her. She doesn't get it. He adds, "You get them divorce papers served?"

Lucy nods. "And signed."

"That's good."

"Why do you ask?"

"I made it a rule a while back not to hit on married women."

She blushes, her pale skin glowing pink. "Did you?"

"Yes, ma'am, figured it'd keep me out of trouble."

"Keep something like this from happening?"

"Something like that—Say, I haven't seen anything on the news about the dirty cops your husband ran with, but you killing the one trying to kidnap you in front of your house—you keeping quiet about Johnny's confession?"

"For now," she confirms. "Why rock the boat, you know?"

She seems to want to say more but doesn't, so Eduardo lets it go. He figures whatever happened, that attorney had something to do with it. After all, not only was she Dante Smith's attorney, but that cop clown on TV... the Wrench. Maybe she and Lucy came to an understanding.

He wouldn't put it past the woman to work things to her advantage.

He says, "No, but then again, I'm going to end up without a job and insurance when all this is said and done. So I don't have any obligation to tell anyone anything about what you might know. They only asked about Cecil Reyes, the man I shot, the man who shot me—it seems they think he did those robberies his cousin, Lamar's friend, was accused of doing. The gun he shot me with matches the one they saw on the security tapes. Or at least that's the story his attorney's telling on TV. Either way, I think Dante'll get off. Me, on the other hand, I'm going to be bankrupt after this."

Eduardo motions to the room, meaning the hospital.

Lucy reaches for Eduardo's hand, catching it in midair. Her fingers intertwine with his. She squeezes his hand as both hands come down on the bed. "Maybe you can stick around town."

"Maybe," he says. "Been thinking about my opportunities out here." He stares at her for a moment. "Old friend of mine from the service who left the marshals to help his dad out—the guy had cancer or something—has a bondsman business out here. Said I could have a job helping him out if I wanted it—that'll help pay for some of this, maybe."

Lucy's other hand slithers into her pocket, grabs hold of something, and comes back out. She places the object on Eduardo's chest. "Think this might help?"

At first, Eduardo thinks it's a pebble. It's dirty, muddy, dried mud, like something fished out of a river, flaky and dry. He plucks it from his chest with his free hand and rubs the dirt away with his thumb. His eyes focus on it, and he realizes it's a diamond. "This what I think it is?"

Lucy nods. "Know anyone who could turn this into cash?"

"You found—"

Lucy nods again, keeping him from finishing his question. Words, like the answer, don't matter anymore.

Eduardo inspects the stone with one eye closed, checking for quality and color. It's a bit yellow but still a diamond. He says, "Yeah, I know a guy, a... a sorta friend of mine, an old informant. His name's Ruth. He might be able to do something with this..."

Lucy juts forward in the seat, quickly covering the space between the chair and the bed, and pecks his cheek. Her lips are soft and warm. She smells good, and it feels good to have her kiss him.

"You've wanted to do that for a long time, haven't you?" he asks.

Before she can answer, he reaches up and caresses her cheek before she can slip away and say an answer he doesn't want to hear. Again, words don't matter anymore. He kisses her on the lips.

Then she comes out of the chair, shifting to the side of the bed, leaning, no, falling into him, without breaking contact, still kissing him. Hurts some, but worth it.

BOOK CLUB QUESTIONS:

1. What stood out to you most about this book—
   whether it was a character, a scene, or a theme?

2. How did the main characters evolve throughout the
   story, and did their changes feel believable?

3. What do you think the author was trying to say about
   life, relationships, or society?

4. Were there any moments that surprised you or caught
   you off guard? Why?

5. How did the setting—time, place, or atmosphere—
   shape the story?

6. Which part of the book resonated with you personally, and why?

7. Did the ending satisfy you? If not, how would you
   have preferred it to wrap up?

8. Were there any choices the characters made that you strongly agreed or disagreed with?

9. How did the writing style—pacing, tone, or language—affect your experience?

10. If you could ask the author one question about the book, what would it be?

BIO:

MARK ATLEY IS A CRIME STORY WRITER whose characters come to life from real-life encounters on the streets and the vivid imagination in his head. The result is a thrilling and entertaining experience, with dialogue that flows effortlessly, reminiscent of an old pickup bouncing down a pothole-filled back alley. He is the author of *A Bright Young Man* and the *Tulsa Underworld* Series, and his short fiction has been published in *Punk Noir Magazine*, *Bristol Noir*, and other literary outlets.

When he isn't writing or spending time with his family—his wife, two daughters, and four dogs—Mark works as a detective in a suburb of Tulsa, Oklahoma. He graduated from Oklahoma State University with two degrees in journalism. You can follow Mark on various social media platforms at @mark_atley or find him wherever his adventures take him.

Discover more at
4HorsemenPublications.com

10% off using HORSEMEN10